Tom West is the pseudonym for the internationally bestselling author of ten novels. *Private Down Under*, which he co-wrote with James Patterson under the name Michael White, is the sixth book in the Private series. *The Einstein Code* is the second book to feature marine archaeologists Kate Wetherall and Lou Bates, after *The Titanic Enigma*. Tom West lives in Perth, Australia.

THE EINSTEIN CODE

TOM WEST

PAN BOOKS

First published 2015 by Pan Books
an imprint of Pan Macmillan, a division of Macmillan Publishers Limited
Pan Macmillan, 20 New Wharf Road, London N1 9RR
Basingstoke and Oxford
Associated companies throughout the world
www.panmacmillan.com

ISBN 978-1-4472-1034-4

1 3 5 7 9 8 6 4 2

A CIP catalogue record for this book is available from the British Library.

Typeset by Ellipsis Digital Limited, Glasgow
Printed and bound by CPI Group (UK) Ltd, Croydon, CR0 4YY

THE EINSTEIN CODE

1

Norfolk Naval Base, Virginia. 14 February 1937.

Albert Einstein pulled himself out of the mud-spattered black Oldsmobile. A young naval officer closed the door behind him as the scientist flipped up the collar of his greatcoat to shield his face against the bitterly cold northerly wind and stepped around a frozen brown puddle.

The naval base was undergoing major renovations; there were signs of construction all around. Einstein was escorted along a series of wooden boards placed over the mud and pools of frozen water towards a newly built headquarters, Building K-BB. It was four storeys high with a control tower on the north-west side.

He was met at the double doors to the building by Commander Flynn, a tall wiry man with a head of grey stubble, tired eyes and a cigarette between his narrow, pale lips.

'Professor,' Flynn said, extending a hand. 'I think we need to get you inside, it's like the Arctic out here.'

'I shan't argue with you there, Commander,' Einstein replied. Flynn held the door open and they entered the building followed close behind by four naval officers.

They took the lift to the top floor and crossed a narrow bridge to the control tower. Half of the large circular room had vast windows that looked out onto a panoramic view of the base and westward to the bay. In the foreground a road led to the water and a curved succession of piers, metal frames extending into the dark water. Docked at these piers were a range of naval vessels, two frigates, a battlecruiser, a minesweeper, and to the south, the hulking form of two aircraft carriers, *Yorktown* and *Enterprise*.

The ships dominated the view and dwarfed the piers and buildings clustered around the road to the water; and on this grey dreary morning, the vessels seemed to merge with the dirty grey-brown waters of the bay. Clouds hung low making the whole vista appear as a painting created by an artist using only the dark end of a monochrome palette.

Looking up towards the horizon, Einstein could see that all marine traffic around the bay had been rerouted for the experiment. Poised in the middle distance, perhaps half a mile offshore, stood at anchor USS *Liberty*, an old Wickes-class destroyer, designation DD74; a ship that had first seen service in 1918 and was soon to be decommissioned.

At one end of the room, following the curve of the windows, stretched a bank of control stations manned by five naval officers. The desks were covered with an array of dials, lights and sliders; one of the stations included an oscilloscope screen, a white line stuttering across the glass. A constant babble of conversation passed between the operatives speaking into Bakelite mouthpieces to their counterparts on the bridge of *Liberty*.

Commander Flynn offered Einstein a pair of binoculars. Looking through them he could make out details of the ship, a half-dozen white-clad crewmen working on the main deck.

One of the operatives shifted in his chair to face Einstein and the admiral. 'T minus five.'

'Professor, let's go through the protocol one last time, shall we?' Flynn led the scientist to a table away from the control desks. Two men stood on the far side studying something laid out in front of them.

Flynn saluted and turned to Einstein. 'Professor, Admiral Stevens and Admiral Le Marc. They are here today as observers.' The two men stepped forward and took turns to shake Einstein's hand.

On the table lay a large piece of paper covered with lines drawn in different colours connecting a series of boxes and triangles, each labelled in bold letters. At the head of the diagram was written: 'Project Cover Up. Top Secret'. At the foot of the paper was a rectangle marked 'Control Room'. This was the room they were now standing in. Close to the top of the diagram was a small box designated 'USS *Liberty*'.

From the rectangle representing the control room, a thick red line ran vertically upwards before splitting into two fresh horizontal lines, left and right. These each arrived at boxes labelled 'Conduction Station'. Connected to these and off to each side of the paper two triangles had been drawn. Under each was written 'Particle Beam Emitter'. Two green lines connected these to boxes carrying the legend: 'Generators'. Bright yellow wavy lines came from the particle beam emitters to converge on *Liberty*.

'Could you talk us through it please, Professor?'

'Certainly.'

Commander Flynn handed Einstein a pointer and the scientist leaned in towards the diagram.

'As you know, the object of this experiment, part of the larger project dubbed "Cover Up", is to build a defensive shield about the warship *Liberty*.' He tapped the diagram. 'We hope to do this because of a consequence of a theory I have been working on with a close colleague, Johannes Kessler in Berlin. We call it the Unified Field Theory.'

'With respect, Professor, could we stick to the practicalities please,' Flynn interrupted.

'Very well. From here' – and Einstein tapped the box representing the Control Room – 'a pulse of electricity is fired to these two "Conduction Stations", here and here. This is then amplified and sent via a cable to each of the "Particle Beam Emitters".' He pointed to the triangles each side of the diagram. 'These then fire a beam of particles called protons towards *Liberty*. When the two streams meet, they interact, and, according to theory at least, they will generate a sphere of exotic particles called "neutrinos".'

'And these . . . neutrinos act as a kind of invisible shield against anything fired at the ship. Is that right, Professor?' Admiral Stevens asked.

'That is indeed the theory, Admiral. If the shield is produced properly in the demonstration today, we should see just a slight distortion of the air around the ship, a shimmering perhaps. We then plan to use small arms fire from a launch close by, to test its effectiveness.'

'And with the crew inside?' Stevens queried.

'That was a decision made by our people early on,' Commander Flynn said. 'We want to see what effect the beams have on humans, not just the ship. All the men aboard *Liberty* are volunteers.'

'T minus two minutes,' the same operator at the control panels announced.

'Gentlemen, shall we go over to the observation window?'

Commander Flynn led the way, and as Einstein and the two admirals reached the observation window he pointed to a line of four chairs and handed them each a pair of binoculars.

'T minus sixty seconds. Conduction coils on.'

There was a hush of expectation in the room, a silence broken only by the whirr of machines, the hum of valves.

'Thirty seconds to link up. Particle emitters on.'

Einstein and the naval men watched through their binoculars.

'Five, four, three. Emitters set to full load. Two, one.'

For perhaps two seconds it seemed as though nothing was happening; but then, almost invisible at first, they could see a hazy light flickering around *Liberty*. It looked like distortion produced by hot air. Four sailors were visible on the deck, each manning a station; two more men could be seen moving around on the bridge.

Then a low hum came from across the water. It was impossible to pinpoint the source. Quickly, it rose through the scale to a squeal that seemed to come from all around. As Einstein and the three senior officers watched, the shimmering aura around the ship started to glow. It began as a mellow lemon altering to a pallid green that spread into a dome encompassing the whole ship. A halo of sparkling light hung over it and around the perimeter where it touched the water.

'Holy . . . !' exclaimed Admiral Le Marc, '. . . that light!'

A ferocious blast of noise came from the ship. The sailors cowered. A shockwave skittered across the water. Travelling at the speed of sound, it took less than two seconds to cover the half mile from *Liberty* to the control room of the naval base. It hit the wall of windows, shattering the panes into countless shards that sprayed the room.

*

Einstein came to completely deaf, feeling the pounding of his own heart, his own heavy breathing reverberating through his head. He pulled himself up into a seated position and looked around. Admiral Le Marc was dead, his head a mess of glass and brain, the horrible white of his broken skull just by Einstein's feet. The other two officers were pulling themselves to their feet, their faces covered with dust and blood. Einstein turned towards where the operators had been seated; the closest was rushing over to them, the others gazed around, shock imprinted on their faces.

Einstein let the young naval operator help him up. A horrible stab of pain shot up his right leg and he almost collapsed.

'Easy, sir,' the man said.

But Einstein was not paying attention. He could see through the dust and the shattered window that *Liberty* had vanished.

2

Orkney Islands, north-east Scotland. Present day.

The chopper – an AgustaWestland AW101 – swung east, banking through the low grey clouds a hundred feet above the pristine dark waters of the North Sea. Glena Buckingham, head of Eurenergy, one of the two largest energy resource conglomerates on the planet, drew on her favourite cigar – a fat Bolivar from a private supplier in Cuba – filling the small cabin with smoke. Neither the other passenger, Buckingham's right-hand man Hans Secker, nor the company pilot John MacBride, dared say a word. Secker just coughed quietly and looked out at the violent, freezing water below the chopper.

'Lord knows why we couldn't have built this facility somewhere a little more civilized,' Buckingham said and looked up at the steel roof of the aircraft, watching the swirls of smoke unravel.

'What? Somewhere inconspicuous like central London, Glena?' Secker risked a little levity.

She gave him a withering look and exhaled thick

grey smoke. The trip up from London had been turbulent and the news on her iPad had irritated her enormously. The world's media had worked itself into a frenzy over the Chinese government's secret purchase of a tiny Pacific island called Dalton from under the very noses of the West. Glena would have found it all very amusing except for the fact the new owners were already boasting about the massive oilfields under the island.

'I do want to see what all the money has been spent on here though, Hans,' Buckingham hissed. 'And it had better be bloody worth it.'

'State of the art, I'm assured.'

'One would hope so for . . . what was it in the end?'

'Eight hundred and twenty-five million.'

'Jesus wept! And this!' Buckingham stabbed at her iPad screen and a blaring headline: US FURY OVER CHINESE PURCHASE FROM PRIVATE OWNER.

'It'll come to nothing,' Secker said.

'Oh, really? You're sure about that, Hans? Why the hubris? The Chinese have bought Dalton Island a few miles from Howland in the Pacific and the area is rich in resources. The Yanks wanted to get their greedy mitts on it. The Chinese have swiped it first; some clever deal offering one per cent share of resources profits. What's there to be nonchalant about?'

'I admit we could have been more vigilant.'

'It pisses me off,' Buckingham snapped. 'We could have got that island for a pittance.'

'Which is why, Glena, we need something like this facility.' He nodded out of the window.

Buckingham was shaking her head. She knew he was right. 'We didn't have our eye on the ball, Hans. China's latest acquisition is about as isolated as it gets. The only thing it was famous for was that Amelia Earhart's plane was supposed to have crashed near there in 1937. Who would have thought the place was perched on a shitload of the black stuff?'

The chopper banked again and through the windows the passengers could see the rugged outline of Flotta, a smudge of an island a little over three miles long by a few hundred yards across. It had barely seen the imprint of humanity until the twentieth century, when the Royal Navy had established a massive naval base at Scapa Flow. In the 1970s an oil refinery had been constructed on the island. Eurenergy had bought the far northern tip of the island, one hundred and twenty acres called Roan Head, and two years ago Buckingham had given the go-ahead to build there the most advanced satellite surveillance facility in the world. From this base, technicians controlled a network of forty-one satellites in close-earth orbit, each probe packed with the latest optical and thermal imaging technology and used to accurately detect hidden resources – especially oil, gas and uranium – anywhere in the world.

As the chopper descended through a brisk crosswind, swaying as it came in, Secker and Buckingham could see an array of white spheres and satellite dishes.

The spheres were each fifty yards in diameter, the dishes clustered around a line of a dozen concrete towers. Secker started to count them but gave up at thirty-two as the chopper turned, descended fast and touched down on a helipad.

The two visitors unbuckled and got up from their seats as the door opened, a blast of freezing air rushing into the cabin. Two men in anoraks, fur-lined hoods drawn down about their necks, stood ducking as the rotor blades slowed, the roar of the chopper quietening. One of the men stepped forward and helped Glena Buckingham down a set of metal steps to the tarmac helipad. Secker followed and the two men gestured to follow them into a single-storey building at the edge of the landing pad.

Soon, all four were inside a warm white-walled room lit by a soft glow from some invisible source. A large window opened out to the flat bleakness of the island and the metal towers of the old refinery topped by red flame like Roman candles in the distance.

One of the anoraked men nodded silently and disappeared through a door at the rear of the room. The other, a middle-aged ginger-haired man with a ruddy complexion, strode over to the new arrivals.

'Ms Buckingham, Mr Secker. It is a pleasure to welcome you to Flotta.'

'Dr Freeman?' Buckingham asked.

He nodded.

'You're shorter than I remember you being.'

Unsure how he should respond, Freeman produced a wan smile and gestured towards the door.

They entered a wide, brightly lit corridor, doors opening off to left and right, men in white coats crossing from room to room, a pair of overalled techs carrying a bulky device which they were manoeuvring into a lab to the left.

'This is the main storage and repair area,' Freeman said.

On the wall were signs, black lettering on stark white backgrounds: 'Main Control Hub' straight on, 'Accommodation' to the right, 'Canteen' and 'Ancillary Laboratories' to the left. They followed Freeman through a set of double swing doors, more doors off to each side, and across a junction. Staff passed them disinterestedly.

At the end of the corridor they came to a bank of lifts. Freeman held the door back as Buckingham and Secker stepped inside.

'This will take us down ten floors,' he explained. 'Our sat dishes are positioned about a hundred yards from this building and the signals are fed down to us in the Control Hub via fibre optic.'

'We saw the dishes coming in,' Secker said.

'There's a second, larger bank of receivers on a small artificial island we have constructed off the northern tip of Roan Head.' Freeman nodded to his left.

The lift slowed and stopped smoothly, the doors opened and they were in the Main Control Hub, a circular room like the apse of a cathedral, a vaulted ceiling strewn with lights and gantries. From the gantries hung four massive flat screens arranged as the sides of a square. Below these were arranged two banks of control panels. Four men and three women sat at one of the banks, another pair of men in white coats stood close to the other.

As Freeman stepped out of the lift with Buckingham and Secker, the people at the desks stopped working. Freeman waved a hand towards his team and made the introductions.

'As you know, we have only been online three weeks, but already my group are gelling,' he said to Buckingham as they walked towards a bank of control panels.

'I'm amazed they don't go stir crazy on this tiny island,' Secker observed.

'They are dedicated scientists,' Freeman responded. 'They are working with the best equipment available and employed for a noble cause – to find hidden fuels for future generations. Besides, they have access to amazing facilities and they're on a civilized rotation, here for three months then home for a month.'

Freeman stopped at one of the banks of controls. 'But I guess you're not here just to meet the staff, Ms Buckingham.' Freeman eyed the CEO cautiously. 'We've prepared a demonstration for you.'

Freeman leaned in to talk to the operative at the nearest control panel and then stood back beside Buckingham and Secker. 'OK, we have the satellites at your disposal, Ms Buckingham. Where in the world would you like to take a look? Any hunches?' He turned with a smile to see Buckingham's set expression.

'Pacific Ocean,' she said, staring at the big screen hanging from the ceiling. 'Dalton Island, the place the fucking Chinese have just bought for a few cents!'

Freeman walked over to the panel and gave the operative instructions. The screen turned blue then flicked back to an image of the earth from space; the view from Satellite 21 in geosynchronous orbit above the equatorial Pacific. The image seemed to grow on the screen as the camera zoomed in, the edges dropping away as the satellite honed in on the coordinates punched into the mainframe of the station computer, 0° 46' 16"N 176° 35' 03"W.

The centre of the screen displayed a green oblong. According to a scale on the side of the monitor, it was a little over three hundred yards north–south, sixty yards east–west at its widest point. A mere pinprick in the vast ocean, a featureless dimple skirted by sand.

'Dalton,' Freeman said. 'Doesn't look much, does it?'

'It is what's beneath it that's interesting,' Buckingham said. 'What's that?'

The image shifted westward and refocused. They could see a large drilling vessel.

'I would say that is an exploratory drilling rig. The Chinese must have got permission from the owners of the island to do some test boring . . . to see what they were buying.'

'Now it's theirs they can do want they want. I

imagine the heavy plant will be on its way from the port of Shanghai as we speak . . . the bastards.'

'OK, let's see what's down there,' Freeman said.

The view on the monitor changed, the satellite image moved south-west to close in on the expanse of ocean near the island, probing the depths to the ocean floor. The data on the screen informed them the rocky seabed lay at an average depth of 2,450 feet. The camera showed an undulating seascape of coral rich in a variety of marine life.

'Switch to hi-res ultra spectral,' Freeman told the operative. 'Watch,' he added to Buckingham and Secker.

The screen filled with a red glow. Freeman whistled. 'A whole lot of oil.'

'Pan back out,' Buckingham instructed, 'keep focused on the top end of the spectrum.' The operator followed orders and they all watched as the image expanded, pulling outward to show an area of some ten square miles of sub-terrain. The red shape filled half the field, shimmering, iridescent.

'That has to be at least a couple of billion barrels,' Secker said, barely able to believe what he was seeing.

'OK, Freeman, zoom back in,' Buckingham said calmly. 'Skirt around the edge. I want to see if we can get an idea of its depth.'

Freeman helped the operative at the control panel and the image on the screen changed once more. Flicking back to a normal spectrum, the camera zoomed in, breaking the surface again and descending towards the ocean floor.

It was then that a strange object flitted in and then out of view.

'Stop!' Buckingham said.

Freeman looked confused, but the operative had halted the pan.

'Back. Same speed, about three, four seconds.'

The image shifted, the panning slowed and they shot past the object again.

Buckingham did not need to say anything, the operative knew. He nudged the controls, panning back at a crawl. The ocean floor flowed across the monitor, rocks, coral, a giant school of small fish . . . and stopped. There on the screen they could all see a white object like a distorted cross.

'Jesus fucking Christ!' Buckingham exclaimed.

3

Off Howland Island, Pacific Ocean. The next day.

'Oxygen at ninety-eight per cent, Kate,' Lou said and pulled round to face her.

'Same,' she said, checking his tank, giving him the thumbs up before turning to the two junior team members, Gustav Schwartz and Connor Maitland. 'Keep comms open at all times, guys. We'll be at seventy feet so we only have thirty minutes at the wreck.'

'Cool,' Gustav said.

Lou Bates and Kate Wetherall sat on the side of the exploration vessel *Inca*, an eighty-five-footer leased by their employers, the Institute of Marine Studies in Hampton, Virginia. The boat was in the shallow reefs off Howland Island in the mid-Pacific close to the equator. The pair, along with two of their team from the institute, had boarded in the Gilbert Islands, three days away. They had been anchored here for the past twenty-four hours, preparing for the first in a planned series of dives to an old wreck, the *Victoria*.

A few miles to the west of Howland lay the tiny atoll of Dalton. Kate and Lou and the crew of the *Inca* had been following the news on the BBC website concerning international outrage at the recent Chinese purchase of the island. Earlier that day they had heard the boom of shallow ocean explosions resonating from Dalton. The BBC had shown aerial photographs and satellite images of Chinese exploratory vessels already beginning to exploit their new acquisition.

Falling backwards into the water, Kate and Lou were instantly cocooned in the near-silent world of the Pacific Ocean, the sunlight shimmering on the surface above them, the coral-laden reef below. They were experienced divers who had explored dozens of wrecks during the three years they had worked together. To date, their most important work had been their key role eighteen months ago in finding a radiation source buried in the wreck of the *Titanic*. They had been brought into the investigation by a commander at Norfolk Naval Base, Captain Jerry Derham. What had begun as an incredible adventure exploring the inside of the *Titanic* had turned into a tangled drama in which the couple had skirted death several times in the space of a few days. Jerry Derham had saved their lives on at least two occasions, and they had grown very close to him.

Lou and Kate's involvement with tracking the source of radiation from the *Titanic* and the sensational story behind it had propelled them briefly into the public spotlight. They had been interviewed by *Time*, appeared on breakfast TV on both sides of the Atlantic, and they had just delivered to their New York publishers the first draft of *Messages from the Deep*, a co-written account of their adventures. Now, though, it was nice to be working on a small project – something a little out of the way. And this was special for another reason. They had married a week ago in Maryland, making this a working honeymoon.

The *Victoria* lay in seventy feet of water, with Dalton the nearest land. Beyond that was the island of Howland, and the nearest habitation was the Gilbert Islands, some 800 miles to the west.

The precise location of *Victoria*, a British trading vessel bound for Hawaii, had remained a mystery since it sank in a tropical storm in August 1889. Only two of the seventy-nine people aboard the ship had survived and reached the Gilbert Islands. They claimed to have been slaves, two of twenty-four men and women taken from the island of Vanuatu.

The British governor of the Gilbert Islands, Sir Jonathan Southling, had refused to believe their story because slavery had been abolished throughout the British Empire over fifty years earlier. The two men, known only as Daniel and Alfred, had been sent back to Vanuatu without compensation and forgotten about until their story was rediscovered soon after the end of the Second World War. During the 1950s, British marine archaeologists had begun to wonder about the validity of Daniel and Alfred's claim. But it was not until a year ago that the wreck was spotted by a NASA satellite and the Institute of Marine Studies in Hampton acquired funding to investigate the wreck.

The *Victoria* was in a very poor state. It had been an old ship when it had sunk and the warm waters and rich marine life in these parts had not treated it kindly. The timber hull and decks had gone completely. All that remained was the steel framework of the vessel resting on the reef like the carcass of a dead animal. Around it was strewn a miscellany of objects, clumps of coral-encrusted metal boxes, steel crates and remnants of the main mast.

The safest way to enter the wreck was from directly above, in through the bow. From here they could see the ship's metal skeleton stretching out across the coral and sand floor of the continental shelf. At a depth of seventy feet almost ninety per cent of light from the surface was absorbed, but large powerful lights on Kate and Lou's helmets and arms illuminated the site.

'I'm going to take it slowly,' Lou said through his comms.

'Right behind you,' Kate replied.

Lou flicked his comms to link with *Inca*. 'Gustav? Connor? Everything OK with you?'

'No probs, Lou.'

'We've reached the wreck and are about to go in through the bow end.'

'Copy that.'

The bow was pointing south-west and raised slightly above the rest of the ship. This part of the old vessel was nothing but a metal lattice and the beams of their helmet lights cut through the dark to reveal an interior coated in multicoloured oxides and crustaceans.

They moved back along *Victoria*'s spine and found the remains of a deck framework covered with corroded steel sheets. Here there was an opening about ten feet across leading into the bowels of the ship. They swept their lights about trying to understand the layout of the interior. Slowly, they swam down to the bottom of the ship to what had once been the vessel's hold.

Lou scanned the hold with his helmet light then moved down to swim two feet above the base of the hull.

'Well, what d'ya know?' he said through his comms.

Kate was there beside him, staring down. 'No mistaking that.' She moved in close to inspect a row of corroded steel shackles, ankle and wrist braces connected to the remains of the floor by thick crumbling chains. They ran in two lines, twenty-four pairs along the spine of the ship. 'Daniel and Alfred were telling the truth.'

She removed a camera from a pouch on a utility belt and started to photograph the objects. Lou had a video camera built into the sleeve of his suit and began filming, beaming the images directly to *Inca* seventy feet above their heads.

'You guys getting this?' he asked through his comms.

'Crystal clear, Lou,' Gustav replied.

Kate was the first to sense the vibration in the water, a strong current pulling her away from the floor where she was taking close-ups. 'What the hell! Lou, you feel that?'

He straightened and lowered the video camera. 'Yes.'

Kate swung her light beams around cutting through the gloom. They could see the water filled with rust and flecks of metal. Something had shaken the wreck and dislodged loose oxides coating the framework.

'Up to the main deck . . . now!' Kate hollered and turned away from the metal shackles, Lou immediately behind her.

'Guys, can you see anything unusual?' Lou called through the comms as he swam fast through the water back up to the hatch and the open framework of the wreck above.

'No, Lou,' Connor replied. 'What's up?'

They did not answer, just propelled themselves upward, emerging through a gap in the deck. Ten feet from the edge of the wreck they could see a huge metal object protruding from the sand and sediment of the ocean floor.

4

The debris-filled water foamed wildly. Pebbles and small pieces of detritus landed on them as they scrambled under the cover of a ragged piece of steel.

'What was that?' It was Connor aboard *Inca*.

Kate and Lou panted into their masks as the water convulsed silently around them.

'Guys? You OK? Kate, Lou, come in.'

'We're all right . . . I think,' Lou managed to gasp.

'What's happened?'

'Not sure,' Kate said. 'Some sort of object has emerged from the ocean floor close to the wreck. Don't know what it is. We need to let the sediment and sand settle before we take a look.'

'How about you come straight back up?' Gustav suggested.

Lou looked at his chronometer. 'We've got nearly ten minutes. Now we're down here, we should try to see what happened.'

He turned to Kate and they peered over the edge of the steel cover. The water had begun to clear. Still turbid, the larger pieces of material had settled. Pulling out from the shelter, Kate took the lead.

It was only as they came within ten yards of the side of the thing they could make out what it was.

'My God!' Kate exclaimed through her comms. 'It's the fuselage of a plane.' They floated a few yards away from the starboard side of the object.

'Look, its wings have been ripped off almost back to the engines.' Kate manoeuvred through the water to reach within arm's length of the shattered aeroplane, pointing to a bundle of frayed and tangled wires.

Lou turned towards the cockpit, pulling himself up from under the side of the plane and grappling his way over the curved metal. He glanced round, spotting Kate immediately behind him.

'I recognize the shape of this plane,' she said. 'It's a Lockheed Electra. Twin engine.'

'Looks pretty old.'

'First used in the 1930s.'

They reached the glass of the canopy. The hatch was unlocked and vibrated a little in the current. The top was shattered, an opening about a foot wide ran half-way across it. The insides of the rip were discoloured with green slime.

Lou leaned over and peered inside. He was silent for a few seconds then pulled back. 'No bodies.'

He tugged carefully at the jagged glass. The canopy crumbled at his touch, shards of glass tumbling away, falling slowly through the water and exposing the inside of the old cockpit.

It was in surprisingly good condition. 'I think most of the damage to the canopy was recent,' Lou commented. 'Look.' He picked up a dagger of glass left jammed in the metal edging around the rim where it joined the fuselage. 'No slime or any other organic material along the joins. The break in the top is old, smeared with the usual crap.'

'That split would have been enough to have let marine life in to consume the bodies. Wouldn't take long.'

'The hatch of the canopy was open though,' Lou observed.

'Oh yes, strange.'

Kate pulled herself up through the water and turned so she could get a good look inside the cockpit. Lou filmed her and Kate used her camera to get some close-ups.

Lou checked his chronometer. 'Two minutes, max,' he said.

It was a wide, shallow cockpit; two seats, two control wheels, a pair of throttle levers. The instruments looked old-fashioned: large, round dials, heavy Bakelite switches. The leather of the chairs had been almost completely eaten away, just a few slimy brown patches left untouched. Kate poked around the control panel. It was covered with crustaceans.

'Definitely no trace of human remains,' Lou observed, panning the micro camera around to take in the details. 'Better go,' he said.

Lou saw Kate tuck her camera away, then glance back at the inside of the old plane.

'Hang on . . . there's something caught in the foot-well.'

'Kate. Gotta go.'

'One sec.' She slipped head-first into the cockpit until she had almost vanished, only her feet remaining above the canopy rim. Lou could hear her breathing heavily through the comms.

'Damn it!' she hissed.

'Kate . . . please! I don't want you spending the rest of our honeymoon in the tank.'

Kate had reached the footwell and stretched to reach her quarry. 'Almost . . . Got it.'

She curled round gracefully and came into view. Lou could see her smiling through the visor. She was holding up a corroded metal cylinder about the size of a relay runner's baton. 'What're we waiting for?'

5

'I don't think there's any doubt whose plane it was.' Kate surveyed the faces of the three men around the table at one end of the lab aboard *Inca*. At the other end of the small room stood workbenches, specialized equipment bolted down, files in high-sided containers, three swivel stools firmly attached to the deck. Gustav Schwartz was flicking through some stills of the wreck on an iPad.

'You really think it is Amelia Earhart's plane?' Connor Maitland said.

'It stacks up,' Lou said.

Kate flicked on a flat screen on the wall above Lou's head and clicked a remote. The monitor lit up with the film they had shot of the tangled remains of the aeroplane unearthed beside *Victoria*.

'It is definitely a Lockheed Electra. Both wings have very nearly been sheared off, but the engines are still in place. You can see, here and here.' Kate tapped the screen with her fingernail.

'What about the age of it though, Kate? You said when we were down there that the Electras were first put into service in the 1930s. When did Earhart's plane crash?'

'The morning of the 2nd of July 1937, about 8.30. She and her co-pilot Fred Noonan were attempting to land on Howland Island. Their last known position was close to here.'

'You seem to know an awful lot about Amelia Earhart,' Lou commented.

'Early teenage obsession,' Kate replied. 'My mother kept these wonderful old annuals. *The Crackerjack Girl's Own Book, 1959* had this brilliant feature about the great heroine, Amelia Earhart. I was hooked!'

'Cute.' Lou grinned at her.

'So, this is a Lockheed Electra. But there were a lot of different models, right?' Gustav asked.

'I did some checking on Google.' Kate brought up a new screen. It showed the schematic of a twin-engine, stub-nosed aeroplane. 'A 1936 Electra,' she said and superimposed it on a picture they had taken of the wrecked plane. They matched almost perfectly.

'This is a model 10E. Earhart and Noonan were flying a heavily customized model 10E. But here's the clincher.' She clicked the remote to show a picture of Amelia Earhart standing beside her plane taken just before she left Darwin to begin the final stages of her attempted circumnavigation.

'The serial number of Earhart's plane was NR 16020. It was written on each wing. You can't see the wing markings here, and of course the aircraft we've found has lost most of its wings anyway. But look . . .'

She pointed to the screen.

'What?' Lou asked.

'I'll close in.'

Kate tapped at the remote and the image expanded. Then she closed in on a portion of the picture just to the right of Amelia Earhart's hip. They could all see a designation painted into the fuselage. 'NR 16020'.

'Now look at this.' Kate brought up some of the film they had shot. Freezing it on a frame showing the damaged fuselage side on, she refocused the image and zoomed in. They could all see a ragged line of corroded metal running diagonally across the monitor, and to the right, degraded, but still legible a letter 'R' followed by a distorted '160'.

'Shit!' Lou exclaimed and pushed back in his chair, bringing his palms down on the table. 'This is the discovery of the century, Kate!'

She beamed.

'So what now?' Gustav asked. 'Another trip down?'

Lou opened his mouth to reply but Kate cut across him. 'Unfortunately . . .'

'Unfortunately what?' Lou and Connor said in unison.

'I put a probe down there a couple of hours ago. Everything is now too shaky down there. The Electra has destabilized the wreck of *Victoria*. It could fall apart at any moment. Way too dangerous to go down to the plane or the ship again, at least for now.'

'Damn it!' Lou exclaimed. 'You sure, Kate?'

'Well, yeah . . .'

'Sorry, of course you're sure. So, what do we do? Use remote probes like the one you sent down? Get the best images we can? Maybe samples?'

Kate nodded and looked around at the three men. 'That's about it.'

They fell silent for a moment, then Gustav said, 'What caused the plane to rise out of the silt?'

'I've been thinking about that,' Lou replied and gazed around at the others. 'The Chinese.'

'The explosions we heard,' Kate said.

Gustav looked confused.

'Amelia Earhart's plane must have come down close by,' Lou explained. 'The Chinese testing during the past twenty-four hours could have dislodged it.'

*

'Amazing,' Kate said. She got up and walked over to the bench at the other end of the lab. When she returned to the table she was holding a sealed plastic bag containing the metal cylinder she had retrieved from the cockpit.

'What have you and Gustav found out about this?' she asked turning to Lou.

'Well, there was no way we could open it,' he replied and glanced at his assistant. 'That'll have to wait until we get back to the States. But we did every test we could on it.' He slid an iPad across the table and she studied a collection of graphs and tables of data.

'It's a standard steel cylinder, 10.4 inches long, 8.1

inches in circumference. No exterior markings. Plenty of corrosion, as you'd expect, ferrous oxide primarily. As you can see, we stripped away the crustaceans and the rust to look for markings and took detailed photos and film footage every step of the way.'

Kate nodded and looked up, rested her chin on her hand, elbow on the table. 'You took X-rays?' She returned her gaze to the iPad screen.

'Yep, full spectroscopic analysis and thermal imaging. The cylinder is hollow, the steel shell less than an eighth of an inch thick, and there's only one thing inside.'

Kate looked up again.

According to the analysis, there is a single sheet of paper inside the cylinder. It looks to be in good condition. From the dimensions, it appears to be a page from a regular stationery pad.'

'No chance you could read anything on the paper?' Kate asked. They could tell from her tone that she expected nothing.

'Well actually . . .'

'No!'

'I consider myself a humble genius.'

'Lou Bates!' Kate exclaimed.

'I modified the X-ray. Managed to position the cylinder at just the right angle, cut out the internal reflections and . . .'

Kate was shaking her head, eyes like slits. 'What does it say, Lou?'

'Just three words: "REMEMBER JOAN'S PLACE?" in capitals.'

6

'It's only Asti Spumante, I'm afraid.' Gustav held up the bottle as Connor rummaged in a cupboard and came up with four teacups, which he held aloft.

'That will do just fine,' Kate replied. 'We can celebrate in style when we get home.'

'To Amelia,' Lou said and they all clinked cups.

Lou was sitting beside the ship's radio, punching in a call code. A moment later a crackle came from the speaker and a familiar voice spilled into the bridge of *Inca*. It was Cherie Elaine, their French lab tech at the institute.

'Kate, Lou?'

'It's us,' Lou responded. 'Surprisingly bad network connection out here! Had to use the radio.'

'What's up? Is there a problem?'

'Nope, Cherie,' Kate replied. 'In fact, it's all brilliant. We've just made the discovery of the century.'

Cherie was quiet. Lou smiled at Kate. They both knew how reserved their assistant was, how she was not easily excited by big talk.

'OK.'

'We're not certain, but we have strong evidence to suggest we have located Amelia Earhart's plane.'

Another, longer silence.

'What evidence?'

'The right serial number, obviously the right model, a Lockheed Electra 10E.'

'That is, well . . . surprising.'

Lou laughed. 'No . . . really?'

'Where is it? What shape is it in?'

Kate leaned in and explained what had happened. 'We're going to head home, we have some materials that need to be studied.'

'What kind of materials?'

'Rather not say over the radio, Cherie. We're catching a seaplane to Tarawa. Gustav and Connor will stay here for a bit, tidy up loose ends. It'll still take us a couple of days to get back though.'

They cut the connection.

'Let's tell Jerry.' Lou was buzzing.

'Why?'

'He's our best man, Kate. He knew we were coming out here for our . . . what did he call it? "Scientific honeymoon"! He would be thrilled to know what we've found.'

Kate shrugged and stood up, found the wine and topped up their glasses, draining the bottle. Lou dialled in the number on the ship's radio-phone. It rang five times and then clicked over to an answer-machine message: 'Captain Jerry Derham. Please leave a message.'

Lou checked his watch. It was late in Norfolk. He

thought of calling Jerry's mobile. Instead, he kept on the line and said: 'Hey, Jerry. Exciting news. Something really cool – can't talk now though. Kate and me are heading back. Give us a call tomorrow. By then we should be once more in the bosom of cell-phone technology.'

7

Princeton. 7 March 1937.

'Your call is now connected, professor,' said the operator.

'Ah, ah, yes, thank—'

'Albert? Albert, are you there? This is Johannes Kessler.'

'Johannes,' Albert Einstein said, clutching the phone close to his ear as though he were afraid his words would not otherwise cross the Atlantic to Germany. He stared at the two men in uniform sitting the other side of his smoky study. They could hear the conversation through a small speaker the tech guys had set up at the front of Einstein's desk. The two men looked anxious.

'Albert, this is extraordinary.'

'Indeed it is, Johannes, and it's a pleasure to speak to you, but we can marvel at this technology another time. I have to be quick.'

'I understand, Albert.'

One of the men across the room, Major Peter Oakland, head of the intelligence taskforce working with

Professor Einstein on Project Cover Up, uncrossed his legs and leaned forward on his elbow, fingertips to his chin. He and his colleague Hugh Gaynor had set up this secret call, a hi-tech link-up across the Atlantic via radio. They only had a window of three minutes.

'The first test produced an unexpected result,' Einstein said cryptically. 'I cannot emphasize how helpful it would be if you could come for a *visit*.'

The line fell silent.

'Johannes? Are you . . .?'

'Yes, Albert. I am here. I'm afraid a visit would be out of the question. Marlene is too ill to travel.'

'I'm sorry to hear that.'

'I cannot imagine how such a thing could be arranged. I'm . . . I'm being watched.'

It was Einstein's turn to fall quiet. The two army officers stared at him unblinking.

'I see. I imagine you are a very valuable asset to those now in power.'

'It would appear so, Albert. I cannot leave Germany.'

Einstein sighed. 'I need you, Johannes. *We* . . . need you.'

There was a sudden crackle down the line. The two army officers looked at each other, but then Kessler's voice came over the speaker.

'I'm flattered my old friend, but I cannot come.'

'What are we to do?' Einstein looked lost.

'Can you elaborate, Albert?'

Einstein peered up at the ceiling and took a deep breath. 'There is something missing in my equations. I wish I knew what it was, but, although on paper the theory seems to be without fault, it will not translate into practice.'

'Can you say what happened with the test?'

Einstein looked at the two men. Oakland shook his head.

'Unfortunately . . .'

'Very well. You had the juice?' Kessler asked, using one of the code words they had developed when they were young post-docs working together in Berlin.

'The juice flowed, reached its destination.'

'And the green balloon went up?'

'It did.'

'My God, Albert!'

'That is where it deviated from the ideal, let us say.'

'Look, Albert. I will do all I can to help you. This work is important, not just to you and your friends.'

Einstein gazed at Oakland and Gaynor. They were far from being friends to him and all three men knew it.

'But how, Johannes?'

'I've not been entirely idle, old friend. I have been giving our old ideas a lot of thought recently. I could send you my work.'

'Too dangerous, Johannes. It could fall into the wrong hands.'

Kessler fell silent again.

'Unless,' Einstein said. 'This is just an idea. Could you encode the work?'

Kessler cleared his throat. 'Well, yes, yes, I could.'

'Then that would be the best option other than you being here in person.'

'It would have to be as unbreakable a code as possible.'

'I'm sure you could manage that,' Einstein answered.

'What about the cipher? How will you . . .?'

'We can sort that out.' Einstein glanced at Major Oakland, who gave his colleague a brief questioning look then nodded to the professor.

'Very well. What next?'

Oakland caught Einstein's eye and tapped his watch.

'Johannes, time is running out. We will get instructions to you.'

'Very well,' Kessler said again. 'I will await—'

'Johannes? Johannes?' Einstein pulled the phone away from his ear and stared at it. The line was dead.

8

The two army officers, Major Peter Oakland and Captain Hugh Gaynor, walked along the path from the door to Albert Einstein's home at 112 Mercer Street and opened the gate onto the pavement, where their car was waiting. A young private was at the wheel. He jumped out and opened the back door for the men to enter, snapping to attention as they shuffled in.

It was a bleak, cold afternoon, rain clouds tumbling in from the east. Oakland offered Gaynor a cigarette and lit one himself, drawing on it hungrily. Keeping it perched between his lips, he lifted his briefcase from between his feet and pulled a Manila file from inside, snapped the bag closed and returned it to the floor. Flicking his ash into the tray on the back of the driver's seat, Oakland passed the file over to Gaynor.

'You can keep this,' he said. 'They're carbons.'

Gaynor looked at the blue single-spaced type.

'It's everything we have on Johannes Kessler.'

Captain Gaynor read through the first couple of pages. Oakland gave him a running commentary.

'A super brain, apparently. Gives old Albert a run for

his money, some say. Kessler and Einstein were close colleagues in Berlin. Einstein was director of the Kaiser Wilhelm Institute for Physics. Kessler is ten years younger, but he was one of Einstein's top people there. They did a lot of work together; nothing published, but fellow scientists have talked about what close friends they were and that between them they cooked up some amazing ideas.'

'I see.' Gaynor looked up from the file. 'But Kessler has no intention of leaving Germany?'

'He's not Jewish, Hugh. And is highly regarded by the Nazis. But he has made it very clear, secretly of course, that he has no allegiance to them. Friends claim he hates the Reich, but cannot leave. He certainly does not suffer from self-doubt when it comes to his intellect – probably with good reason.'

'This stinks, sir. I'm sorry, but can we really trust these guys? A couple of Krauts. And one of them is still in Germany!'

Major Oakland couldn't help laughing. 'You're talking about two of the most respected scientists in the world, Captain. And, strictly speaking, Einstein is not German, he's a Swiss citizen.'

'Still Krauts.'

'All right, you're entitled to your opinion, but the simple fact is we've been told we have to make this work. Our job is to ensure the whole thing runs smoothly, no leaks, no betrayals. I know a fortune is being pumped into Project Cover Up. I'm not privy to details of course, but it's clearly pretty hot. We all know war is coming, Hugh. We might not like it, but that won't stop it happening.'

'So what do we do?' Gaynor asked, grinding his cigarette into the metal grille of the ashtray.

'We make sure there's a tight lid on anything Kessler is exposed to. Can't let him have anything we unearth this end. It's gotta be a one-way street. Get Kessler to send Einstein the material, but he must not send anything back. We can't even let Kessler know if tests start to work or not.'

'OK, but how do we get anything out of Kessler without the Nazis learning about it?' asked Oakland.

'That's the big question. The two of them were talking about codes. If anyone can create an unbreakable code it would be those two, but how do we get it over here without risking it falling into German hands?'

Oakland looked out at the flat almost featureless landscape as rain started to hit the glass. 'Just have to hope one of the high-ups who so desperately want this project to succeed comes up with a foolproof way to get Kessler's work here, or else the whole scheme is dead in the water.'

9

London. Present day.

It was off-peak, a rainy spring Thursday when the three of them stepped into the capsule of the London Eye and ensured no one else would occupy the same space. Two men and a woman. The woman was Glena Buckingham, the older of the two men was Hans Secker. The younger man, bespectacled and bearded in a rather fusty tweed jacket, was known to the other two under a false name, Herman Toit. All they knew about him was that he was South African, purportedly thirty-four years old and an ex-mercenary who had worked in Angola and Eritrea. A trained killer, Toit had secretly served Eurenergy for close to fifteen months and was the replacement for a man called Sterling Van Lee, who had headed up Eurenergy Security before him.

Glena seated herself facing east towards Docklands as the vista of London began to spread out before them. Toit settled into one of the row of seats across the capsule opposite her, though Secker remained standing.

Buckingham had made an effort to merge into the background by opting for jeans and a plain cotton jacket. Large sunglasses covered about twenty per cent of her face. Secker was dressed in his usual exquisitely tailored, slightly old-fashioned suit and Windsor-knotted spotted tie. He could have easily passed as a banker or City broker.

'So what is your news, Herman?' Buckingham asked.

Toit didn't look at the woman for a long moment. Instead, he contemplated the clear horizon: Kingston, Richmond, Teddington.

'It could be very important, or it could be nothing of great value.' He had retained a faint Afrikaans accent. 'I have received intel from a reliable source that MI6 has acquired reports that may shed some light upon a strange experiment conducted during the 1930s.'

'Sounds like the sort of shit Internet conspiracy theorists get into a foam about,' Secker replied.

'What sort of experiment?' Buckingham cut in.

'The cranks refer to it incorrectly as the Philadelphia Experiment.'

Secker couldn't hold back a grin. Buckingham snapped round and gave him a hard look. His expression straightened.

'And?'

'It appears some version of the experiment did indeed occur and was run by a very senior and respected scientist. It was not conducted in Philadelphia, but in Norfolk, Virginia and a few years before the date set by most "experts" on the subject. I'm still trying to establish who the scientist was.'

'The Philadelphia Experiment is considered to be an urban myth, Herman. Why should we countenance the story?'

'I know,' Toit replied and pulled himself up from the seat. He towered over the diminutive Secker. 'But apparently Six are taking it seriously.'

'OK,' Buckingham said. 'But what relevance does it have to anything?'

'I only have a brief report to go by, but two things about it jumped out at me. The first is that the experiment was considered at the time to be one of utmost importance to the US military.'

'When was this exactly?'

'1937.'

'Right.'

'The events were secured under a Triple A intelligence rating, which meant that no one had access to the facts for a minimum of a hundred years. Even then, it appears MI6 acquired the information by fluke.'

'How? What sort of fluke?' Secker asked.

'I have no idea.'

'The second fact?' Buckingham said.

Toit paused again before answering. His eyes turned to the buildings close to the London Eye: the Houses of Parliament across the river, the Admiralty, Westminster Abbey. 'I heard through the grapevine that you spotted something quite extraordinary using the new satellite network controlled out of Flotta.'

'You are well-informed.'

'It's my job.'

'Go on.'

'According to my information, the experiment in 1937 had some close connection with a very famous woman of the time.' He pursed his lips, glanced at his shoes and then turned his gaze straight into Glena Buckingham's eyes. 'Amelia Earhart.'

10

Ignoring each other as though they had not exchanged a word on the thirty-minute journey, as the capsule of the London Eye completed one full revolution and skimmed slowly along the egress–ingress platform, Herman Toit had parted company with his employers. He had then turned left while Secker and Buckingham hung a right.

The Eurenergy executives were met by a chauffeur-driven BMW that slipped onto Belvedere Road en route to the company's Hammersmith headquarters. Toit walked north beside the grey-brown Thames towards grimy concrete steps that led up to Waterloo Bridge.

It had clouded over, the temperature dropping a few degrees. Toit walked at a brisk pace towards the Strand. He turned as a black cab slowed and drew to a stop at the kerb. The driver's window wound down, and a thin man with black hair and dark shades leaned over.

'I have a message for you, Mr Toit.'

Toit, all senses alert, looked back along the bridge towards the Bullring and the Imax cinema. 'I'm all ears.'

'Could we drive a short while, sir?'

Toit glanced into the interior of the cab to see it was empty, then pulled on the handle and slipped inside. The cab drove away before he was seated. Beside him on the leather seat lay an iPad. Toit picked it up and instantly the screen flickered to life.

A heavily pixelated face filled the screen and a man's distorted voice spilled from the tiny speaker.

'You come highly recommended, Mr Toit.'

Toit stared impassively at the screen and noticed the driver concentrating on the road as they approached the Strand.

'We would be interested in employing you.'

'I am already spoken for.'

'But paid insufficiently I would imagine.'

Toit pursed his lips and looked out at the traffic and the stone buildings. 'Go on.'

'We would like to secure your exclusive services for a particular task.'

'I've never been keen on the word "exclusive".'

'I believe, Mr Toit, that in this case, when you hear our terms, you will be.'

' "Our"? I like to know who I'm being propositioned by.'

A short laugh from the speaker. 'That is quite fair. My operational name is Ming Lo. I am a representative of Ling Chi, Minister of State Security in Beijing.'

'I see.'

'We have recently learned that a rather dangerous artefact has been discovered in the Pacific.'

Toit could not hide his surprise completely.

'You should not expect our intelligence people to be any less efficient than your present employers, nor indeed the agencies of the West.'

'I don't,' Toit responded. 'I'm just unclear as to how you have concluded this find is at all dangerous. Is it not an academic matter?'

'If it were of purely scholarly interest why would you meet your employers in such a clandestine manner? And why would Glena Buckingham be so interested in the aforementioned artefact?'

'So, what do you require of me, if your people are so efficient?'

The small laugh again. 'Personally, I like your attitude, Mr Toit, but you would not do well working within the official agencies in my country.'

'Then, Mr Ming, it is fortunate that working in Beijing is not on my bucket list.' He glanced at his watch. 'I've a busy evening ahead of me, so if you could please come to the point.'

The line was silent for a moment. 'We believe the relic discovered by the pair of researchers from the Institute of Marine Studies is more than a trophy for a billionaire fan of Amelia Earhart. I would ask you to study the attached document.'

Toit tapped the screen and Ming's face was replaced with a file. He opened it and sat in silence for a few minutes, reading. He then touched the link once more and the blurred face reappeared.

'Exclusivity is expensive.'

He could see the man's expression change through the digital camouflage. 'We are not poor.'

Toit rubbed his fingers across his chin. 'OK. You have my attention.'

11

Ten minutes after their meeting with Toit, Glena Buckingham and Hans Secker were seated in the back of the black BMW760Li and in spite of the fact that the car had recently been purchased for a little over £100,000, it was stuck in traffic like a jalopy.

Buckingham looked out at the crowds of commuters either side of Pall Mall, the grand grey facade of the Reform Club and the throng of besuited workers crossing the entrances to St James's Square.

'It would be faster to walk,' Buckingham declared. A beep came from a flat screen on the back of the driver's seat. She touched the screen and a man's face appeared. He looked flushed, a bead of sweat nestled in his philtrum.

'Joyce,' Buckingham said to her Deputy Chief of Operations (Southern Region). 'You look positively glowing.'

Joyce took a deep breath. 'Some interesting news, ma'am.' He swallowed and straightened in his seat. 'Just picked up a transmission from close to the new Chinese island, Dalton.'

'Stop before you say anything else. I take it this is a scrambled line?'

'Of course.'

'Go on.'

Secker was leaning to his right to better see the screen. Buckingham could smell his breath.

'My team is aware of your memo, ma'am – about the plane spotted using the equipment on Flotta. They will keep their eyes peeled and ears to the ground for anything linked with it. We only caught fragments of this recent transmission, but we've pinpointed it, and Flotta IDed the caller. It came from a chartered ship, *Inca*, moored off Howland close to Dalton.'

Buckingham raised an eyebrow. 'What was the gist of the transmission?'

'The caller mentioned finding Amelia Earhart's plane.' He glanced at some papers in front of him. 'A Lockheed Electra 10E?'

'Oh my goodness!' Buckingham brought a hand to her mouth. Neither Joyce nor Secker had seen their boss demonstrate such emotion before.

Buckingham nodded as though she were processing the information, then she glanced out at the milling office workers. 'That is . . . excellent news, Joyce.'

'I have some of the message. We caught the tail end of it.' He tapped a key on his laptop. A second of quiet hiss spilled from the speaker of the headrest screen and then a man's laughter could be heard. '*No . . . really?*'

Then a woman's voice, a trace of a French accent. '*Where is it? What shape is it in?*'

A pause, then a different woman. *'We're going to head home, we have some materials that need to be studied.'*

The first woman spoke again. *'What kind of materials?'*

'Rather not say over the radio, Cherie. We're catching a seaplane to Tarawa. Gustav and Connor will stay here for a bit, tidy up loose ends. It'll still take us a couple of days to get back though.'

The transmission ended abruptly.

'This ship?' Buckingham asked. 'Anything?'

'Chartered in the Gilbert Islands five days ago. Booking in the name of the Institute of Marine Studies, Hampton, Virginia. The lead names are . . .' He glanced down again.

'Doctors Wetherall and Bates,' Buckingham interjected.

Joyce looked up, puzzled.

'I'm familiar with the names.' Buckingham turned and gave Hans Secker a frosty look.

'How long ago was this call made?' he asked.

'Two seventeen a.m., our time, sir. I was only informed at noon. I then checked it through Flotta.'

'You did well, Joyce,' Buckingham said distracted. 'Anything else?'

'No, ma'am.'

Buckingham spun on Secker and narrowed her eyes. 'Sounds like we have a little time, Hans.' She checked her Patek Philippe. 'They may still be in the Gilbert Islands even if they left the ship soon after the transmission. I want them found and followed. They must have retrieved something of value from the remains of the aircraft. They hinted at it. Whatever it is, I want it.'

12

Off Howland Island, Pacific Ocean. Present day.

Lou held his hand up to shield his eyes as he stared out over the endless horizon.

'There it is,' he said and turned to Kate.

She saw a flash of light as the evening sun reflected off the approaching seaplane, a Canadair CL-215. They could see its canary yellow fuselage as it came closer and banked round, reaching the surface of the ocean about a hundred feet to *Inca*'s starboard.

Their assistant Gustav was waiting for them in the launch with their luggage and equipment. Kate gave their other junior, Connor, a hug and Lou shook his hand.

'See you back home,' Lou said. 'No sunbathing, we want a full analysis of that wreck before you leave here.'

Connor gave him a mock salute and Lou and Kate descended the ladder to the launch.

*

The flat, pristine blue of the Pacific dropped away beneath them as the seaplane took off towards the setting sun. It was a three-hour flight to Tarawa, the main island in the Gilberts. For most of the journey, Lou and Kate spoke little, Lou absorbed in his book and Kate with her headphones on listening to music.

Lou put his book down on his lap and tapped Kate on the arm. She pulled off the headphones, the music spilling out. Lou nodded to her MP3 player and she switched it off.

'I can't figure out why Amelia Earhart had the cylinder in the cockpit,' he said. 'She must have been involved in something.'

'I imagine she was. There have long been rumours she was a spy and that her plane crash was no accident.'

'Tell me more.'

'Well, she was a very experienced pilot and the attempt to circumnavigate the globe had been planned meticulously. They were flying in clear weather, early in the morning, and aiming to land at Howland.'

'Where were they headed?'

'You don't really know anything about her, do you, Lou?'

He raised his eyebrows. 'I was more into baseball players.'

'OK. Well you know she was probably the most famous woman in the world at the time she died?'

'Err . . .' Lou shook his head.

'She lived at a time when women didn't do things like fly planes. About two years before her death she had started to plan the most audacious flight anyone could imagine – a circumnavigation of the globe. She had a navigator with her, a man called Fred Noonan. They set off from Miami, flying to South America, across the Atlantic to Africa, then on to South East Asia, Australia and Papua New Guinea. Eventually they flew across the Pacific to Honolulu, planning to fly over to the mainland of America and back down to Miami. Needless to say, they didn't make it to Honolulu.'

'And there's no evidence of her being involved in any strange conspiracies? There has to be a reason for the cylinder and the cryptic message inside.'

'I agree.' Kate gazed out of her window to the vast expanse of water, the sun low over the waves. 'There have always been loads of stories linked to her disappearance, obviously. If one of the world's most famous women disappears on a trans-Pacific flight at a time when war was brewing, it's bound to spark all sorts of rumours.'

She pulled out her phone, checked for a signal, was pleasantly surprised to see she had a couple of bars and called up Google. A moment later they were looking at a website called: *Amelia Earhart: 10 Conspiracy Theories*. She scrolled down and they both read the screen.

'Yep, all there,' Lou commented. 'Alien abduction, suicide, murder, captured by the Japanese.'

'And a theory she was a spy for the US government.'

'That's not in the same league as alien abduction.'

'No, it's not!' Kate laughed. 'The US military helped to fund her trip. That's a documented fact. The intelligence service would have wanted something in return, you can be sure of that.'

'All right, well it's all food for thought,' Lou concluded. They felt the plane begin to descend. A voice came over the cabin PA. 'Doctors Bates and Wetherall, we're about to begin our descent into Kiribati. Please buckle up. We should be landing at Bonriki International Airport in about ten minutes.'

*

It was probably the smallest and shabbiest 'international' airport in the world. Consisting of two large huts joined by a glass-covered walkway, it boasted hand-painted signs to 'Customs' and 'Quarantine' and a handful of very laidback staff. From Kiribati, Kate and Lou had to first travel in the opposite direction to their final destination. A 727 took them west to Brisbane, and from there they flew east on a direct flight to Los Angeles.

*

Landing at LAX, Lou opened a fresh text from Jerry Derham, a reply to his answer-phone message asking what the exciting news was about.

'Don't call him again,' Kate said to Lou as they

headed towards the departure lounge for the connecting flight to Norfolk. 'We'll be there in a few hours. You never know who's listening in to mobiles.'

'A little paranoid, isn't it?'

'Maybe, but the paranoid are usually the last to die.'

Lou texted back: 'Can't explain now. About to board flight home. Stopover in Des Moines. ETA Norfolk, 6.05 p.m. Will call then.'

*

They managed to snatch a few hours of fitful sleep. The in-flight food was almost inedible, they had seen all the movies before and they hit severe turbulence half an hour before reaching Norfolk, leaving them unsettled and anxious. By the time they arrived at Norfolk International Airport, night was drawing in. They felt wrung out and jet-lagged.

Passing through passport control in a daze, they collected their cases and loaded a pair of trolleys with their personal luggage and a large metal box containing their equipment and samples. Before leaving *Inca* they had wrapped the canister from Amelia Earhart's plane in bubble wrap and enclosed it in a padded envelope. Lou had put this into his briefcase, never letting it out of his sight.

'We need some good strong coffee before we pick up the car,' he remarked, turning to Kate walking wearily beside him.

She forced a half smile. 'At least a gallon for me.'

They saw the green NOTHING TO DECLARE sign to their right and headed for it. Passing the first manned desk, they approached the second and last and were about to turn into the arrivals lounge when they heard a voice.

'Sir, madam.'

They did not think it was a call to them at first and kept walking.

'Sir, madam.' This time much louder.

They turned in unison and manoeuvred the trolley over to the desk. Behind it stood two customs officers, a tall thin man with steel-rimmed glasses and a stocky woman whose blue officer's blouse was a size too small.

'We have nothing to declare,' Lou said.

The female customs officer ignored him. 'Could you place your bags on the counter, please.'

Lou leaned down and laid the metal box and the two suitcases next to each other on the counter.

'Names please,' the male officer asked.

'Dr Lou Bates.'

'Dr Kate Wetherall.'

The two officers turned their attention to the metal equipment case, trying the latch.

Lou looked at Kate, who was staring at the male officer.

'You have the key?' he said.

'It's scientific equipment,' Kate began. 'We are researchers, just returned from a project in the Pacific.'

'Could you open it, please, sir?' the woman asked Lou.

He shrugged and pulled a key from his jacket pocket, leaned across and opened the lid of the metal box. Inside lay a powerful microscope, a smaller box of samples, a collection of metal lab utensils and a small spectroscopic analyser.

The female officer shuffled along behind the counter and she and her colleague picked up the smaller box.

'Please be careful, those are delicate samples,' Kate said and glanced at Lou.

The male officer poked at the box. 'What sort of samples?'

'From a shipwreck.'

'A shipwreck?'

Lou picked up his briefcase. 'We have a licence to bring samples into the country. Here . . .' He reached into his bag and withdrew a folder of papers.

'These will have to be checked,' the woman said not looking up from the contents of the metal box. Between them she and her colleague shifted the box to a table alongside the counter. She turned to Kate and Lou's suitcases and unzipped the nearest one.

Kate and Lou stood still, silently watching every move the customs officers made. They rummaged through the cases with experienced movements, lifting piles of clothes, feeling around the edges of the cases, flipping open the toiletry bags.

A third officer appeared to their left, leading a Labrador on a tight leash. He walked over to the counter and the dog pulled up to sniff around the bags. The handler then took the dog over to the table and the

Labrador nosed around the instruments and boxes in the metal case, before falling back on all fours and looking up at his master. The two officers at the counter nodded to the third man and he walked off with the dog in tow.

The female officer shut the cases and started to zip them up, Kate and Lou finished the job and Lou was about to lift them off the counter and back onto the trolley when the tall thin man said: 'Could we take a look at your hand luggage please?'

Kate placed her shoulder bag and a small camera bag on the counter. Lou lifted his briefcase from where it had been resting at his feet.

The customs officers emptied out the contents of Kate's bag. A container of make-up, a pen, a purse and a mess of receipts and gum packets spread across the counter. The woman shuffled through the collection and placed each item back into the bag. Next she turned her attention to the camera bag, pulled out a top-end Nikon, felt around inside the bag and then returned the camera.

The male officer pulled Lou's briefcase along the shiny metal surface of the counter. 'Key please, Dr Bates.' Lou pulled a key from his pocket and handed it over.

The man removed the items from the case. A laptop, a file of papers, a copy of *New Scientist* and the padded envelope containing the cylinder from Amelia Earhart's plane. He went straight for the envelope and felt the shape of the object inside.

'What's this?'

'It is connected with our work,' Lou began. 'A sample we removed from a wreck.'

The officer held his gaze. 'Could you open it please, Dr Bates?'

'Sure.' He peeled back the flap of the envelope and removed the cylinder swathed in bubble wrap.

'Keep going.'

Lou glanced at Kate. She shrugged and Lou pulled back the wrapping, then laid it on the counter with the cylinder resting in the middle.

The officer went to pick it up.

'Please,' Lou said a little louder and more aggressively than he had intended, 'it's a delicate item. We are taking it to our lab for analysis.' The two officers gave him a dark look.

The man lifted it with exaggerated care. Lou exhaled loudly.

The officer turned it around end to end and looked closely at its corroded metal skin.

'What is it?' the woman asked.

'I'm afraid that is confidential,' Kate replied.

'Could you open it please?' The man held it out to Lou.

'No!' Kate exclaimed. 'Now this has gone far enough. We have done nothing wrong. You have seen our licence and other documentation. We are on a perfectly legal and legitimate expedition. This is a delicate and precious—'

'Dr Wetherall.'

'I insist—'

'You are not in a position to insist upon anything,' the male customs officer snapped and glared at Kate. He turned back to Lou. 'Dr Bates, could you open it please?'

'Definitely not,' Lou answered. 'It is an artefact from our studies. If I open it, any contents will crumble to nothing.'

The man looked a little taken aback by that. He glanced at his colleague. 'Please wait here, I will have to consult my superior.' He walked away from them quickly.

Lou spotted a sign over a door that said CUSTOMS INTERVIEW ROOMS 1–4, and marched over to it, pushing it open.

Finding himself in a small side room, he saw a woman behind a counter and paced over to it, slapping both hands down. 'What is all this about?' Lou hissed, leaning forward.

'Could you please remove your hands from the counter, sir,' the woman said.

Lou looked down at his hands then back up at the woman. 'This is outrageous. What is all this about?'

'Unless you remove your hands from the counter I will be forced to place you in custody.'

Kate came up behind Lou and tapped him on the shoulder. He straightened with a heavy sigh, and they went back to their luggage.

A door opened and the customs officer entered. Following him was another, older man, and two paces behind them strode an armed guard, machine gun at his waist. The two men walked round behind the counter, the guard stood a few feet to their right eyeing Lou and Kate.

'My name is Mr Manor,' the older man said. 'I am the most senior officer here. I'm afraid we will have to confiscate all your luggage, your briefcases and personal items, including this.' He nodded towards the cylinder resting in the bubble wrap.

'What!' Kate exploded. 'What possible reason . . .?'

'Dr Wetherall, Dr Bates, please, we are required to inspect these items. They will be properly cared for, and if they do not transgress regulations, after we have finished with them, they will be returned to you. You will be placed in custody until our investigations have reached a satisfactory conclusion.'

'That's ridiculous!' Lou said, his face flushed. 'We are not carrying anything illegal. We have permits and licences. Check the damn paperwork, man.'

'We will, Dr Bates. In the meantime we have to take the precaution of confiscating your luggage so that it may undergo close analysis.'

Lou lost it and made a grab for the cylinder. The female customs officer was closest to him and looked startled. Kate emitted a small scream. The armed guard stepped forward, lifted the gun and pointed it at Lou.

'Sir,' he yelped. 'Step away and raise your hands.'

Lou did not react.

The guard took another step forward. 'Step away

and raise your hands.' They could all hear the guard prime the gun.

'Lou!' Kate screamed.

He stepped back and raised his hands.

13

Smithsonian Institute, Washington DC. 25 March 1937.

It was a rare occasion for Amelia Earhart . . . she was wearing a cocktail dress.

'Gosh, I feel so damned awkward in this thing,' she remarked, accepting a glass of champagne from her husband, George Putnam, who stood at the doorway beside a man holding a tray of drinks.

'Feel happier in the old leather jacket and pants, Amelia?'

'Sure would.' She surveyed the crowded main hall of the Smithsonian Castle building on the National Mall. 'I don't know more than one per cent of these people,' she added in a low voice.

'The great and the good, darling. And if the truth be told, ninety-nine per cent of them are not worth knowing!'

Amelia laughed and shook her head. 'You are pure evil, Georgie.'

They stepped into the room and heads turned as applause grew. Amelia smiled and felt George squeeze her hand. The band in the far corner struck up with 'Dixie'. George let go of her hand and walked over to a small group of men. Amelia turned to see the First Lady, Eleanor Roosevelt, looking stately in a grey silk dress, her brown hair in two whirls at her temples. She was smiling at her and clapping decorously.

'Well you do scrub up nicely, my dear,' she said.

'I feel ridiculous!' Amelia kissed her old friend on the cheek and the two women hugged.

'It's a splendid turn-out.'

Earhart nodded and took a sip of champagne as she cast her eyes around the gathering. She leaned in to Eleanor's ear. 'I just hope they're all in a generous mood.'

A tall man in a dinner jacket approached and gave a slight bow to the two women. 'We are ready when you are, Mrs Roosevelt.'

Amelia took a deep breath. 'Well, time and tide and all that.' She gave Eleanor Roosevelt a nervous look.

'Between us we'll knock 'em dead.' The First Lady squeezed Amelia's elbow.

Eleanor led the way across the room, parting the throng as she went. The band was still playing, a more modern tune now; Amelia recognized it, one of her current favourites, Benny Goodman's 'Stompin' at the Savoy'. The gathered wealthy of Washington and New York seemed relaxed, lubricated with free-flowing champagne.

The two women reached a podium at one end of the room and the music faded to nothing. Amelia could hear the hubbub of conversation dwindle to silence. She stood to one side of a wooden lectern and the First Lady walked calmly up to the microphone; it squeaked as she approached. Pausing, she surveyed the hundreds of faces: politicians, business moguls and patrons of the arts and sciences accompanied by their bejewelled wives.

'Ladies and gentlemen.' She had a rather frail, high-pitched voice, but years of experience as the wife of the 32nd president had imbued her with confidence. 'It was with enormous pleasure that I accepted the invitation to be here this evening, in this magnificent setting; and it too is an honour to introduce to you one of the greatest women alive today. This lady is not only a cherished friend of mine and my husband's, but as you will all know, she is one of this country's most respected ambassadors, renowned throughout the world for her pioneering achievements as an aviator, a woman dedicated to pushing back the boundaries of what is possible. To me, it seems unimaginable that anyone could climb into a machine and fly across oceans and continents, but my friend here does it before breakfast. She needs no further introduction. I give you Amelia Earhart.'

Eleanor Roosevelt stepped down as Amelia took the podium to warm applause.

'Well, my goodness!' she began and turned to the First Lady seated at the side of the dais. 'Was that really me you were describing?'

A warm ripple of laughter passed through the gathering and Amelia took a deep breath.

'The reason I'm here tonight is to tell you all about the flight I hope to begin in just a few months from now, in June. And, I must confess, I'm also here to pass around the begging bowl.'

Another peal of gentle laughter and Amelia gazed around, found her husband George a few rows back and focused on him as she started to speak again.

'You would have all heard of the unfortunate circumstances of my first attempt to circumnavigate the globe, and ending up in Hawaii.' She produced a good-natured laugh and pulled a face. 'That was galling to say the least!' She put a hand on her hip and produced a self-disparaging grimace which solicited another laugh from the crowd.

'But we have regrouped and reworked things and we plan to give it another go starting on June 1st.'

Two men in overalls shuffled behind Amelia manoeuvring into place an easel holding a five-foot-square map of the world. Across it stretched a zigzagging red line.

'The journey is scheduled to begin in Oakland,' Amelia explained and tapped the map with a wooden pointer handed to her by one of the men. 'This time we intend to travel west to east, the opposite way to our last attempt. From Oakland, we fly south-east to Miami and then on to Natal in Brazil.' She moved the pointer. 'From there we cross the Atlantic to Dakar, Senegal in West Africa; across Africa, on to Karachi and Calcutta, then Singapore and south to Darwin,

Australia. We then take on the Pacific, perhaps the most arduous stage of the journey. We take a break in Hawaii and hope to fly from there to Oakland.'

The audience was hushed. The ladies looked stunned; some of the men wore sceptical expressions.

'Twenty-nine thousand miles in all,' Amelia went on. 'Quite a trek!' She glanced at the rapt faces. 'Now, I would like to introduce to you my navigator on this voyage, Mr Fred Noonan.'

A tall, elegantly dressed man in his mid-forties with slicked-back dark-brown hair started to walk through the applauding crowd to the podium. Looking rather serious, he reached the lectern and pecked Amelia on the cheek. Turning to the audience, he wore a slender smile. 'Thank you.'

Amelia saw her husband in the throng. He was clapping, a cigar wedged between his teeth.

'I'm very much second fiddle in all this,' Noonan commented. 'Amelia is the star, and rightly so. My job is just to make sure we don't get lost!'

The two aviators stepped down to the floor as the crowd whooped and applauded loudly. With Eleanor Roosevelt, they turned. Amelia could see the faces of her audience, expressions of admiration, scepticism, envy, disbelief from some. Noonan was patted on the back, a respectful path was cleared for the First Lady, and in a few moments the band struck up again. George Putnam appeared at his wife's elbow, an aura of cigar smoke about his face.

'Excellent show, sweetheart,' he said and kissed her

on the cheek. 'You look like you could do with another glass of bubbly.' Putnam turned and collared a waiter, plucked up two glasses from a tray and handed one to Amelia.

'Do you really think it went well, Georgie?'

'I do. A triumph.' He was about to add something when they were interrupted by a man wearing a dark-brown suit and trilby. George gave him a puzzled look.

The man removed his hat, ignored George Putnam and said to Amelia. 'Miss Earhart, I'm sorry to interrupt you.'

'What is it?' Amelia replied, eyes narrowing.

'Could I ask you to come with me?'

She looked startled and turned to her husband.

'I'm sorry, I don't mean to alarm you,' the stranger added. 'It's just for a few minutes. My superior would like to have a brief word with you.'

'Your superior?'

The man leaned into Amelia's ear. 'The president, Miss Earhart. The president wants a word.'

14

George went to object. 'Now look here . . .'

Amelia silenced him with a glance, then placed a gentle hand on his. 'Relax, George. It's OK. I'll be back in a minute.' The man in the suit led the way across the hall. No one took much notice. In a moment they had reached the door, crossed a corridor and were soon out in the crisp, cool night, the noise of the gathering in the hall dwindling to nothing.

The president's black Lincoln was parked across a small lane close to the rear loading bay of the museum. A man dressed in a black suit and trilby was leaning back against the bonnet smoking a cigarette. Amelia could see the driver at the wheel and hear the purr of the big engine ticking over.

'This way please, Miss Earhart.' The agent held her elbow gently, and guided her towards the rear of the car. The man leaning on the bonnet stood up, and opened the back door. Amelia peered inside the car, saw President Roosevelt and lowered herself onto the soft leather seat.

'I'm sorry about the cloak and dagger stuff, Amelia,'

the elderly man said. His voice sounded tired. She looked into his dark eyes and thought he appeared especially unwell this evening. His cheeks were carved with deep worry lines and the skin around his mouth sagged a little.

'I'm intrigued, sir.'

'Good.' He took a deep breath and glanced out of the car window to the darkness laced by a dim glow from a distant street lamp at the junction of a lane and a broader street running beside the main building. He turned back to face Amelia.

'The fact is, we need your help.'

'Well . . . Sure, anything I can do.'

Roosevelt held her gaze for a moment. 'It's an intelligence matter.'

'And I assume you cannot tell me too much about it?'

'No, you're right, I can't.'

'OK. What do I have to do?'

Roosevelt interlaced his long thin fingers on his lap and looked down at them. 'We need you to pick up a package from one of the stopovers on your planned flight. They tell me you are refuelling at Dakar, Senegal.'

'How did you know that, sir? I only just . . .'

Roosevelt held up a hand. 'I told you, Amelia, it's an intelligence matter.' He tapped the side of his nose. 'Dakar would be the best place for you to collect the item. It will be delivered by British Intelligence.'

'What do I have to do with this package?'

'Bring it back home.'

'I see,' Amelia replied. 'Sounds simple.'

'I'm not ordering you to do this, my dear. I only want it done if we have your explicit agreement.'

'That makes it sound bad, Franklin.' Earhart allowed herself the privilege of using the president's first name. She had known him a long time and thought of him as a family friend. 'You wouldn't be saying this if it were straightforward, would you now?'

Roosevelt considered her seriously. 'I won't lie; there is an element of danger. The contents of the package are extremely valuable to us. And of course that means they would also be very valuable to others.'

'Things really are hotting up in Europe then . . .'

Roosevelt turned his gaze back to the night. Still looking out of the window he said: 'They are, but I have absolutely no intention of drawing this country into any damn mess our friends across the Atlantic get sucked into. However, there are some matters of intelligence, some opportunities, let us say, that cannot be ignored.'

'Well, as I said, sir, I'll do anything I can.'

Roosevelt turned back and took Amelia's hands in his. She could see the veins on the back of his gnarled left hand, a cluster of liver spots in the fleshy skin above his knuckles. 'My Secret Service guys have told me you should remember a code word to use if you ever doubt the veracity of anyone you meet claiming they are ours or from the British. The word is: "Pioneer".'

'I see,' said Amelia. 'I'm flattered, sir.'

'We'll make the necessary arrangements,' he said. 'And, Amelia, thank you.'

15

Norfolk International Airport, Virginia. Present day.

It was stifling in the small room. Lou sat on an uncomfortable metal chair bolted to the floor, his legs under a table that had also been bolted into the concrete. There was no window, and the only light came from a stark bulb dangling from a cord. He had been marched off along a corridor straight to this room, catching a glimpse of Kate as she was escorted to another room on the other side of the main hall. Glancing at his watch, he saw that it had been nearly ninety minutes ago.

What had happened back there? Sure, he had been tired and he had always had a problem with authority; but why had they been picked on in the first place? And why had the customs people been so interested in the cylinder? They couldn't possibly know how significant it might be.

He took a deep breath of stale warm air and wondered if Kate was OK. Had they interrogated her? Was that the reason for the wait? Or had they simply wanted him to stew for a bit, get him really worried?

Lou got up from the chair and started pacing the tiny room, in tight circles around the table and chair, head down, thinking, thinking, trying to rationalize, work out a way to get things back on track. He had behaved irrationally, he knew that, lost his cool. Over the past hour and a half though he had pulled himself together, begun to think straight, be logical, be practical. Kate would certainly have made a better showing, he was sure of that. She was always more analytical than him, always the 'sensible, cool one'. She had got him out of many scrapes; maybe she would be able to sweet-talk them. He didn't mind being considered crazy, just so long as he and Kate could be on their way.

The door opened. Lou tensed up. He was standing behind the chair, hands on its cold, metal back. The man they had seen earlier, the senior officer, Mr Manor, stood at the opening. The door was pinned to the wall with his leg. He had a closed Manila file in one hand, and gave Lou a frigid look.

'You may go.'

Lou stared at him.

'You look as surprised as I feel,' Manor said blankly. 'Appears you have friends in high places.'

Lou walked to the door and turned into the hall. From the main room he could hear Kate's voice. An armed guard stood at the end of the corridor, his machine gun lying diagonally across his chest. He was staring straight ahead and ignored Lou completely.

Captain Jerry Derham turned, a grim expression on his face.

'You look pleased to see me,' Lou quipped.

'I think you've made enough wisecracks for one night, buddy.'

Lou saw Kate. She took a step towards him, looking relieved and ran her hand along his upper arm.

The two junior customs officers stood behind the counter. Derham led the two scientists towards a table close to the exit. Their cases and other luggage lay on top. The bubble-wrapped cylinder taken from Amelia Earhart's plane seemed to be untouched. Lou glanced at Kate.

'You checked it?'

She nodded towards Jerry. 'We both have. It's OK.'

'Come on,' Derham said. 'Let's find a trolley and get out of here.'

*

Outside the main doors to Arrivals, Lou, Kate and Jerry stood close to the pick-up and drop-off point, cabs pulling up and exchanging passengers before drifting off into the night.

'So what the hell happened back there, Lou?'

'Actually, Jerry, can we save the post-mortem?' Kate interrupted.

Derham let out a heavy sigh. 'I had to pull out all the stops.'

'And we both really appreciate it.' Kate gave Lou a hard look.

'Jerry, I'm sorry. I lost my cool.'

Derham shrugged.

'It stinks to me though,' Lou added, catching Kate's eye.

'They seemed to know exactly what to look for,' she said. 'That was no random search. We were targeted. They were put up to this.'

'You're probably right. They were very hard work . . . wouldn't play ball, even when I told them it was a military matter. I had to put a call through to Admiral Sharp. Only then did they sit up and take notice.' Jerry ran a palm over his forehead.

'You look all in,' Kate commented.

'I've felt better . . . But, I think it's time you two explained exactly what is in that bubblewrap package, and why someone should tip off customs.'

Kate smiled for the first time in hours and nodded towards Lou. 'He's been wanting to tell you all about it since we were on the boat!'

*

They found Kate's car in long-term parking where they had dropped it before leaving for the Pacific.

Jerry helped them load the luggage. He checked his watch. 'It's 11.45. You have your passes into the base, yeah? Meet there in an hour, my office. I have to drop off some files to one of my superiors in town.'

'At this time of the night?'

'The United States Navy never sleeps, Lou,' Jerry said with a grin. 'Catch you later.' He walked off across the car park, skirting a giant puddle in the middle of the road.

Although they had only been away for just over a week, to Kate and Lou it felt a lot longer. It started to rain, smearing the view through the car windows, the water splashing against the sides of the vehicle as it accelerated away through a set of lights, around the airport perimeter, out onto Norview Avenue and then north-west on the freeway.

The traffic was very light on the I64, the six lanes of the highway were swept by gusts of cold rain. Neither of them spoke very much for the first few minutes of the journey, each lost in their own thoughts about the discovery they had made and the recent experiences at the airport.

Eventually Kate said: 'Our radio transmissions from the boat must've been intercepted. How else could anybody have possibly known we had found anything?'

'I guess. But why would anybody be monitoring our signal? Sounds a bit far-fetched.'

'Well, I suppose intelligence traffic is heavier than it would normally be in that part of the world because of the Chinese business.' She turned to look out at the windswept landscape, the grassy banks each side of the road, a few bedraggled trees in the distance. 'I can't believe that one of the team would have said anything to anyone. Connor or Gustav?'

'No way.'

A couple of hundred yards from intersection 278 they saw, coming up directly behind them, blue and red flashing lights.

Lou slowed the car and pulled over to the hard shoulder. 'Jesus Christ! It really isn't our damn night, is it?'

He switched off the engine and they sat quietly listening to the crunch of the cop's boots as he walked towards their car. There came a tap at his window and Lou lowered it. The policeman was a beefy young Latino with a bleached blond crew-cut who looked a few years younger than them.

'Your nearside brake light,' he said, his voice completely expressionless. 'It's blinking, about to go.'

'Thanks, officer. I hadn't realized. I'll get it fixed as soon as I can.' Lou forced a brief smile.

The policeman took in Kate sitting in the passenger seat. 'Can I see your licence please, sir?'

Lou patted his breast pocket, then realized he had put his wallet in the glove compartment. He reached over.

'Sir,' the policeman said.

'I'm getting my licence.'

'Slowly please.'

Lou found the licence, handed it to the policeman and sat waiting with his arms folded across his chest. The officer studied the licence, then handed it back.

'Could you step out please?'

'What? I thought you said I just had a faulty bulb?'

Lou noticed the policeman's right hand move down a few inches to hover close to his gun holster and felt Kate jab her elbow into his side. He glanced back at the officer, sighed again and slowly eased open the door.

The man moved very quickly. The second Lou was out of the car the barrel of a standard-issue .40 Smith and Wesson was digging into his ribs.

'Hey!' Lou shouted and the barrel was pressed in harder. He heard more crunching gravel behind him and saw the policeman give a brief nod to someone the other side of the car. Lou half-turned to see a second officer, tall and bald, opening the passenger door. Kate appeared in half-shadow, the officer gripping her arm as she protested.

Lou glanced back at the police car behind Kate's vehicle and saw a third figure at the wheel.

'Get in the back,' the first policeman snapped and jabbed with the gun again, sending a ripple of pain down Lou's side. The policeman opened the rear door to Kate's car and pushed down on Lou's head with his free hand. Lou saw Kate being shoved into the back seat across from him in a similar way. The doors slammed behind them. The young blond officer pulled into the driver's seat, the bald one sat, half-turned, in the passenger side, his revolver pointed straight at them.

'We're going on a short ride,' he said. 'I don't wanna hear a word from you, understood?'

Lou and Kate sat, mute.

'Understood?'

They both nodded. The driver put the car in gear and pulled back onto the highway followed closely by the cop car, its flashers off.

16

Kate felt for Lou's hand across the seat, found it and squeezed tight. He gave her a quick reassuring glance; the bald cop appeared not to notice, just kept the gun trained on them.

They drove Kate's car extremely fast down the Interstate, the cop car close behind. They skirted Inglenook Park on the left, then, a little further on to the right, they shot past a sign to Southern Shopping Center. Kate and Lou knew it well, they had only been there a couple of days before leaving on their trip. A few miles on, they took a left off the highway and joined a two-lane road heading west. The rain was heavier now, slamming against the windscreen, gushing under the car as they sped along.

They took another left then a hard right onto a country lane, the car bumping along over the uneven surface, slamming through the puddles, muddy water pluming its flanks, tyres struggling to find purchase. It was dark out here, no street lights, the only illumination coming from the headlights of the two cars and the moon full against the inky black. All they could see were the shapes of trees and occasionally scuffed and rain-drenched metal barriers either side of the road.

Finally, the car began to slow and drew to a halt. The police car pulled up immediately behind them. Tessellated shadows fell across the face of the bald cop with the gun. He hadn't uttered a word since warning them to stay quiet back on the highway.

The lights of the cop car behind flicked. A few moments later Kate's door was wrenched open and the third man, plain-clothed in jeans and a scruffy leather jacket, cigarette dangling from his lips, stood on the dark road. He had a gun in his left hand and flicked it to indicate that Kate and Lou should get out.

They had stopped on a driveway, the shape of a large dilapidated building just visible to their right. The rain stung like ice on their faces and soaked through their clothes in a few moments. Lou felt a hand shove him from behind, and he and Kate were frogmarched towards the old building.

It was a disused warehouse. One of the walls had collapsed completely, a pile of soaked, crumbling bricks was all that remained of it. The other three walls held shattered windows, part of the roof yawned open to the leaden cloud-heavy sky. The place stank of diesel. There were oily puddles on the cracked concrete floor. One wall of the warehouse was lined with rusting oil drums.

A small section of the building remained relatively intact, with a boxy office at the top of a flight of metal stairs. One of the men stayed back with the cars, the other two guided them to the foot of the stairs. The blond one took the lead, the other to one side. The door to the office ahead of them swung open and a raw white light spilled out. Kate and Lou were ushered up the stairs.

'Welcome,' said a dark-haired man in a black track-suit. He ushered them into the office. Lou and Kate stood bedraggled, water pooling on the floor. The bald cop covered them with his revolver.

'What exactly is this all about?' Lou said, surprising himself with how remarkably calm his voice sounded.

The man looked from Lou to Kate and back, then indicated to the cop that he should lower the gun. A little surprised for a second, the man complied.

'Who are you?' Kate hissed.

'Well, to answer the pretty lady's question first. My name isn't important. Call me . . . oh, I dunno . . . Pete. Yeah, that'll do.' He turned to Lou. 'This is all about a certain something you have, and we want, bud. Blank looks . . . oh very good. Your best poker faces! Let me fill you in. The two of you – newlyweds, I hear, how lovely, I'm a great believer in the institution of marriage – the two of you have just returned from a charter boat anchored close to Howland Island in the Pacific Ocean, yeah? There, you happened to find Amelia Earhart's long-lost aircraft. And you discovered something else.'

There was a sound behind them at the door to the office. The man in plain clothes who had driven the cop car kept the door open with his foot and struggled through the opening with Kate and Lou's suitcases, one in each hand. The blond guy helped him and they laid them on the floor close to a metal desk.

'There are two more boxes,' the plain-clothes guy said. 'The small one's a sample box or something. Left them at the foot of the stairs.' The blond cop headed through the door. A moment later he was back with Kate's shoulder bag and camera bag, Lou's briefcase and the two metal boxes.

The man calling himself Pete leant on the desk, keeping his eyes on Lou and Kate. The bald man levelled his gun.

'Open them.'

Kate found the keys in her pocket and crouched down to unlatch first one case then the other. Lifting back the lids, she stepped away. The guy in the leather jacket and jeans began disgorging the contents of the cases, tossing clothes aside, searching roughly along the bottom of the cases before yanking open the pockets inside the lids. Finding nothing, he picked up one case, flipped it over, and shook it before turning his attention to the other.

'Nothing.'

Pete kicked the large metal box with the toe of his shoe and nodded to the two bags beside it. 'Get these open.' He turned to the blond cop. 'Go check the car. Take it apart, I want that fucking artefact.' He glared at Kate and Lou. 'It would be much easier if you just told me where the fuck it is.'

Lou shrugged. 'I don't know what you're talking about.'

Pete nodded almost imperceptibly to the bald cop with the gun. He stepped forward, swung his arm and smashed the butt into Lou's jaw. Lou groaned and collapsed to the floor. Kate screamed and grasped his hand as Pete grabbed her arm.

'No!' He spun Kate round, her face inches from his. 'Now, where is it?'

They all heard the noise from the floor of the warehouse. It sounded like a muffled yelp followed by the clang of metal.

Lou was getting up, the side of his face reddening, a line of blood running down to the collar of his shirt. 'Leave her . . .'

The bald cop went to hit Lou again, but Pete stopped him with a wave of the hand. 'Sssh . . . What's that?'

They all gave him blank looks.

'All right, tie them.'

The plain-clothes guy pulled a couple of lengths of cord from the pocket of his leather jacket. Pete crouched down beside the bags and the boxes. Undoing the small bags, he tipped out the contents, rummaged through the side pockets, found nothing. He tried to unlatch the larger box, but like the cases, it was locked. Reaching into his tracksuit jacket, he pulled out a pistol, brought it down heavily on the lock. It didn't give way. He stepped back, fired a single round at the box and the lock gave, the boom of gunfire reverberating around the office.

He eased back the lid. The box was quite empty. He stood, breathing heavily, hands on his hips. Shaking his head, he turned to Kate and Lou, who had been forced to sit with their backs to a wall furthest from the door of the office, their hands tied behind them. Stepping across the office, Pete stretched his neck; the muscles around his jaw twitched.

The blast shook the office.

Three of the windows shattered, the glass spraying the floor. The light, swinging on its cable, flickered off, then on again.

Pete stumbled and managed to grab the edge of the desk. The plain-clothes guy was not so lucky; flying across the room, his head hit the wall near the door.

Pete glared at the bald guy. 'What the fuck was—?'

A second explosion ripped through the warehouse and a jet of flame shot past the entrance to the office at the top of the stairs. Pete didn't wait a moment, darted for the door, surveyed the warehouse floor and was dashing down the metal stairs. The bald cop spun round and followed him, grabbing the stair railing.

Three heavily armed men in black body armour, faces obscured by balaclavas and night goggles ran across the floor of the warehouse towards the bottom of the stairs.

The area was engulfed by flames. Towards the far end of the warehouse, oil drums were ablaze. The bald cop only made it to the third step.

'Stop. Drop the gun,' one of the assault team shouted.

The cop ignored him and peeled off a couple of rounds before he was ripped apart by a shower of machine-gun bullets.

Kate and Lou struggled to pull themselves up, but with their hands tied behind their backs it was almost impossible.

'Help!' Kate yelled and struggled to stand. They could see sparks and orange dust in the air beyond the windows and caught a glimpse of the flames. The air hung heavy with the stench of burning oil. They heard shouts, gunfire, a heavy object tumbling down the metal stairs. Then came the thump of boots on the rungs.

Two men dressed in SWAT gear crashed into the room. The lead figure held a Heckler & Koch MP5 sub-machine gun at waist level, his partner swung a Remington ACR assault rifle one-eighty.

Kate pulled herself in close to Lou. The unconscious plain-clothes guy begun to stir and get up off the floor. A third member of the assault team stormed through the door into the office, saw the man staring at him and swung round his gun, the barrel pointed at the middle of the man's forehead.

'Down!' yelled the leading SWAT officer, his voice muffled. The man put up his hands, sprawling on his front like an insect. Lowering his machine gun, the team leader stepped over.

'I'm here to help you.' He gripped Lou by the upper arm and pulled him to his feet before turning his attention to Kate. The man's partner nonchalantly pushed the Remington across his back, glanced quickly at the third man now covering the door and pulled a black folding knife from a pouch on his belt. Crouching beside Kate, he sliced the cord around her wrists before turning to Lou.

'Who are . . .?' Kate started to ask.

'Let's get you out.' The man turned as his colleague dragged the plain-clothes guy to his feet and pushed him hard through the door.

Down on the warehouse floor, flames flickered along the walls, a sheet of burning oil spread from the stairs to the rear doors. As they reached the bottom of the staircase, a third explosion thundered through the shattered building, propelling Kate and Lou to the floor. Kate cried as a searing pain shot up her arms.

'Get up . . .' the commander of the team said urgently.

The air was being sucked out of the building. Lou and Kate felt the breath squeezed from their lungs, the backs of their throats so raw they couldn't swallow.

Kate was aware of being pulled to her feet by someone and caught a glimpse of Lou rolling on the floor, his face black with ash. The left leg of his trousers was alight. She went to cry out, but no sound came from her mouth and Lou disappeared from view.

Lou felt something heavy and rough-edged slamming against his leg and he almost gagged when he saw his clothes were alight. He dragged himself up and stumbled forward, felt his knees give way and started to fall again. Strong arms caught him just in time, an arm around his shoulders, guiding him to the left then the right, around a stack of rusted oil drums. He glimpsed a patch of black; the night beyond the warehouse, a place where the air was clear and clean and chill and wet. He felt as though he had to get there at any cost, as quickly as he possibly could. That simple patch of sky and the cold wet seemed to him like a distant heaven waiting for him. With a final burst of energy, he shoved aside the pain and the terror and stumbled into the open air.

17

'Oh my God,' Kate exclaimed, stumbling over into a patch of grass and weeds. She was shaking, a foul taste in her mouth, and all around – hanging thickly – the cloying stench of burning oil.

For a moment she couldn't make out the moving shapes around her. She caught a glimpse of Lou not far away; he was getting to his feet unsteadily. She stood up, took one pace, felt a hand on her shoulder and spun round.

'Kate.'

In the dark she couldn't tell who it was, just an outline of a man. A beam of light from a torch carried by one of the others cut through the night and for a second she saw a large figure dressed in black. Her eyes adjusted. The man was six-three with broad shoulders. He was pulling off the SWAT balaclava to reveal a head of damp blond curls, a broad face, prominent cheekbones, large brown eyes. There were black rings of soot around his eye sockets, but Kate recognized him instantly.

'I don't believe . . . !'

The man smiled, almost comically, white teeth against the soot and the black uniform.

'The strangest things happen, Kate Wetherall.'

Kate broke into a smile and fell into the man's arms, clutching him around the waist. 'Adam . . . It really is you . . . What the hell . . .?' She pulled away and held his forearms. He made her feel tiny.

'What the hell am I doing here? After what just happened, I wonder about that myself! It's a long story.'

Kate spun round to Lou. He was standing five yards away. She ran over. He was panting, his face filthy with soot and sweat, his hair matted and clinging to his skin. He looked stunned, like a wild animal cornered and on the verge of panic. He smelled of burned fabric.

'Lou! You OK?' Kate grabbed his shoulder. 'Lou? Your pants were burning. Is your leg all right?'

He looked up, nodded raggedly and winced. 'Yeah.' He ran a hand along the outside of his thigh down to his knee. 'I think so. I feel like somebody's hit me all over with a mallet . . . no, make that two mallets. But aside from that . . .'

The man called Adam had walked up behind Kate. Lou looked up and saw him.

'You won't believe this, Lou,' Kate began. 'This is Adam Fleming.'

Lou looked blank.

'We go back a long way,' Fleming said. He had a deep voice, cut-glass, Eton and Oxbridge.

'We were . . . friends, at Oxford,' Kate said.

Fleming raised an eyebrow. 'I thought we were a bit more than friends, Katie.'

She produced an uncomfortable laugh. 'I think I need to make some introductions. Lou, Adam. Adam, this is my husband, Lou Bates.'

'Ah, apologies. I knew you were both here. The dossier told us doctors Kate Wetherall and Lou Bates were coming into Norfolk International, and we expected trouble, but I had no idea you were . . .'

Lou raised a hand in a gesture of friendship. 'No probs. We've only been spliced a week.'

'Congratulations. You nearly had a very short marriage.'

'You saved our lives,' Kate said.

Fleming looked away towards the flames lapping around the framework of the old warehouse. 'I'm just sorry we were unable to save the item you are carrying.'

Kate glanced at Lou. 'Don't worry about that,' she replied.

'We didn't have it on us,' Lou said. 'We switched briefcases at the airport. Jerry Derham has it. Hopefully, it's safe and sound at Norfolk Naval Base.'

'A very sensible precaution.'

Two men approached, the other members of the SWAT team. They stopped and saluted. 'Sir,' one of them said. 'May I suggest we get the civilians away asap.'

'Yes, of course, Alders.' Fleming turned to Kate and Lou. 'My orders are to get you two to Norfolk Naval

Base.' He looked back at Alders. 'I'll escort them. You and Rodriguez clear up the mess.'

'How on earth did you know we were here?' Kate asked.

'I said it was a long story. I think it can wait.' He checked his watch. 'It's almost 1 a.m. Your friend Captain Derham has just been briefed. He'll be expecting you at the base.' He glanced over towards Kate's car, then considered Lou. 'You both OK? Dr Bates?'

'Please, call me Lou. I'll live.'

18

The clock on Captain Derham's office wall read 2.45 a.m. as a cadet brought in a tray of coffees and started handing out the mugs to Kate, Lou and Adam Fleming. En route, Kate and Lou had grabbed a shower and a change of clothes at their lab at the Institute of Marine Studies, just a few miles from the naval base. Lou had a plaster on his jaw. Fleming had stowed away his body armour and weapons and was now dressed in combat trousers, T-shirt and black boots.

'I've been briefed by Admiral Schnell at the Pentagon,' Derham said, rearranging some papers on his desk. 'But I guess you guys need an update.' He turned to Kate and Lou.

'Might be helpful.'

Derham put a hand out towards Fleming indicating that he should speak. As he leaned back in his chair, the Englishman looked calm and relaxed.

'I'm MI6. I'm over here liaising with a CIA task force. Have you heard of a woman called Glena Buckingham?'

'I've read about her,' Lou replied. 'I think it was in *Time* or something.'

'She's the head of Eurenergy, one of the big fuel conglomerates. Very powerful woman,' Kate said.

'She certainly is. On the surface she's a highly regarded, respected businesswoman heading up one of the biggest companies in the world. A scientist by background, very clever, ruthless, basically everything you would expect of somebody who has reached her position, especially a woman in a man's world. However, all is not what it seems. We know that she has been involved in a number of clandestine efforts over the last few years, which definitely are not above board. She was behind the attempt to sabotage the mission to rescue the Fortescue document on *Titanic* eighteen months ago.'

'You are joking!' Kate responded.

Fleming shook his head. 'We have a fat dossier on her and her cohorts. Trouble is she is very powerful, very clever, as I said, and she has an expert team to protect her. In spite of our best efforts, we still cannot find anything to pin on her. But we will.' His expression had hardened.

'So, OK,' Lou said. 'Can we backtrack a moment? I feel I've missed something. What has this woman got to do with us?'

'I take it you've been following the news about the Chinese? Or did you miss it on your honeymoon?'

'You mean the atoll? Dalton?'

'We heard about it,' Kate said. 'In fact we were right

near there on the boat. Even heard some explosions. Drilling, we assumed.'

'I understand from your transmissions that it was a plane you found, what you think is Amelia Earhart's plane.'

'How on earth did you know that? We've told no one apart from our team back there.'

'That's precisely how we knew about you and what you found,' Fleming said. 'We've been watching Dalton Island carefully, tracking all communications from the Chinese. We picked up your call to the institute.'

'And this Glena Buckingham character and her friends at Eurenergy must have done the same, then?' Kate shifted in her seat.

'OK, so let's get this straight,' Lou said. 'The Chinese have bought an atoll in the Pacific with spare change and everyone is up in arms about it because a) they overlooked it, and b) it's sitting on vast resources. You guys at MI6, and presumably the CIA, the FBI, the Pentagon, the Kremlin etc. etc. have all been listening in to comms between Dalton Island and Beijing and you happened to pick up our transmission about the Lockheed Electra and what we found on it.'

'That's about it.' Fleming looked from Lou to Kate and then Derham. The captain had a stern look on his face but seemed happy just to listen.

'And Ms Buckingham was also spying on the Chinese, I take it?' Kate said.

'That's what we are assuming.'

'So why is she after us and what we have?'

'Well, that's the funny thing,' Fleming said, a wry smile playing on his lips. 'We had no idea either. Then some bright spark in my department who had been scouring through the archive of articles about Buckingham came across an interview she gave to *Cosmopolitan*, of all things, about five years ago in which she happened to mention her lifelong fascination with Amelia Earhart.'

Lou couldn't help laughing.

'It gets better. We believe that there is far more to your discovery than the solution to an interesting historical conundrum. But as far as we know Buckingham was simply using her people to get something she wanted personally.'

'Why is it that MI6 and our guys are so keen to get hold of what Kate and Lou found?' Derham said.

Fleming didn't reply for a moment but looked down at his hands. Sighing, he looked up. 'The fact is, we are not absolutely sure what value there is in the object that Lou and Kate brought up. But the reason I'm here in America is because MI6 and the CIA have been working together to try to build upon a theory one of our people came up with. From hints in letters and using a set of newly declassified MOD documents dating back to the 1930s, he has presented a strong argument to investigate rumours that Amelia Earhart was not only an American spy, but was also involved in one of the most audacious military projects of the era.

'Two years ago, a small team was formed in London with the remit to get to the bottom of our operative's claim. But then, back in March, we lost the scent completely. It was an amazing bit of good fortune, not to mention impeccable timing, that we overheard the comms from your boat.'

'What exactly is this project you're talking about?' Kate asked.

'And perhaps you'd better start at the beginning,' Lou suggested.

'Yes, I'm sorry. I'm getting ahead of myself. Have any of you heard of the Philadelphia Experiment?'

'I've heard of it. Some crazy conspiracy theory, isn't it?' Derham replied.

'I know a little bit about it,' Lou volunteered. 'I was quite interested in that sort of far-out stuff when I was at college.'

Kate gave him an odd look.

'It was a long time ago.'

'Not that long!'

'Five words, Kate. *The Crackerjack Girls' Own Book*.'

She laughed.

'Anyway,' Lou went on. 'I read a few books about that sort of thing – the Bermuda Triangle, UFOs etc. The Philadelphia Experiment was something that was supposed to have taken place in the late thirties or early forties? Wasn't Einstein involved? I remember something about some sort of weird test to try to teleport a ship. Went horribly wrong.'

'Yes, well, there are many different versions of the story, most of them contradict each other and have become ridiculously exaggerated.' Fleming paused for a moment to drink some coffee. 'The truth is far less esoteric than the conspiracy nuts would like, but for all that, no less astonishing. Einstein was indeed involved. The experiment was conducted in 1937. Einstein was working on an extension of his general field theory, a sort of spin-off from relativity – the idea of creating a device employing a rather exotic aspect of his theoretical work. On paper, he had concluded that he could create a quantum field around a subatomic particle. With some serious military funding the idea was developed to the point where he believed he could produce a similar field around a much larger object, effectively making it invisible.'

'That sounds like complete hokum,' Kate said.

'Not according to the secret files kept from the time, which have never been made public, of course. It isn't hokum, but equally, the theory didn't work out very well when put into practice. Einstein conducted an experiment early in 1937 that ended in disaster. He set up a test in this very shipyard and attempted to create a quantum field around a ship, USS *Liberty*. The idea was to create a form of defensive shield, a canopy of pure energy that would stop bullets and shells fired at the ship. Something went awry.

'According to reports, *Liberty* dematerialized for a few seconds. When it reappeared, it was configured slightly differently in space-time. Many of the crew were killed; some of them embedded in the fabric of the ship itself. A shockwave devastated the old control tower killing an admiral and injuring a half-dozen others.'

'They used a crew?'

'I know,' Fleming said. 'Astonishing, but they did that sort of thing back then.'

Derham looked stunned. 'I've never heard of this.'

'Well, the navy weren't exactly proud of it, Captain. Apart from the fact that the work was extremely dangerous, and potentially game-changing in the hands of an enemy, the test had failed utterly, so even senior brass were kept in the dark about the whole thing.'

'I imagine that wasn't the end of the story though,' Lou said.

'No it wasn't. Einstein had developed the original theory with a close colleague, Johannes Kessler, with whom he had worked at Oxford during the early thirties, just after Einstein had left Germany for good. After emigrating to America in 1933 Einstein shifted his attention to other work, and it wasn't until 1936, when things were really hotting up in Europe, that he began to think about his defensive shield again and the navy became interested. Problem was, he needed his old colleague Kessler to make it work. Einstein was able to take some of the physics further, but then he hit a wall. He tried to go it alone, which resulted in the failed test here at the base. That disaster made him realize that he couldn't do it without Kessler's help.'

'Where was Kessler then?' Derham asked.

'Still in Germany. He was working for the Nazis, but he was opposed to them. He couldn't leave, because he had family in the country and he had missed the great exodus of intellectuals a few years earlier.'

'And of course it would have been extremely difficult to correspond in secret with something so dangerous at stake.'

'Precisely. But the team in London have pieced together information which suggests that Einstein, Kessler and the military cooked up a plan. Kessler had to get his latest work over here so that Einstein could incorporate it with his own theories, to mould some sort of improved version of the calculations for a defensive shield.'

'How did they manage that? I assume they did manage it?' Lou asked.

'The MI6 team could find absolutely no evidence of any collaboration between Einstein and Kessler after their Oxford days. There is no paper trail, no record of any correspondence anywhere, and absolutely no clues to show that a second experiment did take place. It seemed that the matter was closed. We concluded that something must have gone wrong with the attempt to communicate with Kessler; or else Einstein did get his colleague's work from Germany but he was still unable to produce a viable defensive shield. But then, six months ago, we had an unexpected breakthrough, thanks, believe it or not, to eBay!'

Fleming pulled an iPhone from his pocket, tapped the screen and passed it to Lou, who held it so that he and Kate could see the screen.

'This is a film that turned up for sale online. One of

our younger agents spotted it and we acquired it without fuss to take it out of public circulation, but just in time, I think. It's a clip two minutes thirty-seven seconds long of Einstein talking shortly before his death in 1955.'

Derham had come round from his desk to stand behind Lou and Kate so he could watch the clip on the iPhone. It was a fuzzy film of Einstein, the classic image of him wearing a scruffy sweater over a buttoned-up shirt, his lined face crowned with frizzy white hair. Pipe smoke rose from the bottom right of the picture, the pipe itself just out of shot. His English was, as always, heavily accented, and because of the poor quality of the recording, it was difficult sometimes to make out what he was saying.

'We had a serious problem. I needed Kessler's work, but we couldn't risk any simple form of correspondence. Between us we came up with what we thought was a watertight solution. Kessler would encode his work with what he and I considered an almost unbreakable code, one we had developed as young men in Oxford before the war. The idea was that he would write his contribution in this code and the document would be taken across the Atlantic by the British. At the same time, the code cipher was to be transported via an entirely different route. In order to use the document, one needed the cipher, but this alone was of no use to anyone at all.

To begin with, everything seemed to work well. Kessler managed to get the encoded documents to the

British. He then succeeded in placing the cipher with a separate, different division of the British Intelligence network. The documents were put on a merchant vessel and separate transportation for the cipher was arranged by an extremely unconventional route. The idea was to get the great aviator Amelia Earhart to deliver it to me.

In 1937, as all this was happening, Earhart was about to embark on a circumnavigation of the world; she was to be the first person to do this. She had planned a route in advance of course, and one of the stops was Dakar in Senegal. The British were to get the cipher to Dakar, where it would be passed on to the famous aviator. She would then take it secretly on the rest of her journey and bring it safely to the United States.'

Einstein drew on his pipe for a second and frowned.

'Of course we all know that sadly Ms Earhart did not make it. In fact, nobody knows what happened to her and her co-pilot. The cipher was lost. Ironically, Kessler's documents were also lost; the merchant ship was attacked by a U-boat in the mid-Atlantic. The captain of the British vessel had been ordered to destroy his ship in the event of being boarded. To this day we do not know whether that is what happened, or whether the Germans got hold of Kessler's document. It made no difference anyway, because they didn't have the cipher.'

Einstein was about to say something else when the film stopped abruptly.

Lou touched the screen to replay the film. After they

had seen it a second time, he handed the iPhone back to Fleming, and Derham returned to his desk.

'So, how can you know this is genuine?' Lou asked. 'It's just that with video-editing software you can do some pretty amazing things.'

'Fair question, Lou. We've done everything we can to verify its authenticity. The film stock is from 1953, two years before Einstein died. It comes from a Kodak wholesaler in Kansas. We've had our guys go over it to check that the images of Einstein have not been tampered with. There are some very clever ways to check when something has been Photoshopped or messed around with in any way. The backroom boys are ninety-nine point nine per cent sure that this film is genuine, shot around 1953, 1954, and that it is definitely Albert Einstein talking. Our voice analysis people have checked that this is his voice and what he says to camera has not been altered or interfered with.'

'How come Einstein was allowed to go on record about this? I would have thought it was top secret, even . . . what? Sixteen, seventeen years after the events.'

'We're pretty sure the military filmed it for their archives and it somehow got out. God only knows how.'

'I was going to ask how exactly this came up for sale, even?' Kate asked.

'A small library in Des Moines was clearing out some old stock; a job lot of hundreds of film clips dating back to the 1930s,' Fleming replied. 'They had no idea what was on the films, nor did they have the manpower to search through them. One of our archivists spotted the ad on eBay and took the films off their hands. Over a period of several months he went through the collection. It was around about the seventieth or eightieth film on his list when he hit the jackpot.'

'Amazing.' Derham was shaking his head.

'Well, no one could have guessed there would be a connection between Einstein and Amelia Earhart, let alone the legendary Philadelphia Experiment,' Lou said.

'Looks like we've got our work cut out for us though. What's next?'

'Unfortunately we've hit another wall. We still have no idea what happened to the Kessler Document.'

19

Dakar, Senegal. 9 June 1937.

'You OK, Amy?' Fred Noonan asked. 'You've had the jitters all evening.'

'Sorry, Freddie, miles away.' They were in the bar of the Imperial Hotel, Dakar. She twirled the ice in her tumbler and stood up from the barstool. 'Listen, Fred. Gotta pop up to my room. I'll be back in a minute, have another iced tea ready for me.'

He went to say something but she was already out of the door.

Along a short passage from the bar, the broad sweeping staircase of the grand old colonial hotel, with its heavily patterned carpet and shining brass stair rods, dominated the entrance. Amelia took the stairs, checked her watch and picked up the pace. Reaching the first floor, she turned left, fished out her key and was soon closing the door behind her.

She sat on the end of her bed, tapping her fingers rhythmically on the counterpane at her side, then checked her watch again. Earlier that afternoon she had picked up a cable at reception. It had simply said '7.30 p.m.', nothing more, no hint of where she should go or who she was to meet.

She felt her stomach churning; she hated all this. She was a pilot, an engineer really. She had not a single political bone in her body, but she was, she reminded herself, a patriot, and when the president, a personal friend to boot, asked her to help, she hadn't needed to think twice about it.

There was a quiet knock at the door. Amelia bolted up from the bed, forced herself to stop and take a deep breath. Brushing imaginary flecks of dust from her trousers, she paced to the door.

'Who is it?'

'Room service, madam.'

Amelia opened the door. A short man wearing the blue livery of the hotel, a white cap placed on his head at a slight angle, stood in the corridor. He held a delicate silver tray in white-gloved hands. On the tray lay an envelope. Amelia stared at it for a second.

'Thank you.' She pulled a couple of coins from her pocket, handed them to the man and closed the door. Leaning back on the wood, she ran a nail along the flap of the envelope and ripped the top, pulling out a single sheet of paper. Opening it, she read: 'Corner of St Germaine Street and Bernice Avenue, 20 minutes.'

*

The sky was darkening, a bolt of orange slicing through the canopy of purple-blue, but it was still busy on the streets of Dakar; traders closing stalls, dusty workmen returning home, children running around. A line of carts trundled along the main street, stopping for a moment to allow a small herd of ragged cattle to cross. The smell of sweat and shit hung heavy in the air.

She checked her watch. She was exactly on time. Turning on her heel she did a three-sixty-degree scan of the area. A rusty bench stood against a brick wall. She lowered herself onto the seat, and watched.

The tap on her shoulder came as a bit of a surprise. She hadn't heard anyone approach. Turning, she saw a small child, a boy of about seven, filthy face, snotty nose, big, brown, almond-shaped eyes. He sat next to her.

'Well, hi there.'

The boy stared at her silently, searching her face. She looked down to see that he was handing her a piece of paper. She unfolded it and read: *Please follow me*.

She looked at the boy again. 'No English?'

He simply stared at her, jumped off the seat and started to walk along a narrow alley away from the main road.

The alley was dark with evening shadows. Washing lines stretched across the narrow space above their heads. The place rang with a medley of sounds; pots and pans clanging, children crying, mothers shouting. The boy moved fast and nimbly and Amelia felt the sweat on her skin under her shirt. Soon, they were far from the main thoroughfare. She saw the boy dash around a corner to their left, followed him and nearly crashed into a door, its blue paint faded and flaked and worn to the wood. The door opened and Amelia followed the boy into a cool, dark hallway.

It took a moment for her eyes to adjust. A faint light appeared in the corridor as a door creaked open.

'This way, please, Miss Earhart.' She could see no one. The voice sounded weary. She walked towards the door.

An old man sat in a low-slung, embroidered armchair wreathed in cigarette smoke. He was wearing a cream linen suit, a tie and a fedora. Amelia noticed his brown brogues polished to a high sheen. He stood up as she entered and he gestured to another chair opposite his. The room was filled with the smell of incense, a blend of patchouli and sandalwood. Half-a-dozen large candles illuminated the room.

The man leaned forward and offered Amelia a cigarette. She took one, he lit it for her with a gold, intricately engraved lighter. She took a long drag and exhaled a plume of smoke.

'We can speak freely here,' the man began. His accent was clipped, English. 'You begin the next stage of your journey tomorrow. Is that correct?'

'Do we not get introduced first?'

The man smiled. 'Forgive me, most rude. However, any name I provide will of course bear no relationship to the one my mother and father gave me.' A faint smile played across his lips.

'I am from British Intelligence. I assume you have been briefed concerning the transaction we are to make this evening!'

She nodded. 'I have, and to answer your question, yes, we do continue tomorrow, 05.00 hours. You have a package for me, I believe?'

He moved his hand to the right of his hip and lifted a rectangular wooden box into the light. 'Like you, I am merely a courier. I have no idea of the contents of this container. But what I do know, is that it must not fall into the wrong hands. I don't know who the wrong hands may be, but you must guard this' – he held it in front of him – 'with your life.'

'I understand.' Amelia couldn't keep the anxiety from her voice. She leaned forward and took the box. It felt warm in her hands.

The loud bang on the front door of the building echoed along the hall outside and Amelia sprang from her seat. She looked wide-eyed at the man in the cream suit. He got up from the chair with surprising agility and grabbed her arm. She looked at his hand and went to speak. Leaning forward close to her face, he brought a finger to his lips.

'Get away . . . now.' He released her arm and pointed towards a door on the other side of the room. 'I'll buy you some time.'

'I don't understand . . . What is this all about?'

'This place is clearly not as safe as I had hoped.'

'But who . . .?'

'Just go . . .'

She turned and another loud bang came from the door. A single gunshot rang out and the door flew open smashing against the wall. Amelia caught a glimpse of a figure turning into the room and then she was through the door in the far wall, closing it and locking it behind her. She paused for a second, heard voices; first the Englishman's then a second man shouting in French. Three gunshots came in quick succession, a cry followed by the sound of boots pounding across the floor of the room. Amelia turned and ran.

20

A safe house, Virginia. Present day.

'They knew, I tell you. They freakin' knew everything! A freakin' SWAT team, armed to the teeth.'

The man in the black tracksuit, Vince Manlow – who Kate and Lou had known as 'Pete' – his face filthy with soot and a smear of dried blood down his left cheek, stared into the camera of the laptop. He could see both Buckingham and Secker seated at the boardroom table of the headquarters of Eurenergy in London. They could see him sitting in a battered metal chair in a bare room, a man holding a Glock beside him.

'And you were the only one to slip away?'

The man nodded.

'Very fortunate,' Secker commented.

'And you say Bates and Wetherall did not have the artefact in their cases?' Buckingham asked.

'I'm ninety-nine per cent sure.'

'Why not a hundred, Manlow?'

'Because, sir,' he stared back at Secker, 'we were

about to open the last pieces of luggage when the bastards hit.'

'Suitcases? Boxes? Which?'

'A briefcase and a small metal box. One of my men thought the box could have contained samples.'

'Oh for fuck's sake, man.' Buckingham glared at Manlow. 'First the useless arseholes at the airport screw up, then you incompetent—'

'We almost had it, ma'am. We had no idea we had been followed.'

'No idea we had been followed,' Buckingham mimicked. 'Fucktard!'

'And you have no idea who the men were?' Secker said.

'They were in full assault gear, sir, night-vision goggles, armed to the teeth.'

'Yes, you said,' Secker spat. 'And you were far too busy saving your own skin.'

'No! I did everything I . . .'

'Oh, shut the fuck up, Manlow. Hans, shut the fucker up . . . I can't bear this. I'm getting one of my headaches.'

Secker gave an almost imperceptible nod to the man standing next to Manlow's chair. He lifted the Glock and fired, sending Manlow across the floor, a plume of blood and brains spattering the wall just out of view.

Secker broke the link to the laptop in Virginia and turned to his boss.

'You have a theory brewing.'

Buckingham held Secker with an expressionless gaze. 'Not a theory exactly, Hans. Toit has missed his last two scheduled call-ins. I'm growing suspicious.'

21

Adam Fleming was staying in a Holiday Inn just outside Hampton. Utilitarian and predictable, it suited his temporary needs without eliciting the slightest enthusiasm.

It was 4 a.m. before he reached his room and although he had been awake for almost thirty-four hours, he did not feel tired. In the shower he touched the red marks already beginning to turn black on his hip and across his chest, injuries from the raid. Moving close to the bathroom mirror he considered his handsome, bruised face, his blond curls plastered to his temple. He dabbed at a cut under his eye and walked back into the bedroom. His mobile trilled.

'Traction, fourteen, obelisk,' said a voice.

Fleming pulled a notebook from the inside of his jacket where it lay on the bed. He flicked through a few pages and found the code for the day. 'Portmanteau, Jeremy, Toucan.' He then flicked a switch on the back of the phone and a pinprick of green light appeared close to the mouthpiece. 'Clear,' he said.

'Must be early for you, old chap.' It was Seth

Wilberforce, a senior assistant to the deputy chief of MI6, Sir Donald Ashmore.

Fleming caught sight of the cheap LED radio alarm beside the bed. 'It's actually very late, Wilberforce. Haven't been to bed yet.'

'Well I have some news for you.'

Fleming lowered himself to the bed. It groaned under his weight. 'Good news, I hope.'

'We think so. A lead on the Kessler Document.'

'A lead?' Fleming was suddenly filled with nervous energy. He got to his feet and started pacing along the narrow stretch of garish carpet between the end of the bed and a wooden unit housing a TV and a mini-bar.

'It's all a bit cryptic, but we've been contacted by someone claiming they know where it is.'

'Well, well.'

'Not sure we can trust it, of course.'

'Understood. But I assume you are doing the checks?'

'As best we can, Adam.'

Fleming sighed wearily.

'The Yanks treating you well?'

'You received my communiqué? The marine archaeologists are safe and well and the artefact is secure.'

'The whole thing almost went arse up at the airport though, I heard.'

'Almost. So, who's behind this lead?'

'No names, just initial contact, someone reaching out to us; calls himself "Zero".' Wilberforce exhaled dismissively through his nostrils. 'Could be a dead end, of course. I've got Serge and MacCabe on it as we speak.'

Fleming was unable to stifle a yawn, tiredness suddenly descending.

'Get some sleep, old chap,' Wilberforce was saying. 'With a bit of luck I'll have something concrete for you when you wake up.'

22

By the time Kate, Lou and the British agent Adam Fleming had left his office, Jerry Derham was on to his fourth strong coffee since midnight and he felt wired. Through his window the lights of the base threw a massicot glow across the horizon dotted with the grey hulks of warships; the stars and a luminous low-slung moon shone in the sky.

Jerry twirled a pen around his fingers absent-mindedly. There was little he could do at this hour. He got up from his desk and walked out into the corridor. It was quiet, just the whirl of air conditioning and the occasional beep of a computer as an email arrived in someone's office. A security guard passed the end of the passage, glanced at Derham and saluted.

In the kitchen, Jerry poured himself a glass of chilled water and retraced his steps back to his office. He placed the drink on a side-table, dimmed the lights and stretched out on the sofa along the wall opposite the window. The last thing he remembered before sleep swept over him was the twinkling of Venus close to the top of the window frame.

He roused himself with a start, caught a glimpse of the wall clock telling him it was 7.34. Rubbing his eyes, he leaned over, took a gulp of the now tepid water on the side-table, stood up and walked around his desk.

'It might be too early,' he muttered, 'but worth a try.'

He tapped the numbers into his desk phone and leaned back as the line connected and rang. He was just about to hang up when a voice came down the line.

'Marsha Edwards, Langley.'

'You're at work very early on a Sunday.'

'Jerry! So are you!' The woman gave a short peal of laughter. 'To what do I owe this honour . . . Captain?'

Jerry loved Marsha's laugh. It reminded him of college days. They had been an item for a while, but now they were happy just being great friends. Not that they saw much of each other since she had been promoted to the rank of senior supervisor at CIA headquarters, Langley. These days it seemed she was at work 24/7.

'Just need some info, Mar.'

'What sort of info?'

'Background check on an MI6 operative.'

'Shouldn't you be calling London for that, Jerry?'

Derham laughed. 'I think that might be stretching the Special Relationship a little too far.'

'I guess. OK. It'll take a few minutes. Lucky you caught me early. Got twenty-six newbies to initiate at eight-thirty.'

'Oh, lucky you!'

It took close to fifteen minutes before Jerry's email

sounded and he opened it to find a file of almost two megabytes Marsha Edwards had sent. One point nine meg of it was a security code which Jerry decrypted with a secure key he was directed to within another encoded website. Twenty minutes after calling his friend, Jerry had a detailed file on Adam Fleming and had begun reading:

CIA File #34565Brit/MI6.
Special Agent Adam Sinclair Fleming.

DOB: 16 March 1983, Norwich, England.
Parents: Brigadier Miles Henry Fleming (deceased) and Dr Mary Louise Fleming (ophthalmologist).
Education: St Paul's School, London; Rugby; Merton College, Oxford (PPE); Sandringham.
Notes: Fleming is perceived as a model agent coming through the tried and tested British Establishment/class/military system. He comes from what the Brits call an 'upper-middle-class family', a military dynasty dating back to the 18th century. A rowing blue at Oxford, Fleming graduated with 1st class honours.
Training and Skills: Qualified as Marksman 1st class, black belt Judo and Krav Maga master. Fluent Russian, Mandarin, Spanish. Pilot's license.

Derham paused in his reading to survey a collection of images of Fleming at Oxford, on exercises at Sandringham, his first ID photograph at MI6, attending a formal dinner dressed in white tie, his blond hair oiled back rakishly.

'Quite the golden boy,' he muttered to himself. 'And the girl to go with it,' he added, noticing Fleming's arm was draped around the bare shoulders of a stunning woman with high cheekbones and large black eyes. He read on:

> Fleming joined MI6 in May 2008. He was recruited by his future wife, Celia Gainsborough.

Jerry stopped again to study more closely the picture of Fleming with the woman.

> Gainsborough was Fleming's superior in British Intelligence. They married in June 2009. Served together in Kabul (July–November 2009) and in Moscow over Christmas that year.
>
> Fleming then worked as senior field operative without Gainsborough in Lebanon, Beijing, and later, Cairo.
>
> Celia Gainsborough was killed on active duty in Mexico, June 2012.
>
> Fleming served three more missions to

Moscow, returned to Cairo and completed two stints in Karachi.

Personal Life: Since the death of his wife, Fleming has had no serious romantic relationships. He seems to have few friends and little time for any social life. He returned to Merton College, Oxford for a reunion in April 2014 and holidayed alone in Malta for the second week of August the same year.

'Wow!' Derham said to himself as he tapped his keyboard and scrolled down to the end of the report. 'Just as it says on the packet!'

There was a gentle tap at the door. Derham looked up and saw in the doorway the man he had just been reading about, his fingers on the handle.

'You free?' Fleming asked. 'I have some news.'

23

Institute of Marine Studies, Hampton, Virginia.
Present day.

'I don't know how you have so much energy,' Lou moaned, sipping at his second cup of strong coffee.

'It's early Sunday morning – the best time of the week. And don't forget I went for a run at six,' Kate replied.

Lou rolled his eyes. 'Obviously you are Superwoman.' He turned back to his monitor.

On the screen was an image of the inside of the cylinder they had found in the cockpit of Amelia Earhart's plane a few days earlier. The piece of paper could be seen clearly, the three words: 'REMEMBER JOAN'S PLACE?' Kate wheeled over her chair directly behind Lou so she could see the screen.

'Handwritten,' she commented.

'This can't be the extent of the cipher Einstein talked about on the film we saw. If it was as simple as that why go through the whole rigmarole of putting the message in this metal container?'

Kate flicked a glance at the rusted metal tube lying on the laboratory bench close by. 'Why not just have somebody commit it to memory and pass it on, or come to that, why didn't this Professor Kessler simply say that over the phone?'

'Agreed. Must be more to it. On the recording Einstein said the code was something he and Kessler had developed when they were younger and working in Oxford together for a brief time before the war. We should have it checked over by a forensic document examiner – confirm it's Kessler's . . . or not. This "Joan's Place" must be something to do with that time, don't you think?'

Kate was nodding, lost in thought. 'More than likely, maybe it was somewhere they hung out, or maybe Joan was a friend, a girlfriend of Kessler's? Einstein was married by 1933, wasn't he?'

'To his second wife, Elsa . . . years before, I think. It could be anybody though, couldn't it? Or *anywhere* come to that.'

'I feel like we're missing something, something obvious. It's really annoying.'

'Look, we've got a lab full of equipment here. I suggest we get started.'

Lou pulled on a pair of latex gloves, picked up the cylinder and held it under a powerful halogen light close to the workbench. Kate joined him, pulling up a stool to the bench.

'We did everything we could with the equipment we had on the boat – we have the basics down: dimensions, weight, description of any markings, condition of the relic.'

'And Gustav ran a full spectrometric analysis as well, didn't he?'

'I suggest the next thing we do is a UV spectroscopic scan, and if needs be, run an NMR on it. I'm pretty sure the paper inside is in good condition. I don't think the object was vacuum-sealed, so there shouldn't be any problems taking it out into an oxygen-nitrogen atmosphere.'

Kate picked up the cylinder and walked over to a plain-looking steel box standing close to the end of the bench. The UV spectrometer was the size and shape of a toaster. She opened the front, placed the cylinder inside the cavity, closed the door and punched a few buttons on the top of the device. A moment later, the image of the cylinder appeared as a brightly coloured graphic on a monitor close to the machine. Kate pulled up close to the bench and began tapping at the keyboard, altering parameters and settings on the device.

On the screen, the image of the cylinder rotated and different coloured lines began to appear on its surface. These denoted fault lines in its metallic structure.

'This isn't telling us anything new,' Kate commented. She retrieved the cylinder from the machine and settled at the bench close to where Lou was sitting.

'Better open it then, I guess.'

Kate gripped the end of the cylinder and attempted to unscrew the metal cap. It wouldn't budge.

'Let me see.'

Kate handed the object to Lou. He tried to loosen the cap but had no more luck than her. Rummaging in a drawer under the bench, he found a pipe wrench. A further search offered up a length of rubber tubing. He cut two short pieces from one end and taped these to the claws of the pipe wrench so the cylinder would not be scratched. Clamping the end of the tube, he gripped tightly and twisted. The cap produced a squeaking sound and began to give.

Small flakes of rust fell onto the surface of the bench, but after three turns on the cap it came loose and Lou placed both the cylinder and the end piece on a pad of cotton wool. Slipping two fingers inside the open end, he pulled out the single sheet of paper.

He handed it to Kate, who rolled it open and placed it on a cotton pad, smoothing it down very gently.

It was a piece of expensive stationery. At the top of the paper was printed: *Regent Berlin Charlottenstr. 49, Berlin, BE 10117, Germany*.

'Ah, hotel stationery. The Regent Berlin, I've heard of that. Quite a classy place – well, it is now. We didn't pick up the header with the scanner on the boat.'

'Kessler must have been staying at the hotel when he wrote this message.'

Lou picked up the cap of the cylinder and rolled it in his palm before studying it closely under the lamp. 'No markings, nothing on here.' He put it aside and moved the cylinder under a magnifying glass on a stand and peered through it. Kate glanced over as Lou turned the cylinder over, end to end.

'Wait,' Kate said. Lou looked at her, surprised.

'Tip it back again.' She took the cylinder from Lou's hands and nudged him aside. 'Yes! I didn't think I'd imagined it.'

'Imagined what?'

'Look.' She tilted the cylinder, catching the inside close to the opening in a pool of light from the lamp.

'Wow! Well spotted. Tilt it back a little bit, can you?'

'Can you make out what it says?'

'Not really. Just a couple of letters. Is it a P? An N?'

'I thought it was a B and then an N,' Kate said.

'You're right.' Lou rotated the cylinder along its axis, and squinted through the magnifying glass.

Kate was an inch away from his face staring at the same magnified image. 'Anything?'

'Nothing.'

'We'll have to use a fibre-optic probe. There may well be some other letters further into the tube.'

It took them over half an hour to set up the equipment. The probe was incredibly slender and pliable. At the end of the fibre-optic strand was a tiny 3D camera able to collect visual data in a 360-degree field and in very low light. It had been specifically designed for use by archaeologists investigating burial chambers and inaccessible parts of ruins. A miniature version had then been adapted to study the insides of delicate, often oddly shaped objects that resisted conventional analysis.

Kate inserted the fibre-optic slowly into the cylinder, taped the end to the opening to keep it fixed in place and pulled up a chair beside Lou at a computer console linked to the probe. Lou tapped at the keyboard, and activated the fibre-optic. For a few minutes nothing changed on the screen as the probe collected data and collated the information to create a detailed coloured image of the entire inner surface of the cylinder. The cursor blinked, a line of computer code slithered across the screen, then a hi-res, full-colour image flicked up on the monitor.

It took a few seconds for the scientists to understand what they were seeing. Then Lou emitted a low whistle, shaking his head in disbelief.

'I didn't expect that!' Kate said.

There was a tap at the door. Kate and Lou looked up in unison and saw Jerry Derham standing just inside the lab, Adam Fleming close behind him.

'It was open,' he said, indicating the door. 'Hope we're not . . .'

'Perfect timing, actually,' Kate said, as she and Lou turned round to greet them.

Fleming pecked Kate on the cheek and shook Lou's hand. The two visitors stood in front of the monitor.

'We've made a breakthrough with the cylinder,' Lou said. 'Look what's written on the inside. We almost missed it.'

'*You* almost missed it!' Kate corrected.

On the screen, three lines of closely packed, seemingly random letters and numbers stood in sharp relief against the dull metallic background of the tube.

'Looks like they're etched in,' Derham said keeping his eyes fixed on the image.

'They are, I think,' Lou commented. 'You can see some faint marks here where the hydrofluoric acid used to create the letters bit in.' He poised a finger over the upper right of the screen. 'A very clever idea.'

'Indeed,' Fleming responded. 'Any clue what it says?'

'We've only just picked it up,' Lou said. 'But it must be the cipher that unlocks the message Kessler sent via the British vessel.'

'And the note: "REMEMBER JOAN'S PLACE?". What was that?'

'A decoy?' Kate offered.

Fleming nodded, lost in thought. 'Possibly.'

'I'll get our encryption expert, Kevin Grant, onto it,' Derham said. 'Remember, he solved the code for the Fortescue document we brought up from *Titanic*?'

'I think this could prove a little tougher.'

Derham raised his eyebrows. 'We'll see. He's very good.'

'So what brings you here?' Kate asked them, lowering herself onto a stool.

'We may have a breakthrough of our own,' Fleming said. 'I was contacted by my superiors in London this morning. We have a lead on the Kessler Document.'

'But didn't it go down with the British merchant ship in 1937?' Lou asked.

'I never said it did . . . Nor did Einstein in the film clip.'

'But there's no evidence that it survived either.'

'Unless our new lead proves to have some foundation. A man who will only identify himself as "Zero" made contact with London yesterday. He says he is working for a powerful Russian named Sergei. He claims Sergei knows the whereabouts of the Kessler Document.'

'A bit of a coincidence!' Kate cut in.

Fleming nodded and glanced around the lab. 'Far too much of one. So, either this Sergei is in Russian Intelligence and they have access to MI6 secrets on this . . . which I doubt . . .' Fleming inhaled loudly and puffed up his chest.

'Of course,' Lou commented. Kate glared at him.

'Or else . . .' Fleming went on, 'what is more likely is that this Sergei character is linked in some way to Glena Buckingham and Eurenergy.'

'That implies she – they – have a very long reach, Fleming,' Derham said. 'I find that hard to believe. You reckoned she had only just learned about Earhart's plane crash site. How could she know Kate and Lou had retrieved anything from the aircraft and linked it with Einstein and the communications he had with Kessler in 1937?'

Fleming shrugged. 'I have no idea, Captain. That's why we,' and he nodded towards Kate and Lou, 'need to get to Moscow asap.'

24

Dakar, Senegal. 9 June 1937.

She ran through the evening, feeling sweat seeping from her pores and the hot air like clammy fingers groping her skin.

The darkness and the light, the colours, the monochrome patches, they all merged into a blur as she tore down a narrow alleyway between two crumbling buildings smelling the urine and the sweat, unwashed clothes and dung.

Out on the main plaza, people milled about, trading, gossiping, drinking, eating. She ignored them all and darted down another passage hardly wider than her shoulders.

This led Amelia to a further, quieter square, a pair of woman arguing solemnly, children, sleepy but still noisy and protesting, pulling at legs. She ducked aside, skirted the square into another almost identical alleyway of stone and sky, and then she was out on the main road, the Imperial ahead on the left.

The sweat had penetrated the fabric of her blouse

and she felt self-conscious as she nodded to the doorman and slipped into the hotel, the wooden box under her arm, across the foyer and into the bar. Fred Noonan was where she had left him an hour earlier.

'Amy . . . Where've you been?'

Earhart gripped his arm, smelt her odour and knew that Fred had too. 'We have to go.'

'Go? Go where?'

'Fred, please don't make a scene, speak quietly. I'm in trouble. People are after me.'

Fred Noonan looked at her uncomprehendingly. His mouth started to move.

Amelia gave the room a furtive once-over. Three tables with seated couples and a lone drinker propped up at the end of the bar staring into his drink. The tinkling of a piano in the far corner doused her words. 'We have to pack and leave right away.'

'Amy . . . You're—'

She pulled his arm. 'Now, Fred!'

*

They met on the landing less than three minutes later, each with a single small leather bag.

'You get a cab out front. Take it round the back. I'll meet you there.'

'You're going to tell me what the hell is going on, right?' Noonan spat. He looked angrier than she had ever seen him.

'Please, Fred. I will. Can you just trust me on this?' She turned away before he could reply.

*

Amelia felt her heart racing and she had to remind herself to steady her breathing. She slipped through a swing door close to the bar's toilets. It opened onto a featureless, barely lit passageway. She reached the end after sidestepping cardboard boxes and a rickety trolley half filled with wooden cartons that gave off the pungent odour of overripe fruit. Beyond the passage lay an annexe to the kitchens. She kept close to the wall and passed into the night air once more, unnoticed. Shouldering her bag, she moved around a corner and saw the cab pull up. Across a stretch of squeaking sand and a pitted pathway, she reached the car and got into the back seat as Noonan directed the driver to the airfield.

25

Moscow. Present day.

The landing at Domodedovo Airport was the bumpiest either Kate or Lou had ever experienced. The 747 came down on the runway hard and started to skid as soon as the wheels touched the tarmac. Women screamed and lights in the passenger cabin blinked off and on. Kate felt Lou's hand grasp hers. She dared not even turn her head to see his face.

For several moments Kate wished she and Lou had not agreed to go with Adam so readily, even if the invite had come out of the blue. Her first question to Fleming had been: 'Why?' To which he had given the reasonable enough answer that higher authorities admired their work, and – as the Kessler Document had supposedly been lost at sea – a pair of marine archaeologists might prove useful.

The skid seemed to go on forever. Through the window, in the corner of Kate's field of vision, the lights of Moscow, like a gigantic fairy castle, lit up the distant horizon. Heaped snow lay either side of the runway and, far off, close to the terminal buildings, a line of snowploughs laboured against the elements.

The plane made a final judder, straightened and decelerated on the tarmac, the engines roaring with a squealing top note like the agonized protests of a stuck pig.

An hour later they were in a cab travelling fast along the Kashirskoe Shosse highway. Adam Fleming was seated in the front studying an iPad, a square-shaped man with a bulbous red nose was at the wheel; in the back Lou and Kate stared out at the bleak snow-girded freeway, cars and lorries streaming past. The cab windscreen wipers worked hard to sweep clear the sludge and spray thrown up from the road. A crimson glow from the setting sun coloured the concrete and bedraggled trees either side of the highway.

'The latest intel from London,' Fleming said, turning in his seat and offering Kate and Lou his iPad. 'Just picked it up after I finally got a signal with MegaFon.'

They read the page of information.

Sergei: We have few hard facts.
Primary source researcher Professor Ian Grady (LSE, 2011) claims Sergei was born Leon Kaminski. DOB: uncertain, 1961–3? Kaminski rose to rank of Major in Red Army (1982–1993). Died in Chechnya, 1993. Name 'Sergei' first reported in 1999. Almost nothing known about this figure. Residence and work-base location unknown.

```
Reported to be anti-Putin; Russian mafia
connections; international links with
oligarchs living in UK, but again, no
hard information. Professor Grady's
assessment considered best background
profile, i.e. Kaminski faked death in 1993,
assumed new identity 'Sergei' and
disappeared off radar. Much of Grady's
construct relies upon single reported
sighting of man who fits rumoured
description of Sergei and bearing an aged
resemblance to Major Leon Kaminski. See
attached long-distance shot at funeral in
Rublyovka in 2010.
```

Kate scrolled down and they both studied an indistinct photograph of a tall, white-haired man in a long black coat, his facial features fuzzy.

'Not very helpful,' Lou commented.

'Agreed, but it's all we or anyone else has, I'm afraid. It'll be no picnic finding the guy.'

'But presumably, if he wants to do business with us he'll want to be found.'

'Not necessarily,' Fleming replied. 'He may only work through intermediaries such as this "Zero" person.'

The car pulled off the highway onto a wide street and across a succession of junctions with traffic lights hanging over the road. The car turned right, then left, before pulling up in front of the grand frontage of the five-star Grigovna Zempska Hotel.

'MI6 must be flush,' Lou quipped.

'Only the best for our specialists,' Adam Fleming replied as he paid the driver.

Five minutes later they had signed in at reception and two liveried bellboys were taking their luggage to a service lift. Fleming checked his watch. '18.05. Shall we meet for dinner? 19.00?'

'Make it 7.30,' Kate said. 'I need some down time.'

'Fair enough,' Fleming said. '7.30 it is.'

*

'Can't complain about the view,' Lou said as he gazed out of the huge bay window of their room.

Kate was in a steam-filled bathroom, the water running. 'What was that?'

'The view,' Lou repeated loudly, half turning back to the room and catching a glimpse of Kate's naked body as she pulled off her robe in front of the mirror. 'But actually I prefer the one in here.' He strode over to the bathroom and held Kate about the waist, kissing her neck.

'Now, now . . . we don't have time for shenanigans, Dr Bates.'

'Oh, I think we do, Dr Wetherall. Unless of course you don't want to keep your ex waiting . . . Katie.'

Kate spun round and frowned at Lou. '*Katie?* You're not jealous, are you, Dr Bates?'

Lou grinned. 'How could I be? You're here naked in my arms and Fleming is in his room, alone.'

'That's absolutely right.' She kissed him, their tongues entwining, a low moan coming from deep in her throat. Lou's hand wandered up to Kate's breast and he felt the hard nipple between his thumb and index finger. Between them they pulled Lou's shirt off as they stumbled into the vast bedroom and fell onto the bed in a tangle of limbs.

*

'What do you make of Adam turning up out of the blue?' Lou asked.

Kate was nestled into him, her head on his shoulder, a single sheet wrapped around them. Propped up on voluminous pillows, they could see through the open curtains that the sky had darkened to a hazy purple, heavy with snow clouds. A glint of neon came from the street below. She propped herself up on one elbow, a look of surprise on her face. 'You sound very suspicious.'

Lou shrugged. 'I dunno, I've never trusted spies and spooks. You'll have to make allowances.'

She laughed. 'Oh, come on.'

'All right, you know the guy.'

'Knew him.'

'Knew him. You seem well, pretty chummy. Do you trust him?'

'Adam was always the keen military type – runs in his family. His father and grandfather were both army, same regiment. You know the sort of thing. I imagine moving into MI6 isn't that strange.'

'What was he like at university?'

'I only knew him in my first year. He was in his final year, PPE at Merton College. We were just friends, in the same crowd for a while.'

'I got the impression he was an old flame.'

'No.' Kate shook her head. 'Men! You always jump to the wrong conclusions.'

'There's nothing wrong with it if he was a boyfriend.'

'I know, it's . . . oh, anyway, why are you suspicious of him?'

'I didn't say I was, you did.'

Lou knocked her elbow so she slipped forward and he pulled her on top of him. She wriggled free. 'I know your game, Lou Bates.' She slid off the bed and clutched at a robe. He made a grab for her but caught only air.

'I have to get ready,' Kate giggled and ran for the bathroom, closing and locking the door behind her.

*

The dining room of the Grigovna Zempska was the epitome of faded grandeur. The hotel had first opened its doors over a century ago and its website claimed that Tsar Nicholas and his family often dined there. Painted in duck-egg blue, with two massive chandeliers hanging from the ceiling, gilt chairs upholstered in a vibrant dark green, it had old world sophistication stamped all over it.

'I've had another email from London,' Fleming said after ordering a bottle of Chablis for the three of them.

'Sergei is still in?' Kate asked.

'Seems so. The message was that Zero would make first contact with us.'

'When?'

'No idea.'

The wine arrived and the waiter poured measures into fine crystal then retreated after depositing the bottle in an ice bucket.

'To our mission,' Adam said, raising his glass.

'Well, I didn't expect to be in Moscow this evening,' Kate commented.

'Life is full of surprises.' Adam took a sip. 'I certainly didn't expect to bump into you a few days ago, Katie. Nor did I expect to meet you, Lou.' He took another sip. 'This isn't half bad. So, tell me, how did you two meet?'

Kate looked across the table to Lou.

'She's my boss,' he said.

'Oh, don't be daft . . .'

Fleming nodded. 'She is definitely the domineering type.'

'Indeed. I have the bruises to prove it.'

'*Actually*, I like to think it was inevitable that we would meet,' Kate said. 'We are both in the same very narrow business. There aren't many people working in marine archaeology.'

'Not at your level,' Fleming said, turning from Kate to Lou. 'You are renowned as the very best in the field.'

'Thanks,' Lou said as the waiter approached and asked if they were ready to order.

A moment later, the orders taken, the waiter retreated after topping up their glasses. Fleming ordered a second bottle.

'And you, Adam? Kate tells me you read PPE at Oxford, a couple of years ahead of her.'

'That's right. I only knew Katie in my final year. A shame really. We met at a party on Divinity Road. You been to Oxford, Lou?'

'I spent one semester there in 2003. I know Divinity Road. I was in a house on Hurst Street a short walk away.'

'Really? I lived in a street off Hurst. Amazing! What a small universe. So, yes, I come from an Oxford/army family: father, grandfather. My great-grandfather fought in the Boer War. I graduated, and of course it was then Sandhurst, but when I finished I didn't actually want to go into the army. My father died while I was at Merton, and so I didn't have anyone forcing me. I decided to go through Her Majesty's recruitment programme. That was, goodness . . . seven years ago now.'

Kate turned as the waiter approached her chair. He was holding a bouquet of flowers. The two men looked at him, puzzled.

'Wow!' was all Kate could manage. 'Who . . .?' She took the flowers in both hands.

'Would you like us to keep them in water for you, madam?'

'Yes, that would be . . . they smell fantastic.' Kate leaned in to sniff the blooms and noticed a card. She grabbed it as the waiter took the flowers away.

She stared at the small blank envelope. 'Is this your doing, Lou?' She beamed at her husband.

Lou had his hands raised. 'Not guilty.'

Kate looked confused, opened the envelope and pulled out a tiny card.

'Who?' Lou asked.

Kate handed him the card. It said: 'FA$HION, Red Square. Midnight.'

26

FA$HION was a nightclub a mere hundred yard walk from the hotel.

Close to midnight, Red Square was still alive with Western tourists and revellers braving temperatures hovering around minus 20 degrees. The domes of St Basil the Blessed were lit up by the street lights and the warm glow of a full moon low to the horizon.

There was a long line outside FA$HION but Fleming stepped over to an enormous doorman wearing a black suit and bow tie and showed him something inside a credit card-sized leather wallet. The man took the wallet, turned it surreptitiously to one side out of the light and then returned it to Fleming as he waved the three of them in.

'How did you manage that?' Lou asked.

Fleming tapped the side of his nose. 'I couldn't possibly divulge trade secrets, Lou. But, put it this way, a couple of American banknotes rarely fail in Moscow.'

The place was packed but thinned a little as they moved further into the club to approach a brightly illuminated dance floor at the centre of seating alcoves spread around the circumference of a vast, circular room.

The music – heavy trance morphed with classic fifties songs by a rarely glimpsed DJ in a metal cage hanging like a postmodernist chandelier above the middle of the room – pounded so loudly that it felt to Kate like the bass was reverberating inside her chest.

They made for an empty alcove, a semicircle of shiny pink PVC. A woman who looked more like a catwalk model than the average waitress came over and took their order. Kate glanced at her watch. It was 11.55. She turned her wrist to show Lou and Adam and they nodded. A few minutes later, the waitress returned with a tray containing three brightly coloured cocktails embellished with paper umbrellas and fluorescent straws. She placed them on drinks mats, handed Adam a slip of paper and turned. Adam glanced at the bill. At the foot of the slip, just below the price were the words: 'Second floor storeroom'. He looked up too late to see where the girl had gone; she had vanished into the pressing huddle of bodies.

Adam held out the bill for Kate and Lou to see and was out of the alcove in a second. Lou managed to empty half his glass with a single pull on the straw before spinning round as Adam and Kate were sucked into the melange of clubbers.

Between a pair of alcoves there was a door out to a passageway. Twenty feet along a corridor packed with more revellers, they found a spiral staircase. This ascended to a narrow mezzanine level that allowed for a bird's eye view of the dance floor and the DJ's cage a few feet lower than the balcony. From here the crowd looked like exotic fish in a pond, all bright colours and skittish movements. Along the narrow balcony they came to a second door. The word 'Staff' was written on it in Russian.

Beyond the door they were completely alone.

'Christ! I can hear myself think again,' Adam said, shaking his head. 'People actually come here voluntarily?'

'It would seem so,' Lou replied. 'So, how do we get to the second floor?' He looked around.

Adam took the lead as they walked quickly along a worn red carpet following a slight curve. They passed two doors on their right and a third on their left. A few paces on they found a lift, but the control panel close to the doors was key-code operated. An open door next to the lift led to a narrow, closed-in ascending staircase. Lou found a light switch, flicked it on and they could see stairs stretching up to the second floor.

The door to the storeroom was scratched and discoloured. Adam swung it inwards. Inside, a single bulb hung from the ceiling. Around the walls stood metal racks filled with boxes and metal drums. Leaning against the back wall of shelves was a very thin man. He had bird-like cheekbones and a patch over his left eye.

'Thank you for coming. My name is Zero.' His English was almost perfect. He extended a hand.

'You have the information?' Fleming asked.

'Of course, my client is a highly professional individual and a process for the exchange has been organized. I hope it will be to everyone's satisfaction.'

'A process?'

'We have placed the material on a heavily encrypted website. To activate the site and acquire the first half of what you are buying you must deposit an agreed sum of money into a Swiss bank account. If your people agree that we are genuine, the second half is released to you via a second encrypted site *after* you deposit the second instalment. Is that clear?'

Fleming glanced at Kate and Lou, who were studying the man. Zero was perhaps six-two but weighed no more than a hundred and thirty pounds. He had wispy blond hair, a pale, almost cadaverous face, and then there was the patch.

'I'm afraid that will *not* do,' Fleming said. 'We do not work on that basis—'

'Yet we haven't even begun to discuss figures—'

'And we will need to see a sample of the document, a photocopy will do,' continued Fleming.

'That is not a basis upon which my boss would work.'

'In that case, I regret it, but you have wasted our time.' He turned, catching Lou's eye. Lou and Kate fell in behind him and the three of them strode towards the door out to the corridor. Fleming was through the door and it was closing behind Lou when they heard Zero.

'Very well.'

Fleming paused for a moment then came back in. Lou and Kate hovered by the door.

'We need to talk numbers,' Zero said, fixing Fleming with a hard stare.

'Let me offer a working programme,' the MI6 man suggested. 'I have my instructions, also.'

Zero nodded and clasped his hands in front of him and waited.

'I have been authorized to offer Sergei three million pounds sterling. We will need a sample to study first and then we can go along with your rather elaborate system of receiving the document in exchange for the fee.'

Zero said nothing for several moments, his expression unreadable. For a second, his gaze wandered to Lou and Kate. 'I can see this is not going to be easy, Mr Fleming. When two parties such as your superior and mine come together and are so far apart in their thinking, it takes great patience and subtlety of mind on both our parts to even begin to reach a satisfactory conclusion.

'Let me be clear. My employer requires thirty-five million dollars for the Kessler Document, which I believe at current exchange rates equates to twenty-two point seven three million sterling, give or take a few thousand.' He waved a hand nonchalantly.

'Well, that is a pity,' Fleming replied. 'I hate to be a bore, but I will have to repeat what I said earlier – it seems you have wasted our time.' He started to swivel on his heel.

'I'm sure your employers will be very disappointed if you return empty-handed to London, Mr Fleming.'

'They will be disappointed, but they are grown-ups. They'll get over it.'

'And you do not feel that this historic document, one that offers so much promise and potential is worth more than a trifle like three million pounds?'

'It is not my place to judge, Mr Zero. As I said, I have my instructions.'

'And three million sterling – which is under five million dollars – is your best offer?'

Adam said nothing. The storeroom was silent save for, far off, the residue of a bass drum beat wafting up from the club two floors below.

'I need to make a call,' Zero stated. He slipped past Adam, and Lou opened the door for him.

'Christ!' Kate exclaimed. 'You're not even on the same chapter, let alone the same page.'

'Patience, Katie.'

After a while the door opened and Zero strode back in.

'Sergei is not best pleased.'

'I'm very sorry to hear that.'

Zero gave Fleming a cold look. 'I have been given very precise instructions. We are able to provide you with a copy of a fragment of the document within the hour and we are willing to accept nothing less than ten million pounds sterling which is almost exactly fifteen point six million dollars. Our terms of exchanging information for cash remain the same. I am informed that if this does not meet with your immediate approval, I am to walk out of this room. A car is waiting for me outside.'

Fleming studied the man's face, following the lines of his prominent cheekbones, the beak of a nose, the patch. 'That is acceptable,' he said. 'I expect to see you at my hotel in exactly one hour.'

27

It had started to snow while they were in the club and by the time they left it was coming down so heavily they had to catch a cab for the hundred yards back to the Grigovna Zempska.

'You plan to trust that guy Zero, Adam?' Kate asked as the taxi slithered away from the kerb.

'About as far as I could spit a goat. Don't worry, we have mechanisms in place to make sure we don't give anyone millions of pounds for nothing.'

'Glad to hear it,' Lou said. 'This Sergei guy sounds like a pretty shrewd operator.'

'Without a doubt. We know almost nothing about him, but one thing we are sure about is that he can hold his own with the better-known Russian oligarchs.'

'Probably made his first few hundred million when communism fell and the Soviet state transformed itself,' Kate remarked.

'Extremely likely.' Fleming looked out at the driving snow, the slurry splashing as high as the windows as the car made a sharp left, its rear wheels protesting and losing traction on the ice.

When they pulled up, they could see the lavish foyer with its marble columns and rich red carpet. It was lit up like a Christmas grotto. Fleming paid the driver and caught up with Lou and Kate in the lobby. 'Just need to do something,' he said and they followed him to a vast mid-nineteenth-century teak and gilt reception desk. Three pretty, black-haired women in identical tight blue two-piece suits sat behind the counter each tapping busily at Apple computers.

'Good evening, sir.'

'Good evening . . .' Fleming glanced at the receptionist's name badge '. . . Natalia. I would like to change rooms . . . immediately.'

Natalia looked puzzled. 'I'm sorry, Mr Ambrose, sir. Is there something wrong with . . .' she tapped her keyboard as she spoke '. . . your room? 545?'

'Yes, I specifically booked a room with a view over Red Square. I was too busy earlier to mention it, but I was most disappointed with the room you have given me.'

'I see.' She was scanning the monitor as she typed. 'I can find no mention of . . .' She reread a few lines of the booking. 'Your secretary Ms Smith made the booking from London.'

'Correct, and she assured me she had booked a room with the appropriate view.'

Natalia fell silent for a moment and concentrated on the mouse, the keyboard and the screen.

'I'm sorry, Mr Ambrose, but . . .'

'I'm sorry too . . . Natalia. I have stayed here quite a

few times and my company places all our executives here when we have business in Moscow. I'm sure the other board members at Ambrose and Finch will be irritated by this slip-up. It is such an annoyance having to change regular venues for our visits and conferences in Moscow.'

Natalia was staring back at the screen and shuffling a little in her seat. Kate looked at Lou and raised her eyebrows.

'Ah, yes, hang on a second, sir.' The receptionist tapped earnestly, eyes scanning the lines of writing on her screen. 'We . . .' tap, tap '. . . do have . . .' tap, tap, tap 'one room . . .' tap '. . . with a very nice . . .' tap, tap 'view directly over the square. Yes . . . 907, a junior suite. We can do this for . . .'

'The same price as my existing booking.'

Natalia looked up from the computer, searched Fleming's face for a moment. 'A minute, please, Mr Ambrose.'

The receptionist picked up a cordless phone, keyed in three digits and started to speak in very fast Russian. '*Da* . . . *Da*,' she answered, nodding. She clicked off the phone, gave Fleming a broad smile and flicked a friendly glance at Lou and Kate. 'That will not be a problem, sir.' She tapped some more keys on her computer, withdrew a plastic card from a drawer and slipped it into a narrow slot in a metal box to one side of the computer. The machine beeped and spat out the plastic. She handed the card to Fleming. 'Do you need some time to repack, Mr Ambrose?'

'No, I have just one small bag.'

'Very good.' She nodded to a porter standing stiffly just beyond the end of the counter. He approached, stopping a respectful distance from Fleming's right. Natalia gave him instructions in Russian and he waved Fleming, Lou and Kate towards the lifts.

'Thank you for your help, Natalia,' Fleming said.

*

'You didn't say you were unhappy with your room,' Kate said as she and Lou found armchairs to settle into and the door closed behind the porter. Room 907 was twice the size of 545 and came with a sitting room. The view through the massive bay windows was like something from Google Images, a perfect snapshot of the Kremlin and St Basil's Cathedral.

'I wasn't,' Fleming said, withdrawing a small device the size of an iPhone from his pocket. He paced around holding the contraption at arm's length, thrusting it into each corner, under the chairs, around a fruit bowl, the minibar and the TV. 'I wanted to be sure we had a fresh room for our chat with Zero.'

'Bugs?'

'Precisely.' He checked the device in his hand. Satisfied, he tucked it back into the pocket of his overcoat.

Kate and Lou watched as Fleming unpacked a small suitcase, removing a laptop and two small, anonymous metal boxes. He placed them on a table close to the kingsize bed dominating the room, wired them up and powered them, using a plugboard and an adaptor. He then ordered two pots of coffee from room service and they walked through to the sitting room adjoining the bedroom.

A waiter arrived with the coffee and placed it on an ornate marble and gilt table, arranged delicate china cups and saucers and was just exiting when Zero arrived at the door to room 907. He was wearing a calf-length fur coat and matching ushanka hat, the ear flaps dangling down, the whole ensemble drowning his face and body. As he removed the hat and coat to reveal a suit and tie, he looked like an astronaut slipping out of his EVA suit.

Fleming checked his watch. It was 1.16 a.m. 'Very punctual,' he remarked and led the man through the bedroom to the living area, where Zero shook hands with Lou and Kate before lowering himself into one of the four chairs around the table. Kate poured the coffee and handed Zero a cup and saucer.

He thanked her and took a sip. 'That is very good.'

'So, what do you have for us?' Fleming asked.

Zero slipped a hand into an inside pocket of his suit jacket and withdrew an envelope. He opened it, removed a single piece of paper from inside and handed it to Fleming, who scanned the contents and passed it on to Lou.

'What exactly do we have here?' Lou asked and offered the piece of paper to Kate.

'A photocopy, naturally. The original document is four pages in length,' Zero began. 'The paper is damaged in places and very fragile, but it is all legible. It is kept in a temperature-regulated chamber built specially to house and protect it. This is a copy of page one. Only a single copy of the original was ever made, some ten years ago.'

'And how did Sergei acquire the document?' Kate asked.

'I'm afraid I cannot divulge that information, Dr Wetherall.'

Adam Fleming was studying the man silently.

'How long has it been in your boss's possession?' Lou said.

'Again, I cannot say. I'm sorry, Dr Bates, Dr Wetherall.' Zero turned to Fleming. 'I cannot answer any other questions concerning the Kessler Document. Now, Mr Fleming, you said you would need to have the authenticity of this verified?' He nodded towards the piece of paper.

'Yes.' Fleming stood up and walked around to Kate's chair. She handed him the photocopy. 'I'll be as quick as I can. London is expecting me. Please help yourself to more coffee, Mr Zero.' He turned and left the room, closing the interconnecting door to the bedroom.

The lock had barely clicked into place when the door flew inwards, smashed against the wall and started to swing back. Fleming was standing in the doorway assuming the Weaver stance, gripping in both hands a Glock 17 with a silencer, the barrel pointed directly at Zero's head.

'What the fuck!' Lou was out of his chair.

Fleming did not waver an inch. 'Sit down, Lou,' he said calmly.

Zero raised his hands, staring straight into the MI6 agent's eyes. 'Bad news from London?'

'Who are you?' Fleming snapped.

'My name is Zero. I work for Serg—'

'Nonsense.' Fleming took a step forward.

'What is this all about, Adam?' Kate said, her eyes darting from Fleming to the Russian. 'Can someone please explain?'

'Katie, this man is a fraud. I was able to take his photograph in the storeroom. I sent this to London with my phone as we were driving back here in the cab. Zero is actually Arseny Valentin, an FSB agent, or should I say a *former* FSB agent. He did not show up for work at the Lubyanka Square HQ on Monday. An alert was put out yesterday. You're a wanted man, Arseny.'

'It is nice to be desired.'

'So what about the document?' Lou exclaimed. 'Is it fake?'

'Indeed. I imagine it goes something like this: Mr Valentin here somehow learns MI6 is following a lead to Sergei; he sees an opportunity and grabs it with both hands; he cobbles together a plausible story and a document and tries to pass it off as the real deal.'

Valentin lowered his hands and clapped slowly, softly. 'Excellent work, Mr Fleming. So, what now? You will kill me and dump my body in the Moskva?'

'That is one option.'

'Adam!' Kate stood up. Lou took her hand and guided her back down to her seat, shaking his head in warning.

'Not a wise one though, I fear,' Valentin said.

'You sound remarkably confident for a man with a pistol pointed at his head.'

'Do you really think I would embark on an adventure such as this without insurance?'

Fleming took a deep breath.

'I have placed a note with a trusted friend,' Valentin went on. 'If I mysteriously vanish she will post the letter to my superiors in Lubyanka Square. It contains everything I know about the Kessler Document and about you.' He turned from Fleming to glance at Lou and Kate.

'But that could all be a bluff of course,' Fleming said.

Valentin shrugged. 'Poker happens to be my favourite game.'

'Not convinced,' Fleming said icily and his finger whitened on the trigger.

'No, Adam!' Kate screamed.

Valentin seized the moment, surged forward and grabbed Fleming's wrist. The gun went off almost noiselessly, the bullet smashing a light fitting and ricocheting into the plasterwork beside a Louis XIV-style mirror above a grand stone fireplace. The FSB agent was lean and very fast. Fleming lost his balance, stumbled back against the door and fell to the carpet. Valentin kicked him savagely in the head and rushed through the doorway into the bedroom.

Kate ran to help Adam to his feet.

Fleming scrambled for the gun, snatched it up. 'I'm fine,' he snapped and pelted after the Russian.

The door out to the hall was slamming shut. Fleming crossed the room in a second and was out in the hallway. Valentin disappeared around a bend in the corridor. The MI6 man ran after him. An empty stretch of carpeted corridor fell away left and right. At the end of the passage to the left there was an emergency exit. Fleming raced towards it, through the door, and into a concrete stairway. He stopped, holding his breath to hear any sign of Valentin. Nothing. He took the stairs three at a time, reached the sixth floor and stopped again, panting for breath. 'Fuck!' he spat.

28

'What the hell just happened?' Kate said. She looked drained as she pressed an ice pack improvised from a face towel and a handful of ice from the minibar against Adam's left temple. A large bruise was spreading down his jaw.

'We're after a very desirable item. We aren't going to be the only ones interested in it.'

'But how did you know Valentin was faking?' Lou said. 'Sure, he was FSB, if London said he was, but maybe he had acquired the real document.'

'I wasn't sure until he arrived here and gave us the photocopy.'

Lou handed Fleming a cup of coffee. 'Explain.'

'The Einstein film I showed you back at Norfolk had actually been manipulated.' He smiled faintly at Kate and Lou's surprise. 'Not in any major way,' he added. 'It is indeed a real film of the scientist explaining what had happened in 1937, but we cut out a section in which he described briefly what form the document took on its journey from Germany.' Fleming topped up his cup. 'We did it deliberately in case the film fell into the wrong hands or its contents leaked, which they clearly have. As soon as Valentin said the photocopy was one page of a four-page document, he gave himself away. The original written by Kessler was etched into a single sheet of tin foil. This was rolled up and placed in a redundant pipe aboard the merchant vessel SS *Freedom*. There never was a paper original.'

'That's very clever,' Kate said and sat in one of the chairs across the table from Adam. 'So, what do you think happened to the document? Was it really lost with the ship?'

'Possibly,' Fleming began and took a sip of coffee, wincing as he drank. 'But it's also possible that the Germans got hold of it. There are only two ways that could have happened. The merchant ship must have been boarded, then either it was taken back to Germany and dismantled piece by piece, or the crew were tortured and eventually gave away the location of the document before they were killed and SS *Freedom* sunk. We might never know.'

'The Germans must have had pretty good intelligence to go to all that trouble. They must have been sure the document was on the ship.'

'Agreed. Presumably, they had acquired some concrete information through their spy network.'

'And it was also a daring thing to do politically,' Lou added. 'Britain and Germany weren't even at war in 1937.'

'But war wasn't far away. Everyone knew that,' Kate said.

'Yes. The spy network in Europe was already working overtime on both sides,' Fleming agreed. 'We and the Germans wanted to get any possible advantage as early as possible.'

'Could Kessler have been tortured, or at least threatened?'

'I don't think so,' Fleming said. 'If that had happened, the Germans would have had a lot of material towards developing their own shield, and there's no evidence to support that, at least as far as we know.'

'But the Nazis would only have had Kessler's contribution anyway. Einstein's work was at least as important,' Kate interjected.

'True.'

'What did happen to Kessler?'

'He continued to work in Germany throughout the war and died in 1946. As far as we know, he never left his homeland again; never saw Einstein again. There's also no record of the two men ever communicating after the failed attempt to get the material Einstein needed for his experiments. The tests in America were called off, the project scrapped.'

Lou yawned. 'Sorry.' He looked at his watch. It was almost 2 a.m.

'So where does this leave us?' Kate asked. 'Back at square one?'

'Not entirely,' Fleming replied. 'Zero, or Valentin, was impersonating a Sergei contact. I had no hint from him that he had ever met the man. It is quite possible

Sergei or one of his minions will still contact us. I think right now the only thing we can do is get some sleep and hope things fall into place tomorrow.'

29

Lou woke to the sound of the shower running. He sat up in bed and saw a trail of running gear leading into the bathroom; then he glanced at the clock. It read 06.54.

'Fuck me!' he said to the empty room and flopped back down with the covers drawn over his head.

Sixty seconds later, the phone rang.

He groaned and reached for the receiver; dropping it, swearing and plucking it up to his ear.

'Lou? Adam. We have a breakthrough. The two of you get down to reception asap.'

'But . . .'

Adam had hung up.

Kate was at the door to the bathroom looking decorous in nothing but a flimsy white gold necklace. She gave him a questioning look.

'Adam. In reception. There's some news. Wants us downstairs *asap* apparently.'

'Better get a move on then.'

Lou jumped from the bed. 'Not so fast . . .'

Kate laughed and spun back to the bathroom shutting and locking the door.

'You have to let me in,' Lou said through the wood. 'I have to get ready, remember?'

'Not till I'm dressed.'

Lou turned, leaned back on the door and produced a weary sigh. 'I'm going to have to do something about that lock.'

*

Adam was in reception looking fresh and rested.

'Great, let's go for a walk,' he said. 'Wipe away the cobwebs. I have a lot to share.'

'Fabulous,' Lou said. 'But can we at least have breakfast first?'

'No need.' Adam lifted a pair of Starbucks cups. 'Very convenient, just a block away.'

Kate laughed and squeezed Lou around the shoulder. 'Come on, Eeyore.'

*

It was almost frighteningly cold outside, the sort of sub-zero temperatures that make you wonder how you can still keep moving. The sky was a grey-black, the sun some way from rising; the red pinprick of Mars could be seen above the trees lining Teatralny Proezd, the main thoroughfare beyond the revolving doors of the Grigovna Zempska Hotel. They walked at a brisk pace west towards Maly Theatre.

'I wanted us to walk. It's the safest way to keep

things between just the three of us,' Fleming said, steam billowing around his mouth in the chill. 'London got back to me after I filed a report this morning. My team are working around the clock and have what we believe is a genuine contact with Sergei.'

'They contacted your people?' Kate asked.

'A few hours ago. The guy representing Sergei is called Max. No surname. He expressed outrage that Sergei should be misrepresented as he was by Zero and sent through some details about himself, including a head shot. My team have matched the image to one of the background figures standing behind Sergei at the funeral in Rublyovka five years ago – the one and only clear ID of Sergei we've had in recent years.'

He handed Kate a photo of the man.

'Another ugly bastard,' Lou commented peering at the picture of Max in the half-light – a flabby-faced bald man with large protruding eyes and no eyebrows.

'Quite so, but hopefully more genuine than our friend Zero.'

They had reached the end of the main road and turned right, heading towards Ploshchad Revolyutsii, the Revolution Square Metro station, its impressive pillared frontage and art-deco friezes standing in sharp relief against the gloom. Straight ahead stood Resurrection Gate, the entrance into Red Square. Sixty seconds later, they were through the gate with the stunning panorama of Red Square spread out before them. The bricked ground was decorated with a patina of frost and snow left behind after a snowplough had, minutes earlier, swept away the worst of the overnight fall. Snow draped the line of bedraggled trees edging the plaza and lay banked up close to the State Department Store GUM, which took up most of the north-eastern side of the square. At the far end, some three hundred yards away, stood the onion domes and tent peaks of St Basil's.

'Has this guy Max suggested the next move?'

'He has promised a direct meeting with Sergei before any negotiations or mention of money changing hands.'

'A good sign,' Lou commented.

They walked across the plaza in silence for a while, overawed by the view. Fleming had been to Moscow many times, but this was a first for Lou and Kate. Neither of them could have guessed as they stood on the deck of the *Inca* that, a few days later, they would be walking across Red Square with temperatures in the minus double figures.

'It is an encouraging step forward,' Fleming said, stopping. They stood together close to the centre of the square. 'But I have to make some things clear. Sergei is a renegade. He won't be helping us. He is only interested in himself and he knows he possesses something valuable.'

'Well, he claims he does,' Kate said.

Fleming nodded and stamped his feet in a futile effort to get warm. 'My team are confident he is genuine. Sergei is a busy man. He runs a mini empire. Twenty or thirty million dollars is not a lot of money to him, but it is worth him getting out of bed for. And who knows? Maybe he has a personal agenda, some other reason to communicate with us and to spend some of his precious time negotiating an exchange.'

'So what's the plan?'

'We're due to meet Max at 9 p.m. at Moscow State University, Building 6. He hasn't said what he wants to do after that, but we should expect the unexpected.'

30

Building 6 of the Moscow State University in the suburb of Ramenki, about three miles from the centre of Moscow, was a four-storey anonymous block of concrete and steel: utilitarian, predictable, with small windows, stains running vertically down the sheer walls, snow heaped at its base. Girdled by a galvanized steel fence, it nestled up against a busy road, Michurinskiy Prospekt.

The cab pulled away and Fleming led Kate and Lou towards a gate in the metal fence. The building housed off-campus geophysics labs. A few lights remained on and they could hear the strains of a Coldplay song tumbling down from one of the windows overhead. The traffic was lighter than usual: CSKA Moscow were playing Spartak in a crucial semi-final game in the Russian Cup.

The path was slippery and they took it slowly to the reception area on the ground floor of the block. The reception itself was closed up, the place quiet except for the hum of fluorescent strips overhead and the far-off thud of a generator. The clock on the wall said it was 20.59. A corridor to the left of reception led to a set of double doors. Against the east wall stood a row of well-used grey plastic chairs.

They were about to walk over to the chairs when a short man wearing a fur-collared greatcoat appeared at the door. He beckoned them over. 'I am Max. Come . . . please. I have a car outside.'

It was a Mercedes CL500. Fleming climbed into the front passenger seat. Max shook hands with him and turned to offer his hand to Kate and Lou in the back. The vehicle was warm and comfortable and lit with gentle, expensive light. From beyond the windows the sound of cars churning the sooty snow was muffled very effectively.

'You are extremely punctual,' Max observed. 'I like that. This is perhaps not the most salubrious meeting point, I know, but I was going for discretion. I hope you approve.'

Nobody replied.

'The way this works is that I will take you to my boss's home,' he continued. 'You will of course appreciate that this is a massive privilege and it comes with some . . . process.'

'Process?' Lou asked, searching Max's face.

'Sergei allows very few to enter his realm. He trusts no one.'

'Realm?' Kate said, giving the Russian a puzzled look.

'Forgive me,' Max said quickly. 'Habit. In some senses we think of it as a realm. I know my boss Sergei does, and I think it is a justifiable tag. Soon perhaps you will be able to make your own judgement on the matter.'

'OK,' Fleming said impatiently. 'Where to first?'

'The Metro station, Universitet,' Max replied and opened the door. 'It's not far, just along the street.'

It was almost deserted, the entrance a single-storey circular building standing on a large traffic island. Across the street stood a row of tatty electrical stores; along the opposite side, a block of apartments, faceless and bedraggled. A young couple dressed in similar brightly coloured parkas with fur-lined hoods zipped up to their cheeks came towards them in the freezing night. Inside, an escalator descended one floor to a small ticket hall. Curved stone walls funnelled into a corridor lined with blue ticket machines and a row of grilled booth windows.

The ticket offices were all closed. Max stepped towards the nearest machine and in a few moments he had tickets for all of them. He handed them round and led the way along the tunnel, through a turnstile, down a wide staircase to a stark platform lined in brown concrete, over-lit and oppressive.

A train thundered into the station, its flat silver snout emerging from the tunnel beyond the platform and out into the neon brightness.

The carriage was almost empty with no more than a handful of figures in overcoats hunched up in their seats.

'We only need to go one stop . . .' Max said, clinging on to a leather strap dangling from a suspended rail above his head as the train rocked on its axis. '. . . Prospekt Vernadskogo.'

The train had barely stopped accelerating when it began to slow; the flash of the multicoloured conduit and junction boxes of the tunnel interior gave way to neon and concrete as they pulled into the station.

They were the only ones leaving their carriage and spotted two other passengers disembarking further along the train. They walked quickly along the platform and disappeared into a side tunnel. Max led the way towards an exit.

As they took a left and then a right, the passages were eerily quiet. Max stopped abruptly. On the wall to their left was plastered a poster for a new Tom Cruise movie and they could just make out next to that the outline of a door sunk into the brickwork. Max had a key in his hand; he leaned in and twisted it in a small partially hidden lock.

A middle-aged man in a trilby and heavy coat and carrying a leather briefcase rounded the corner.

'Tom Cruise . . .' Max said as he began shuffling away from the door and pointing to the poster. The others huddled together as though they were old friends who had stopped for a moment to discuss the movie. The man in the trilby ignored them and in a moment he had disappeared around a bend at the end of the passage. Max glanced round, pulled the door outward and beckoned Fleming, Kate and Lou into the opening.

Max ducked inside, pulled the door to and flicked on

a light switch. They were in a maintenance tunnel running parallel to the passenger route. It was illuminated by a low voltage strip light embedded in the ceiling. The floor was scuffed and worn concrete, oil smears decorated the walls, and from nearby they could hear the sound of dripping water. It smelled of damp.

'Well, this I didn't expect,' Lou said, looking around.

'Perhaps I should have explained,' Max said. 'Sergei is not what you might consider a conventional man. While some in his political and financial position establish themselves abroad, others are persecuted and imprisoned by our so-called rulers. Sergei has found a unique solution that allows him to stay in his homeland and the city he loves but far removed from his enemies.'

'Explain some more, please, Max,' Fleming said. He couldn't straighten up in the maintenance tunnel for fear of hitting his head on the ceiling.

'This' – Max waved a hand around in the half-light – 'is one of many entrances to the outer ring of Metro 2.'

'Metro 2?' Fleming exclaimed. 'You're telling me there really is such a thing?'

Kate looked at Lou and then said: 'Could one of you please tell me what you are talking about?'

Fleming tilted his head and put out a hand towards their guide, who said: 'Metro 2 is the popular name for a vast network of tunnels and chambers lying beneath the Moscow underground system. It was built by Stalin's minions, beginning in 1947, just as the Cold War began. Some of it has not been explored in recent times and was sealed off in the early 1960s. In the mid-1990s, my boss, Sergei, began making a section of Metro 2 habitable. The periphery of the network is more or less public. Excitable teenagers and various cranks calling themselves "diggers" make forays into Metro 2, thinking they will find hidden treasure or perhaps nuclear silos. There are even organized media tours that can be booked secretly on the Internet. None of it is officially sanctioned of course. In fact, the government continually insists there is no such thing as Metro 2.' He produced a gruff laugh. 'Sergei tolerates these people because it is easier for him to do so. But none of them has a clue about the real subterranean places he has occupied, expanded and made habitable in the lowest reaches of Stalin's network under Moscow – what I referred to earlier as Sergei's realm. Security is incredibly tight and our own intelligence team, headed up by a former KGB bureau chief, is world class in the art of disinformation.'

'Unreal,' Lou said.

'May I suggest we move along?' Max said. 'You look very uncomfortable, Mr Fleming.'

He took them along the narrow tunnel. 'Watch out,' Max said. 'The ceiling dips even lower here.'

At the end of the section they came to another locked door. It was card-operated. A metal rectangular box with a small slit at the front hung on the wall next to the door. Max ran a card along the groove, there was a low hiss and the door slid open. They passed through into a wider corridor with a higher ceiling and better lighting. It stretched away into the distance, sloping downwards very gradually so that the end lay out of sight.

Fleming rubbed his neck. 'Thank God for that!'

They walked on for several minutes until the corridor opened out into a roughly circular space. The light here was fainter, the neon strips left behind, replaced by a pair of ceiling lights that did not quite illuminate the corners and crannies. Three corridors led away from the room.

'I'm afraid I have to insist on a security measure,' Max said. 'You will of course understand that I cannot lead you straight to Sergei. The route to the inhabited zone must be revealed to no one. You will have to agree to be blindfolded for a while.'

Fleming stared into the man's little eyes. 'I'm not comfortable with that.' He glanced at Kate then Lou.

'Be that as it may, Mr Fleming, I have very clear instructions. If you wish to meet Sergei you will have to abide by his terms. This is his domain. It is merely a security precaution. We have not preserved our home for almost a quarter of a century by being careless.'

'How long do we need to be blindfolded for?' Kate asked.

'Ten minutes at the most,' Max replied. 'It is just so that you may not retrace the journey.'

Lou shrugged. 'Whatever.'

Max fixed the blindfolds to each of them, a strip of

black cloth tied at the back of the head. He then started to bind Kate's wrists.

'Hang on, you didn't say anything about tying our hands.'

Kate spun round and lifted her blindfold.

'I'm sorry, but I have my orders. Forgive me, but we have only just met. I have no way of knowing I can trust you to keep the blindfolds in place.'

'Shit,' Lou hissed, pulling his blindfold off. 'I have a bad feeling about this.'

'Well, if you do, Dr Bates, I can take you back to the Metro station. From there you may return to your cosy hotel room.'

Lou gave the man a fierce look and felt Kate's calming hand on his shoulder.

'Please, put yourself in our position,' Max went on, his voice softer. 'I'm sure you would feel the same way. The government has been trying to bring Sergei before a rigged court for decades. They want his money. I assume you have heard of Mikhail Borisovich Khodorkovsky? He was the richest man in Russia, imprisoned in 2004 on trumped-up corruption charges, his assets seized. My boss does not have the luxury of freedom of movement about the city, the freedom you probably take for granted. But at least he is not in jail or exiled.'

'Very well,' Fleming said. 'Ten minutes, not a second longer.'

Max tied their wrists behind them as loosely as possible, tied their blindfolds back on, and then joined each of them together with a length of rope so they could walk single file behind him.

At first they made slow progress and kept tripping over each other's feet, but soon they found a rhythm. Max shouted back instructions as they came to bends, and then they slowly descended a long flight of stairs. They stopped at every junction and Max turned them round a few times so they had no idea in which direction they were then taken.

'This is not my idea of fun,' Kate hissed.

Lou heard her. 'Mine neither. You OK?'

'I guess.'

They stopped for a moment.

'I have to open another set of doors with my card. It may take a second, please be patient. We are nearly through to the release point.'

'Sounds like you've done this before,' Lou observed.

'A few times. It is a necessary evil, and again, I apologize.'

They heard Max tap a set of metal keys and the slither of the card through the reader, then came the sound of him tugging on what must have been a large handle followed by the creak of a door opening away from them. They felt a draught of warmer air hitting them in the face.

Lou was ahead of Kate and behind Fleming. He felt the rope go slack ahead of him, then heard the sound of someone stumbling around.

'What's happening?' he yelled.

'Lou?' Kate shouted.

'Lou? Kate?' Fleming's voice boomed around the confined space. 'Stay still, or we'll . . .'

Lou spun round and almost lost his balance as he bumped into something or someone. 'Adam?'

'Ow!'

'Kate?'

They both stood still, listening. Nothing.

'Fleming?' Lou called. 'Max?'

No reply.

He tried again, louder. Kate joined in. 'Adam . . . Max . . .' then panicking, 'Shit . . . Shit!'

'Kate, keep calm. Where are you?'

'I'm here. Don't move away.'

Lou followed her voice, shuffling slowly to his left. They bumped together again.

'OK,' Lou said. 'Bend forward. I'll move my head down – you feel for the blindfold.'

He felt her knock against him and leaned forward.

'Move your fingers until you find my face.'

Kate touched his shoulder and shifted position, bending down and across. She grabbed the blindfold and lifted it up and over Lou's head. He then stepped round and did the same for Kate.

They looked around. They were in a dimly lit corridor with rough stone walls and floor. To their left water ran down the hewn rock in a narrow rivulet. Lou tried to loosen the ropes about his wrist. After a moment of struggle, he managed it and then untied Kate.

'Where are the others?' she said. 'What the hell's going on?'

Lou could see the fear in his wife's eyes. 'I wish I knew.'

31

'What now?' Kate said.

Lou put his fingers to his forehead. 'God knows. We could be anywhere.' He pulled out his mobile and glanced at the screen, expecting very little. Kate gave him a questioning look and tried hers.

'Absolutely nothing. I reckon I lost the signal before we even entered Metro 2.'

'Me too.'

'We could backtrack and try every alternative turning. That way we could maybe get back to the entrance door off the subway passenger tunnel.'

'Yeah but that doesn't help us find Adam, or Sergei.'

'No. We have to move on, keep track of every step, draw some sort of map.'

'You got a pen? Some paper?' Lou asked, rifling through his coat and jacket pockets.

Kate produced a couple of pieces of paper, letters she had kept in her bag for days. Lou found a pen in the inside pocket of his jacket.

'OK, which way?'

'Take your pick. Fifty–fifty chance, I guess.'

They headed off along the corridor. It continued for at least a hundred yards, featureless, curved stone walls to each side, wet with damp. The corridor swung left and they reached a junction. Kate drew the path they had taken on the back of one of the letters, keeping it small – they had no idea how far they had to go.

'Right,' Lou said. 'The only thing we can do is make random guesses, try a route for maybe ten minutes, see what we find. Then we have to make a decision to either backtrack to here and set off in the opposite direction, or keep going.'

The next ten minutes offered a succession of bland passageways, each pretty much the same as the other. They made random choices, turning left or right. Twice they came to a junction with three options and just had to make an unscientific guess. At the end of a long, winding corridor they emerged into a large open space, the floor made of brick. The light was brighter here and they could see thick metal pipes running along the walls. Two closed doors stood at the far end of the room.

'Well, this is a good sign,' Kate said. 'It certainly beats plain corridors anyway.'

'The pipes indicate we're near machinery. They look heavy-duty, maybe the water supply for Sergei's community?'

'Possibly,' Kate agreed. 'This place Max was talking about. It would need water, electricity, air. There must be a ducting system, from the surface. These services would be guarded and there must be many independent redundant systems or the whole thing could be easily sabotaged. If Sergei and his people have been down here for the best part of a quarter of a century they would have built in safeguards and defence systems.'

The pipes disappeared into the far wall between the doors. They paced over. To the left stood a solid-steel fire door. Lou tried the handle. The door was locked. 'Nope,' he said.

Kate tested the handle of the other door and eased it towards them. It opened into a low-ceilinged room, racks of shelves just visible. Kate ran her hand along the inside wall and found a switch, a single low-voltage bulb snapped on and lit up the room to reveal floor-to-ceiling metal shelves to the left and across the far wall. To the right, the pipe from the large room jutted from the wall close to the ceiling and stretched away, curving under an archway.

They walked across the room ignoring the empty shelves and took a right under the arch and into another anonymous corridor. The pipes ran above head-height along the wall. Kate noted it all down.

The corridor ended with an archway that led into a vestibule. Directly ahead stood a closed door. It opened inwards to reveal a room lying in darkness. It took a moment to find the light switch, an old Bakelite affair on the wall. Lou flicked down the round-ended switch and a row of fluorescent tubes began to flicker into life, splashing bursts of garish light into the room and clicking loudly in the silent confined space.

More metal shelves. These were packed with boxes,

papers spilling from them. More papers and files lay stacked next to these boxes. There was a strong smell in the room, the unmistakable odour of old, damp paper.

'It would be fascinating to take a look at some of these papers,' Kate said. 'Maybe another time.'

'Where have the pipes gone?' Lou asked.

Then they saw them disappearing from the room through a rough-hewn hole above an open doorway. They passed through into a passage that sloped steeply downwards, curving to the left. Immediately around the bend they were brought up sharply. The tunnel opened out onto an abandoned Metro platform.

The place had not been used in decades. The wall opposite the platform was covered with peeling posters, communist propaganda – faded pictures of healthy wholesome-looking children and happy peasants; images from a place and time that had never really existed. There was a layer of dust underfoot and lines of lichen at the edge of the platform; green tendrils of slime hung from the ceiling accompanied by an all-pervading stench of damp. The words *Stantsiya Nomer Odin*, written in Cyrillic and Latin script, were just visible on a corroded metal sign.

Kate pointed to two huge openings in the ceiling, one close to either end of the platform, left and right. 'Must be air vents, do you think?'

'Yeah. This whole network is amazingly ventilated.'

Kate wandered along the platform, the sound of her boots echoing in the silent cavernous space. Turning on her heel and walking slowly back towards him, she said: 'When do you think this was closed down?'

He was standing close to the entrance they had emerged from, gazing at the ruined ceiling and the stained walls.

He shrugged. 'From the look of these posters' – he nodded towards the wall – 'I'd say mid-twentieth century, maybe early sixties.'

'Certainly smells like it,' Kate said and stopped abruptly.

'What?'

Lou strode over.

'An old emergency equipment post. Could be useful.'

'Too right it could,' Lou said, peering through the filthy glass to the inside of the box. Using the sleeve of his coat, he wiped the cover clean. Then, pulling off his boot, he held the ankle leather and smashed the heel against the glass. It shattered into daggers that scattered across the concrete close to his feet. With gloved hands, he tugged away the remaining shards and pulled out an axe, a coil of rope and a torch.

'I don't imagine for a minute this works,' he said searching for the 'on' switch of the torch. He found a protuberance halfway along the metal tube and a pale light burst from the end. 'Christ!' he exclaimed and switched it off. 'Fantastic!'

'Look at this.' Kate was pointing to a torn remnant of a Metro map in a shattered frame pinned to the wall close to the emergency kit box.

'Not much of it left.'

'No, but look here.' She pointed to the lower left corner. 'It's the Sokolnicheskaya line; the one we were on with Adam and Max. See? There's Universitet and Prospekt Vernadskogo.' She ran a finger down the paper. 'The last stop on the line should be Yugo-Zapadnaya, but look, there are three more stations on this old map: Stantsiya Nomer Odin, Stantsiya Nomer Dva, Stantsiya Nomer Tri: which must mean "Stations One, Two and Three". This is Station One.'

'How very Soviet.'

'Yes, but don't you see? It implies this is the first of three abandoned stations, the others, Station Two and Station Three must be further into Metro 2.'

'OK. So we follow the track south-west?'

At the end of the platform they found a set of three concrete steps that led down onto the tracks. The opening to the tunnel stood a few yards away.

'Feels creepy,' Kate said.

'The tracks won't be live,' Lou replied, nodding towards the rails. 'Look how rusted they are for a start. They haven't been used for years . . . decades.'

'Can we make sure?'

Lou searched around the tracks. It was littered with pieces of brick, plaster and metal; a few lengths of wood. Trudging back along the side of the track, he eventually found what he was looking for, a metal rod about five feet in length and half an inch in diameter. It looked as though it had once been used as a piece of trim or maybe part of a light fixture.

Walking back to Kate, he stood at the very edge of the opening where the tracks lay.

'What are you going to do?' Kate looked worried.

'Watch.'

He laid one end of the rod on the outer rail. 'If this track was still operational, the middle rail would be live,' he said. 'Universal design. If I drop this metal across the gap between what was the live rail and this outer rail' – he nodded at the metal strip running left to right close to their feet – 'it'll short out – lots of sparks and fuss.'

'OK.'

He let go of the metal pole. It fell a couple of feet and landed on the central rail, the other end still lying on the outer rail. Nothing happened.

'Stone dead,' Lou said.

'All right. Makes sense.'

'Of course it does.' Lou stepped forward, put his foot on the middle rail and started shaking frantically, emitting a horrible sound.

'Lou!'

He stopped and grinned. 'Got ya!'

Kate punched him hard on the shoulder. 'Don't ever . . .'

'Oh, come on!'

'No, Lou . . . Not funny.'

'Shit . . . sorry.' He shrugged.

They stepped into the space between the outer and middle rail and started to walk towards the black hole of the tunnel entrance. Kate reached into her pocket and pulled out the map she had been drawing. Lou waited for her to catch up. But then, as she thrust her hand back into her coat pocket to retrieve the pen, the paper flew out of her hand.

'No!' she exclaimed. The paper hovered in the air, rose a little. She grabbed for it. Lou did the same. It rose higher. He made another desperate leap for the paper as it caught the updraught from the air duct directly overhead and disappeared upwards into the shaft.

'Goddam it!' Lou yelled.

Kate closed her eyes, her face drained of blood. She let out a sigh. 'I thought we were getting too many breaks!'

32

The torch was weak, the beam dispersed and pallid, but it provided just about enough light to see a few yards ahead.

'It's weird,' Kate said. 'I'm not at all scared thousands of feet beneath the surface of the ocean, but this bothers me.'

'It's because you know that underwater no one can jump out on you.'

'Oh great! Thanks, Lou.'

He laughed. 'I didn't mean it like that!'

'At least we don't have any decisions to make. It's a straight track.'

'But we could walk right past a door that leads us into the heart of Metro 2.'

'Yes, but we can't try every one of them, can we? This track must lead deep into the hidden Metro network. Why else would the stations have been shut down half a century ago?'

'Yep, and if it's any consolation, if the schematic back there is in proportion, I don't think the distances between Stations One, Two and Three are that great.'

He checked his watch, moving his wrist down to catch the torchlight. 'It's past midnight,' he said and stifled a yawn. 'Perhaps we ought to get some rest.'

They went to the side of the tunnel. Lou handed Kate the torch and bent down scooping away the track ballast, the sharp stones packed beside the rails. A few inches beneath the surface lay a tarmac base.

'You rest first,' he said, pulling off his overcoat and rolling it up to produce a makeshift pillow. 'Not quite the Grigovna Zempska I'm afraid.'

'I'm exhausted,' Kate said. 'Will you be all right?'

'Of course. I'll wake you in two hours.' He cleared a patch of ballast and leaned back against the side of the tunnel. It was uncomfortable, impossible to find a patch of wall that wasn't either pure rock or covered with cabling and pipes. He kept the torch on, figuring there was little point in him being awake and on guard if he could see nothing.

It took only a few moments for Kate to drift off and she started to snore quietly. 'Must be tired,' Lou said to himself, his voice swallowed by the still air. He stared around the barely lit tunnel. Their eyes had adjusted to the low light levels quite quickly but there was a limit to how well the human eye could see in such darkness. It was eerie, there was no denying that, but just knowing Kate was there beside him was reassuring.

He slipped seamlessly into a dream-filled sleep like stepping through a doorway. It was a vivid dream. He was in a car driving along an unmade country road, rough frozen mud and icy water all around. His body was shaking. He awoke with a start and it took several moments before he realized he could hear something, a muffled thud.

'Kate,' Lou whispered and gave her a gentle shake. 'Kate.'

She awoke with a start.

'It's OK, babe.'

She pulled herself up and he gave her a reassuring hug and helped her to her feet. She was dazed and disorientated.

'I heard a sound.'

She saw him put a finger to his lips in the faint light.

Nothing.

'Wait,' Lou said and tilted his head.

The thudding sound came again.

'There.'

'Where's it coming from?'

'I can't tell. Behind the wall?'

He picked up his coat, shook it and pulled it on. 'Let's walk on for a bit.'

They headed along the tunnel in the direction they had been walking earlier. For a few moments the sound did not seem to change in volume, but then they noticed it becoming a little louder.

'Moving in the right direction,' Kate said.

A dim light appeared further along the tunnel. They approached it warily, edging forward in the darkness, keeping close to the left wall. As they moved closer they could pick out the sound of a drill. It stopped and started. In the quiet periods, they heard voices, a man shouting orders in Russian.

Drawing nearer, they caught a light spilling from a crack between an ovoid metal door and its frame. They slid along the wall close to the opening and Lou peered round, doing his best to keep out of sight of whoever was on the other side.

He could see a large room lit by powerful arc lights. Four men were working in the room. They were dressed in mucky overalls, hobnail boots and metal hats. Two of them were screwing boards over bare stonework, a third was stirring cement in a mixer, the fourth covering a patch of floor with wet cement.

Lou pulled back. 'Workmen,' he said.

'At this time of the morning?' Kate glanced at her watch. '3 a.m.?'

Lou turned back to the view and watched as the men continued working. He heard a muffled sound close to his ear and whirled round. Another man in a metal hat and overalls, with a filthy face, soot and grime around his eyes and nose, had a chunky dirt-smeared hand around Kate's mouth, a knife to her throat.

'*Kto ty?*' he spat.

Lou put his hands up. 'I don't speak Russian.'

'English?' the man said with a heavy accent. He kept the knife precisely where he had placed it, his hand steady. 'What you do here?' He flicked his head up, chin thrust forward.

'I, we . . . we got separated from our friends.' He

wasn't sure what to say, so he decided to tell the truth. 'We were on our way to see Sergei.'

'Sergei?' The man looked surprised.

'Please . . . Can you let my wife go? We mean no harm.'

He gripped Kate tighter, moved the knife a fraction of an inch along the white flesh of her neck. Lou could see the point digging in, close to breaking the skin.

'What's your name?'

'Why?'

'Because I ask.'

'I'm Lou Bates, Dr Lou Bates. This is my wife, Dr Kate Wetherall.'

'Why you see Sergei? How you know Sergei?'

'We were brought down here from Prospekt Vernadskogo.'

'Who brought you?'

'A man named Max. There were three of us with him, us and our friend, Adam Fleming. He has disappeared. I . . . we don't know Max's surname. Please . . . could you let her go?'

The man took a deep breath, slowly pulled the knife away and loosened his grip so Kate could slip away. Lou grabbed her and pulled her close.

'Need check for weapons,' the man said stepping forward, putting the knife between his teeth and frisking first Lou then Kate.

'We are unarmed,' Kate said.

'Maybe, maybe not.' Satisfied, he stepped back and gripped the knife in his hand. 'ID?'

Lou pulled out his passport from an inside pocket of his jacket. Kate found hers in a pocket of her jeans. They handed them over. The man flicked through them.

'So, what you want?' he said.

'What's your name?' Kate asked.

He stared at her for a few moments before answering. 'Milov. Boris Milov, foreman of this work group. I know Max and . . .' He paused for a moment and puffed out his chest. 'I know Sergei. He is my master.'

'Master?'

'My boss. He is big boss.'

'You live in Metro 2?' Kate asked.

Boris nodded. 'Again . . . what do you want?'

The door from the room opened and a man stepped out into the tunnel. He saw Lou and Kate and gave Boris a quizzical look.

Lou glanced at the man and turned back to Milov. 'We were due to meet Sergei to discuss . . . a deal.'

Boris caught the other man's eye. 'Hear that, Peter? A deal.'

Peter produced a crooked smile; his teeth were a mess.

'How we know you not government spies?'

'You don't,' Kate said matter-of-factly. 'But I imagine Sergei would not be pleased if you were to take matters into your own hands, to make false assumptions.'

'You threaten me?' Boris said and took a step towards them.

'Just pointing out the obvious . . . Boris,' Kate snapped back.

He fixed her with a cold stare. His eyes looked small and very dark. Then, to their surprise, he broke into a smile. 'How do you people say it? Pluck. You are pluck, young lady. I like that. Come on, follow me.' And he pushed past them, swung the door open and stomped into the room, the drill screeching and then stopping abruptly.

'This part of new extension. East Wing, Section 4. That probably means little,' Boris said and nodded to the workmen. They turned back to their labours. 'We are at outer edge of Metro 2. You must have followed very strange route from Prospekt Vernadskogo.'

'We have no idea how we got here,' Kate said. 'We were blindfolded for part of the way.'

'Of course.' Boris was nodding.

'But then we were . . . dumped and separated from our friend and from Max,' Lou added. 'We started to draw a map, but lost it.'

Boris stopped. 'The tunnels are our protectors. Many people have died trying to find way out. You lucky.' He turned into a small room containing a metal desk strewn with papers, an ancient wood-fuelled heater stood in another corner. A single weak bulb dangled from the ceiling by a coiled wire.

'Hungry?'

Kate shook her head.

'I have cheese and strong coffee.'

'I'd like a coffee,' Lou said and looked at Kate. She nodded.

It was strong too, syrupy and sweet and delivered in

a chipped enamel mug. Lou and Kate felt its invigorating effects almost immediately.

'Are you allowed to talk about Metro 2, Boris?' Kate asked, watching the foreman as he reclined in a battered old chair, feet up on the desk, mug of black coffee steaming in his hand.

'Depends.'

'We know Sergei is a recluse and Metro 2 is his . . . well, Max called it his realm.'

Boris barked a laugh. 'Max is a romantic! Reads too much, watches too many old Soviet movies! Sergei is very different. He is practical man, like me. Most of us practical men, that is how we survive.'

'How many are you?'

'How many? No exact number. Maybe . . . how you say? Two thousand, three thousand . . .'

'Wow!' Lou exclaimed. 'We had no idea.'

'I come here 1997. My three children born here. We have four doctors now and a good hospital. We want for nothing.'

'How do you keep going?'

Boris gave Kate a puzzled look. 'We work hard.'

'Yes, but . . .'

'We each have our jobs to do. Some go to surface if we need supplies. We grow food.'

'How?'

'I don't know word. There are light shafts from surface. We build in recent years. We also use lamps. We have air . . . I don't know word again . . . Sent down here?'

'Ventilation. We saw some heavy piping.'

'That may have been air or electricity.'

'And there are families living down here?'

'You sound surprised!' Boris gave Kate a testy look.

'I wasn't judging.' She had her right hand up, clutching the coffee with her left. 'Quite the reverse, Boris. I'm amazed at your ingenuity. But why? Why are you here?'

'I cannot speak for others. But there was nowhere for me up there.' He pointed a blackened fingernail towards the ceiling. 'I got into trouble . . . found my way underground. That was long time ago.' He got up from the chair. 'Come, we are close to finishing shift. You wish to be taken to Sergei? Then you must come with us . . . or tunnels will suck you in and never spit you out.'

Boris led the way along a narrow passageway that opened out into a large rectangular high-ceilinged space. The workers had gathered there, and Kate and Lou could see an old carriage on a single track. It was a dumpy, corroded thing fronted by an electric locomotive.

A rail ran along the spine of the carriage from which a series of leather straps hung. The train pulled away slowly accelerating to a sedate twenty miles per hour, before plunging into a tunnel; the only light, a sparse reflection along the walls from the rather dim headlights of the locomotive. It made an awful noise, clattering along the tunnel shaking and rolling like a jelly on a dessert trolley.

'Not far,' Boris shouted over the racket. 'Old train . . . but this best way. After long day it good!'

The train emerged from the tunnel into a well-lit station. Lou spotted a sign as it slid past: '*Stantsiya Nomer Tri.*' He nudged Kate and pointed towards it.

Boris noticed. 'We build loop, cutting off Station Number Two just past where we worked today. Part of network for these electric trains. It feeds off main power grid of regular Metro. We get around faster than on foot. And it costs us nothing!' He gave them a gappy grin.

The train slowed and pulled to a stop at the end of the platform of Station Number Three. The men jumped out and headed off along the platform chatting and joking among themselves. Boris hung back with Kate and Lou.

'I don't know your business with boss,' he said. 'It is none of mine . . . I shall take you to him now.'

They followed him along the platform and turned into a narrow passageway, through a door and down a long, wide spiral staircase that opened out into a corridor. A man came towards them pushing a cart laden with sacks, another man dressed in workman's overalls carried a huge hoop of electric cable over his left shoulder, a metal toolbox in his other hand. He strode past them without a second glance.

Down a side passage they saw two women hanging their last items of washing on a line. Kate, Lou and Boris edged past the women and headed along the corridor, made a left and a right and stepped into another wide open space. In front of a heavy wooden door with a large brass handle two children were playing with a pair of handheld Nintendos. Boris shooed the kids away, stepped up to the door and rapped the handle.

A few moments passed and a man in military fatigues appeared at the door. He had a Kalashnikov over his shoulder and a holstered handgun in his belt. He gave Kate and Lou a hard, questioning look and then noticed Boris.

'Anton Viktor Dubovnich, these two are here to see Sergei,' Boris said in Russian.

Dubovnich looked them up and down. 'I'm sure they are,' he sneered, holding his gaze on Kate's breasts a little longer than was polite. 'I take it you have checked for weapons? Checked ID? Followed protocol?'

'Of course. Unarmed. Their IDs fit their story.'

'Which is?'

'They are here to see Sergei on business.'

The militiaman sneered again. 'Business?'

'They know Max.'

Lou recognized the word and jumped in. 'Max brought us into Metro 2 . . . to meet Sergei.'

The man stared coldly into Lou's eyes.

'Max brought them down. They got separated and lost,' Boris said.

Dubovnich considered Kate, then Lou. He unshouldered his Kalashnikov, the barrel a few inches from Lou's guts. 'You should know better than to bring strangers here, Boris Gregorovich Milov. People don't just get separated from Max and "lost" in the tunnels. These two are either spies or they were meant to be ditched. Either way . . .' He stepped forward, swung the rifle round with lightning speed and slammed the butt into the side of Lou's head, sending him sprawling across the floor.

33

Lou came to staring blankly at a wooden floor, a throbbing pain beginning at the side of his head and running down his neck. He lifted his head and the pain screamed. Slowly he began to focus and touched his temple. His fingertips came up red.

'Lou . . .' It was Kate.

He looked up at her and gradually his vision cleared. First getting up onto one elbow, he rose slowly, Kate helping him to his feet. 'You OK?'

He did not answer. Instead, he rubbed his eyes and looked round. The barrel of the Kalashnikov hung only inches from his face.

A man stepped over and took his arm gently. Lou looked round and saw Adam Fleming. He had a black eye and a gash across his cheek, the latter patched up with a row of Steri-Strips.

'Take it easy, Lou.'

'What the fuck . . .?'

Fleming stepped back and Lou could see they were in a large room lit weakly by a chandelier containing a dozen candles. In the centre of the room stood a long heavy oak table. At the head of the table sat a large man in a leather coat. He had spiky salt-and-pepper hair, prominent cheekbones and a vivid scar running from the corner of his left eye in a meandering line to his chin. To his right sat Max; still dressed in his fur-collared greatcoat, he was staring at the oak table.

'Please sit,' Max said. He indicated to three other seats at the table. Fleming strode over to the chair to the left of the man at the head of the table.

Lou took two steps towards the table, the rifle still levelled at him. He stopped suddenly. 'Fuck this,' he spat. 'Why should I sit?'

The stranger at the table raised his hand and Dubovnich backed off.

'Dr Bates, we would appreciate it if you would sit with us,' said Max. 'We apologize for what has happened – a misunderstanding.'

'Misunderstanding?' Lou shot back. 'Then why is this ape still pointing his rifle at me?'

The man with the scar signalled to Dubovnich again and the guard at last lowered the Kalashnikov. Lou glanced at Kate, took a deep breath and lowered himself slowly into the chair next to Fleming, while Kate sat down opposite him.

'There,' Lou said acerbically. 'Sitting down. Now can you tell us what is going on?'

The man with the scar spoke at last. 'My name is Sergei.' And he glanced round at Fleming then Kate, 'You wish to speak to me.'

Lou sighed and shook his head. 'Nice introduction.'

'Forgive us,' said Max. 'It was a necessary precaution.'

Fleming went to interrupt.

Lou raised a hand. 'No, wait a minute. Kate and I could have been killed, lost in those tunnels. And what happened to you?' He glared at Fleming.

'I removed the rope tying him to you, then took him to a different tunnel before removing his blindfold,' Max said.

'What was all this for?' Kate sounded exhausted. 'I don't—'

'We had to be sure you were not Russian government spies,' Sergei said.

'It's standard procedure. If you were agents you would have called for assistance once you were lost in the tunnel system. You didn't do that.' Max waved a hand towards Adam. 'Nor did Mr Fleming, who arrived just before you two. He took a tumble. We patched him up. He has a remarkable sense of direction and amazing resilience.'

Lou glanced at the Englishman and turned back to Max. 'So, you're saying it was a test?'

'In a way.'

'Please, let us move on . . . yes?' Sergei said, holding court. 'You must be famished and parched. I have not broken my fast. Would you do me the honour of sharing a meal with us?' Sergei's expression was unreadable. He clapped and a young man appeared beside his chair. 'We are ready to eat.'

The food was surprisingly good: steak, fruit, crisp bacon, eggs, cereals, coffee and juices.

'This is wonderful,' Kate said as her coffee was topped up. It was a strong Brazilian blend with no trace of bitterness. Very different from the stewed workman's coffee Boris had given them.

'You sound surprised,' Sergei remarked. 'I am a billionaire after all, Dr Wetherall! What did you expect? Rice and rough vodka fresh from the still?'

'No, I . . .'

Sergei produced a fulsome laugh. 'I am teasing you,' he said. His English was almost without accent, smooth. 'We try to live well here. This breakfast is nothing too grand. We eat like normal wealthy people. We try to do everything others do.'

'But you must miss the space, the air, the sun?' Lou said.

'Yes, of course, we have to accept some drawbacks, but no one is forced to stay here and some people do leave after a while. Each to his own. I believe the pros outweigh the cons, for if I were to be apprehended by the authorities I would be kept in a far more confined space than we have here.' Sergei extended his arms to encompass his personal fiefdom. 'And, most importantly, I would not be a free man. My world here under Moscow may have some limitations but I sleep in my own bed at night, I eat and drink what I wish. I am free to talk to anyone I choose. I have the latest Internet and telecoms here.' He waved a hand. 'This is merely a work space. My home is large and I have a garden watered and illuminated by advanced technology. Most crucially, it is mine. I spend good time with my children and my wife every day, and if I decide to, I can, and do, travel to the surface incognito. Money buys whatever you wish for.'

'And you are prepared for us to come here. Aren't you concerned we could reveal the location of Metro 2?' Kate said.

Sergei laughed, shaking his head. 'Hah! You can try! Why do you think we took such precautions? The authorities are quite aware of us and even know roughly where we are, but we've made it extremely hard for them to touch us . . . and believe me, they try.'

'And you are amenable to talking to us, to arranging a deal over the Einstein–Kessler material?' Adam Fleming said before taking a sip of coffee. He looked from Sergei to Max.

'I am, my friend. But not now. I'm sure you are all exhausted and in no mood to discuss business.'

'Well, I'm . . .'

'Good,' Sergei said and started to rise from his chair. 'We are agreed then. I apologize again for the very shaky start to our meeting. But I sense you accept that we could do little else.'

'I'm sure—' Fleming tried again.

'I hope you find the accommodations to your liking. Shall we meet again here this evening? Seven p.m.?'

34

Lou and Kate were so tired they took little notice of the journey to their quarters. They noted without comment that the rooms were spacious and comfortably furnished, the bed large and welcoming, and they fell asleep to the sound of birdsong piped through hidden speakers.

Lou awoke first, feeling refreshed. He glanced at a bedside clock and saw that it was almost 6 p.m. He crept out of bed leaving Kate asleep while he looked around.

The suite reminded him of an old movie he had seen as a kid – *Planet of the Apes* – in which the ruling caste of orang-utans lived in luxuriously appointed caverns. The bedroom led on to a large living area, which he had no memory of passing through some ten hours earlier. It was furnished with two modern leather sofas, a widescreen plasma TV on the rough stone wall, and in the corner stood a desk, a Mac and a printer. Curious, Lou flicked on the TV with a remote and surfed through the channels – everything from local Moscow TV to BBC World and CNN. 'Amazing,' he said under his breath.

Kate appeared in the doorway to the bedroom. She stretched and yawned.

'How'd you feel?' Lou asked.

'Like I've just had a great sleep after a week of insomnia.'

'Me too.' He waved around the room. 'Sergei wasn't kidding when he said that they had everything normal wealthy people took for granted. I've just tried the TV, they have CNN.'

'Oh, well fancy that!' Kate replied and looked at him as though he were a four-year-old before stepping forward and kissing him affectionately on the cheek.

*

At 6.55 a man in a green paramilitary uniform knocked on the door. He did not give a name and spoke abruptly in accented English. 'Come with me, please.'

Lou and Kate followed him along a series of passageways. They passed people going about their business: two repair men fixing a fluorescent strip light, a young mother scolding two small children who were clearly not keen to learn that it was their bedtime.

Emerging from a wide corridor, they entered a spacious courtyard – lines of single-storey apartments with curtained windows and flowerpots outside. Seeing these, Kate looked up and noticed three large circular lights recessed into the roof. Each of them was at least four metres in diameter and they gave off a soft orange light. She pointed them out to Lou as they followed the anonymous guard. 'Must give out a broad spectrum including UV; simulated sunlight, basically.'

They arrived at a set of double doors. The guard knocked loudly. The doors opened inwards and he ushered them inside before retreating without a word.

'Good to see you both,' Sergei said, moving away from where he had been talking to Adam Fleming and Max and walking across a smooth stone floor towards them, a hand extended. 'I trust you slept well.'

'We did,' Lou replied.

'Come, sit,' Sergei said and led them to an arrangement of sofas and chairs around an ornate coffee table. Adam settled into a chair to Sergei's left. Kate and Lou made themselves comfortable on a wide sofa. Sergei looked relaxed as he reclined in a modern wingback chair and ordered coffee from the same young man who had served them breakfast that morning.

'So,' said Fleming, turning and considering Sergei. 'Where should we begin?'

'I understand you have had the inconvenience of an impostor, this Zero character.' Sergei gave Fleming a hard look. 'You won't have any such issues with me.'

'Glad to hear it.'

The coffee arrived and they were distracted as it was poured and the cups handed out.

'We each have something the other can provide,' Sergei said, bringing his cup to his lips and surveying the faces of his guests over the rim.

'Zero was talking about absurd amounts of money.'

Sergei waved away the remark. 'I am a businessman,

Adam . . . may I call you Adam? But, and this is very important, although I like money – like it very much – it is not the only thing in my life. You would have learned already that I am not the most conventional man you have ever met, no?'

He turned to the scientists, then pointed to Lou. 'What do you think matters to me almost as much as money, Lou?'

'I would say, Sergei, that you like to stick it to the authorities. With this document you have something your government would like to get its grubby hands on, and although you are a patriotic Russian, love for your country goes only so far. Getting one over on the Kremlin and the promise of greenbacks into the bargain is a serious temptation.'

Sergei laughed his heavy bass laugh and clapped, smacking his big meaty hands together like slabs of beef on a butcher's block. 'Right on target!' he exclaimed and drained his coffee cup. 'So, make no mistake, I do want to be paid for what I have for you, but I will also derive great satisfaction from denying our beloved leaders upstairs access to the information.'

'OK, what is it you have for us, precisely?' Fleming said. 'You have the Kessler Document?'

'You mean the etched metal sheet secured within the piping system of SS *Freedom*?'

Fleming didn't flinch. 'Well at least we know you are not an impostor. But how did you know about that? You have the original?'

'Ah, all in good time.' Sergei placed his empty cup on

the table and stood up. 'Come, drink up. I have something to show you.'

'Sergei,' Max said, 'I will see you later. I have to do my regular inspection of the periphery with my men.'

Sergei nodded and Max turned to the others. 'I hope I will see you later.'

The four of them boarded a vehicle that closely resembled an oversized golf cart. Another man in paramilitary uniform lowered himself into the driver's seat and released the brake. It glided quietly along the corridors. People stepped smartly out of its path. None of the passengers spoke as they travelled perhaps four hundred yards before pulling up outside the entrance to a tunnel. Sergei disembarked and strode ahead. At the end they stopped at a massive door. Sergei leaned in to a combination lock positioned in the centre of the door, turned the dial anticlockwise, paused, twisted it further another few notches, paused, flicked it clockwise and then back again. A low clank came from a lock on one side and he pulled on a handle easing the door outwards.

Nothing prepared Kate, Lou and Fleming for the sight that met their eyes. The door opened onto a room the size of an aircraft hangar. Beyond a small clear area close to the door thousands of yards of metal shelving in dozens of rows stretched into the distance. The ends of the racks stood at least a hundred yards away, close to the far wall. Each row of shelving stretched to the ceiling some thirty feet above their heads. From where they stood, they could see that the shelves were filled with thousands of boxes, files, ledgers and books. All three were struck dumb.

'Impressive, no?' Sergei said unnecessarily.

Along with the soldier who had driven them, they followed Sergei into the room, dwarfed by the sheer dimensions of the place, their boots echoing around the cavernous space.

'What *is* this place?' Kate asked, gazing around at the gigantic stacks. 'It's incredible.'

'Metro 2 was originally built by Stalin's people. You probably know that. It was meant to be a vast fallout shelter for the glorious leader, his ministers and their families. There was a direct rail link to it from the Kremlin. I had that sealed up before moving here and I have constructed a decoy system to stop the authorities opening it up again. Stalin's successors kept up the maintenance of the entire network, but, and I'm not sure why, they lost interest in it during the 1970s. It was then the party technocrats realized that if they kept storing paper in the Kremlin and other archives at the rate they were, Moscow would soon be submerged in triplicate! They remembered Stalin's folly and well . . .' He waved a hand around.

'This is one of a dozen and a small one at that. But it is the most interesting for our purposes.'

'Why?' Lou asked. 'What sort of documents are kept down here?'

'A vast range.' Sergei stopped, turned to the nearest rack and pulled down a box. It was cardboard and coated with grey dust. He blew across the lid before lifting it. Inside sat a pile of papers. He pulled out a sheaf and scanned the top page, rifled through a dozen pages and tossed them back into the box. 'Merchant shipping schedules from January 1948 for Zone 3; that's the Baltic shore.'

'Fascinating!' Lou responded.

'So, are you telling us the documents we are after are in here somewhere?' Fleming asked and held Sergei's gaze.

'Well, I wouldn't be so cruel as to just dump you here and leave you to it. There is a system.'

'You can't just point us to the document?' Kate said.

'And how do we know it's actually here? I assumed you had it to hand.' Fleming could not disguise his irritation.

'Why should I make it easy, Adam? Whenever is anything worthwhile easy?' His smile vanished. 'I'm really not in the business of making things easy for Western Intelligence agencies!'

'But . . .' Lou began.

Sergei raised a hand. 'I'm not trying to be deliberately obtuse. The Kessler Document is not here.'

Fleming exhaled loudly.

'But that does not mean you will leave empty-handed. Far from it. I know where it is. However, it would be much better for you if you followed a paper trail and discovered what happened to the document yourselves. And besides, that's what you two do, isn't it?' He turned to Kate and Lou. 'Research? Exploration?'

'Yeah, but . . .' Lou began.

Kate caught Fleming's eye. He looked barely able to control his anger.

'We could just walk away,' the MI6 man said stiffly. 'After all, you could be wasting our time completely.'

Sergei knitted his brows. 'Why on earth would I do that?'

'A game? You said yourself you're an unconventional man. Maybe it's your idea of fun to get us down here and then lead us on a wild goose chase.'

'And pass up millions of dollars?'

'Loose change to you.'

Sergei nodded and pursed his lips. 'Yes, I understand your reasoning, Adam. But you are actually quite wrong. I'm being perfectly genuine. I could sit you down and tell you a third-hand story to explain how this' – and he swept his hand around again – 'could lead to the Kessler Document, and then hand over what my people have unearthed. But where's the fun in that?'

'Actually . . .' Fleming began, but Sergei held up his hand imperiously again.

'No, really, Adam . . . please humour me . . . And actually, I have my more serious reasons.'

'And they are?' Adam snapped.

Sergei tapped his nose and left, flanked by his armed assistant.

35

'Fuck!' Fleming hissed as the door closed behind Sergei and his driver. 'This is ridiculous. He's a lunatic!'

'I guess when you have a few billion and have to live down here you get your kicks wherever you can,' Lou commented.

'No. This is malicious.'

'It's not, Adam,' Kate said, exasperated. 'Stop being so paranoid. Sergei said he had serious reasons for doing this.'

'And we should simply trust him?'

'Any better ideas?' Lou asked. 'Anyway, I like a challenge.'

Kate read a couple of labels on the nearest shelves. 'I suggest we take . . .' She stepped back towards the door and counted the rows. 'Four aisles each, see if we can find some sort of pattern.'

'I don't know about you, Kate, but my Russian is a little rusty,' Lou said.

She pulled out her phone and started tapping. 'Aha.'

'What are you doing?' Fleming asked.

Kate turned her iPhone to show Adam and then Lou.

'No conventional above-ground provider of course, but we can hook up to the community's Wi-Fi network. I knew there had to be one. I noticed it on the computer screen in our room just before we were taken to see Sergei. We can use Google and a translation app. I know your Russian is pretty good, Adam, but I only know a few words.'

Lou grinned. 'You're not just a pretty face are you?'

Kate gave him a phoney smile. 'First, we're going to have to try to track down the section of the archive that is relevant. Then we can narrow it down until we have something manageable . . . agreed?'

Lou pointed to their left. 'I suggest we number the rows, one through twenty-four, two rows each aisle, starting that end. See the rows are divided into sections? We need to note down the row, the section and the shelf, starting with number one at ground level, going up to . . .' He counted under his breath. 'Eight . . . Jeez! There are . . . one hundred and sixty shelf sections in each row, and . . . what? Something like a dozen boxes in each. Almost fifty thousand boxes!'

'Yeah, but the shelf sections must be organized in some way. They won't be random. We have to narrow it down to what?' Kate glanced round at Lou and Fleming.

'Military, 1937 to . . . when did Sergei say this archive was first used?'

'The 1970s.'

'That's probably only . . . what?' Lou groaned. 'A thousand boxes, maybe?'

'No time to waste then,' Kate said.

'Fine,' Fleming said giving a heavy sigh. 'I'll take rows one to eight, yeah? Kate, you search nine to sixteen. Lou, seventeen to twenty-four. Meet up at the end.'

Each row had a moveable ladder that slid along on castors. They quickly found the labels were well organized and comprehensive; each with a category, subcategory and date.

With the help of the online translators they soon identified keywords: *voyennyy*, 'military'; *grazhdanskogo*, 'civil' and *sovershenno sekretno*, 'top secret', and the app could transpose from Cyrillic to Latin script. They simply had to scan the words with the phone and the app did the rest. Half an hour after starting, they met up at the far wall of the vast room.

'OK,' Kate said. 'What do we have?'

'Mine were all pre-World War Two files, nothing after 1935,' Lou said.

'Opposite problem,' Fleming added. 'All 1960s onwards to about a year before the date Sergei said the authorities constructed the archives.'

'I thought I would come up dry too,' Kate said. 'I started in the low numbers, but by aisle fourteen I hit the right zone. The collection is clearly listed chronologically. I found 1937/Military/Naval.'

'Cool,' Lou said.

'Only about fifty boxes.'

Lou exhaled loudly. 'Lead the way.'

They brought all the appropriately labelled boxes to the floor. There were forty-one of them.

'Best if I go through this, isn't it?' Fleming said as they stared at the piles despondently. 'You can't check every title of every document on your iPhone!'

'Good point. But actually, how could the Kessler Document have ended up here anyway? I don't know why we haven't questioned that before.'

'I have thought about it,' Fleming said. 'The Germans got the document from SS *Freedom* and tried to make something of the research data, but obviously failed. The Russians must have appropriated the document in 1945. Remember, the Yanks captured von Braun and the whole Peenemünde crew who built the V1 and V2? The German research into the defensive shield must have been carried out in a region of Germany the Russian Army overran at the end of the war.'

'In that case, maybe we should be looking for files written in German.'

'Actually, yes, that's a very good point,' Fleming said. 'Lou, you take those piles.' He pointed to a collection of some dozen or so boxes and swung round. 'Kate you can handle those, and I'll go through these.'

They were halfway through their assigned piles of boxes when Lou walked over to Kate with a file. 'This could be it.'

Fleming straightened up from a carton he had just opened and joined them.

It was a thin and faded Manila folder with Sovershenno Sekretno, 'Top Secret' stamped across the top third of the cover. Beneath this was written: LEGNICA ISSLEDOVATEL'SKAYA BAZA (1937–1944).

'What is it?' Fleming asked.

Lou held out the folder. 'Legnica is a place: a town in Poland, fairly close to the border with Germany, I think. It was absorbed by the Reich when they invaded in 1939. The Russians would have taken it very early in 1945 as they advanced on Germany from the East.'

'"Issledovatel'skaya Baza" means "Research Base",' Fleming responded. 'And the year is right . . . 1937.'

Lou opened the file. It contained a single slip of paper stapled to the back cover and a few hand-written words: *Perenapravljajut B-19-4c.*

'This must refer to the archive we're in,' Kate said. 'The people who set up this place used their own system to categorize the boxes and shelves. We called them rows one to twenty-four, they designated a letter of the alphabet. Then the stacks were divided into numbers along the rows and up the levels.'

'Very clever,' Lou remarked. 'So this is aisle B, stack nineteen along and up on the fourth level.'

They swung into the first aisle on the far side of the massive space. Kate tugged on the end ladder as they ran along counting the segments, slowing as they reached the fifteenth, sixteenth . . .

'Here,' Kate announced and started to climb. Reaching the fourth shelf of boxes, she could see 'segment c' a little to her right and indicated to Lou to shift the ladder a few yards. A moment later, she had a box in her hands and was descending the ladder carefully until she could pass it down to Fleming.

They rifled through the box. It was filled with more Manila folders and they created a pile of them to their left. Halfway down they reached a thick file again stamped: 'Top Secret'. Beneath this: LEGNICA BAZA (1937–1944) hand-written in large capitals. Inside lay a thick wad of papers held together with a chunky metal clip. Across the front page, the title: *A Litany of Errors: My Misguided Role in the Treachery of Dimitri Grenyov, Chief Scientist at Movlovyl Research Base, and His Attempts to Apply the Theories of Johannes Kessler* by Michael Caithness.

36

A Litany of Errors: My Misguided Role in the Treachery of Dimitri Grenyov, Chief Scientist at Movlovyl Research Base, and His Attempts to Apply the Theories of Johannes Kessler by Michael Caithness

My name is Michael Caithness, prisoner X-R34, Camp 16, Kemerovo. I am told the date is 3 October 1954, but I only know this is true because the guard has vouched for it. Outside, the temperature is -12 degrees centigrade and the night is only just beginning to close in. Tomorrow I shall die; it has been arranged, the money passed on to the commander of the camp. It will be a mercy killing because men such as I, educated in a minor public school and then Cambridge, a man best suited to a soft desk job and a smart bachelor apartment in

Knightsbridge, drawn into espionage in a moment of drunken weakness and then quickly trapped by both sides, could not countenance struggling for each breath in this vile place until I waste away. No, I procured the funds from good friends in Britain and they have paid for my death . . . hence this confession. I know it is not as it should be, but I have never considered myself a wordsmith. Nevertheless, it is an honest account. I have tried to recreate in this piece the events as they unfolded at the time, as true to life as I can be. So if I'm occasionally inconsistent or you spot imperfections of style, I apologize in advance.

I first heard of the Kessler Document soon after starting work at my aforementioned job as an MI6 pen-pusher. It was just a name that would have passed me by if it had not been for a strange confluence of events that began to unfold without my bidding. As I said before, I was ensnared at a weak moment and entrapped.

One of my juniors got wind of communications between Westminster and Washington in which the name Albert Einstein cropped up. He knew the great scientist was then living in Princeton and working at the university. He also knew I had read Physics at Cambridge. Now, you should know straight away that I am not a proper scientist; I have done no research, written no learned papers. I went straight from a science degree into the intelligence business. However, I've always had a fascination for many scientific disciplines, read widely, and of course, the name Albert Einstein is almost totemic. Indeed, I used to be something of a dinner party bore in London when recounting how I had once met the most famous scientist in the world in a lift when he visited Cambridge in 1933, and how I had shaken the man's hand.

The young chap who had heard a rumour about Einstein and some vague intrigue between us and the Yanks did not know much but just enough to pique my interest. I conducted a little surreptitious digging and learned of a recent aborted attempt to complete some mysterious set of experiments that had involved Einstein and a former colleague of his in Berlin, one Johannes Kessler. According to the intelligence I managed to unearth, a set of secret papers acquiring the epithet 'the Kessler Document' had been en route to America aboard a British merchant vessel. The ship never arrived, the documents were mysteriously lost.

At the time, no more could be ascertained about the scientific papers or the intriguing experiments. The war came along and I forgot all about it.

Until, that is, my first major error to which I have already alluded. A friend I had not seen since we were habitués of the same staircase at Trinity invited me out to dinner at Claridge's.

He understood that deep down I had grave misgivings about the integrity of the West; that buried beneath layers of British reserve, upper middle class conformity and the bullying of my true blue father, I was actually a closet Commie sympathizer without myself being fully cognizant of the fact. Too much rather good Saint Emilion followed by a Cognac that dated from a time when Queen Victoria was newly widowed and I was open to all sorts of offers. That night, 4 April 1948, I became a double agent.

The first six months in this new role were actually rather dull. I passed on bits of information and received a payment in cash. The stuff I had access to was pretty low grade. I knew that and my handler knew that, but what I had not suspected was that acting the traitor was the best thing I could have done for my career. It was only later I discovered that the counter-espionage network of which my Cambridge friend was an integral part had tendrils extended deep into MI6 and this network moved me up the ladder, in part to reward me, but also to gain me easier access to more useful material.

Almost exactly a year after being recruited to betray my country, I was taken on my first trip to Russia. Officially I was there in the guise of a Whitehall official assigned the task of putting out feelers for negotiating a behind-the-scenes thawing of trade barriers between London and Moscow. Unofficially, the trip had been arranged by my Soviet masters, a stage in the further indoctrination process for young double agents.

And, somehow, the fact that I had studied science and maintained an abiding interest in exotic physics had gone before me, so that on only my second night in Moscow at a showy state banquet to which I was invited as a very junior delegate, I was introduced to the man at the heart of my story, Dimitri Yury Grenyov, Chief Scientist at Movlovyl Research Base. This is the man who has led me, just a few years later, to a Siberian labour camp and to this, the eve of my prearranged death.

Grenyov was immediately friendly, which at first surprised me, but as I drank more champagne I became less concerned by this and I genuinely warmed to the man.

He was a very plain-looking fellow with wispy grey hair, drooping eyelids over small eyes of a quiet indistinct colour. He had bushy eyebrows, thin lips and a pallid complexion. His handshake was limp and he spoke in uneven metre, quick bursts of energetic monologue and then a silence as though he constantly needed to recharge before the next burst. I found him hard work, but then, as he drank more, he relaxed and became surprisingly good company, and especially interested in life at Cambridge. He had been only once a few years before the war and retained fond memories of the place.

The two of us ended up back at my hotel room where we cracked open a bottle of vodka and carried on talking and drinking well into the small hours. He finally made his exit about four o'clock and we agreed to meet up for coffee at eleven as I was not expected at the trade department until after lunch.

I passed out in my only suit and woke at nine to find I had vomited down the front. I felt so bad I was convinced I would never walk again, but twenty minutes under a cold shower and I started to come round. I cleaned the jacket of my suit with soap and water knowing that there was no laundry service at the hotel. I managed to make a half-decent job of it, changed my shirt and went for a brisk walk around Red Square hoping that the sub-zero temperatures and some air would do something for my hangover. Arriving early at the prearranged venue – a cafe close to Red Square – I ordered a pot of extra strong coffee, and after two cups I began to feel almost human again.

Grenyov's first reaction when he saw me was to laugh. 'Ah! Perhaps vodka is not your drink, Michael!'

I groaned and watched him pull up a chair and order more coffee from the waiter.

I had time to think about the previous night as I had trudged through the snow edging Red Square, and without further ado I said to Grenyov: 'So, tell me, Dimitri, what is all this about?'

He gave me a puzzled look that slipped into a friendly smile. 'I've been too obvious?' He took a deep breath and thanked the waiter as the man placed a fresh pot on the table. 'I have been asked to talk to you and get to know you . . . Not,' he added quickly, 'that it hasn't been a pleasure, Michael. I find your company genuinely stimulating.'

'Oh, good,' I said, my tone a little brittle. 'Obviously your engagement with me was sanctioned. What puzzles me is why?'

'We each have an association with Cambridge . . . beyond Trinity being your alma mater,' Grenyov said, glancing around.

'I see.'

'I indicated last night that my work lies within the domain of particle physics. I should now say that it is actually a project first begun by Einstein years ago; work he started with a German scientist called Johannes Kessler . . . You look a little startled,' Grenyov said and drained his coffee cup.

'I have heard about Einstein's experiments in the United States before the war. You are talking about those, yes?'

Grenyov nodded and refilled his cup.

I checked the tables near us. Closest was a young couple who were clearly only interested in each other. Behind the scientist, a single woman, middle-aged, soberly dressed, sat reading a book. 'I was led to believe the Kessler Document was lost.'

Grenyov winked. 'It was lost . . . to the British and the Americans at least. The Nazis got hold of it. But it wasn't easy for them. After a fight they boarded the British ship.'

'SS *Freedom*?'

'Yes . . . you know a little of the story?'

'A little.'

'The crew were killed and the vessel towed back to Ifnl in Morocco a then-secret naval base the Germans built in the mid-thirties.'

'This is some two years before the war began.'

'Which illustrates the value the Germans placed on finding the document.'

'So what happened then?'

'They stripped the ship to its bare bones like hyenas on the savannah. They eventually found the document inside a redundant part of a cooling system.'

I shook my head in disbelief. It seemed extraordinary that anyone would go to such lengths over a scientific document. 'So,' I said, 'having gone to so much effort I assume the Germans tried to make something practical from the theoretical physics; tried to understand what Einstein's contribution would have been.'

'That's precisely right. They constructed a

dedicated research facility in occupied Poland, a place called Legnica. A very good scientist, Herman Gottleib from the University of Berlin, was put in charge and some of the best particle physicists in Germany were recruited. I've no idea how much money was thrown at the project, but it would have been considerable – at least until other demands on the Reich's science budget cut the effort. Whatever the cost though, they got nowhere.'

'Only one Einstein, I guess.'

'Yes and no. Einstein is a consummate genius, of course, but there are many other great minds in his wake.'

For a second, Grenyov looked a little affronted and I realized that beneath the affable persona, the Russian had an indelible self-respect and a clear awareness of his considerable ability and achievements.

'Do you have any idea what the document contained? What the Germans were trying to do? What Einstein was trying to do, come to that?'

He leaned in towards me across the table. 'Of course I do, Michael. Surely, your memory is not that short.'

I must have looked very confused because Grenyov grinned.

'It was just over four years ago when the Red Army occupied Poland. The army took the researchers at Legnica by surprise. The scientists had little time to destroy their files – the work of almost seven years.'

'And you have continued with the work?'

'Yes. I was appointed head of the project in January 1946.'

I said nothing for several moments, just studied Grenyov's strange face.

'Very well, I can accept all this. Indeed, it makes perfect sense. So maybe it's time you actually told me what has occupied Einstein, the Germans and yourself for so many years?'

'Two words,' Grenyov said. 'Defensive shield.'

I repeated the words back to him. My expression must have been one of blank incomprehension because Grenyov began to explain straight away.

'Imagine if a nation at war had the ability to fit a device to its ships, tanks and aircraft that could repel any weapon thrown at it. Imagine a ship being attacked by a more powerful vessel that launches torpedoes and shells that all come bouncing back at the attacker. It would be useful, no?'

'But how could that be possible?' I said.

'You are familiar with the idea of trying to unify Einstein's theory of relativity with quantum mechanics?'

'I left university before the war,' I responded. 'I've tried to keep up with new work, but it's . . .'

'Yes, yes, I understand. Well a refresher

then.' Grenyov looked at his empty cup, buying a little time to phrase properly what he had to say. He topped up his cup with the last of the coffee. 'So . . .' He had his hands out, palms up. 'On the one hand we have relativity – Einstein's great discovery.' He moved his left hand up and down as though weighing a fruit. 'This deals exclusively with phenomena on the large scale – solar systems, galaxies, the speed of light, etc.' He raised a questioning eyebrow.

'Yes,' I said.

'Then on the other we have quantum mechanics.' And he mirrored the earlier action with his right hand. 'This deals with only the very small scale – at the level of atoms and sub-nuclear particles.'

'Right.'

'For years now physicists have tried to find a way to combine the two, to create what they call a unified theory. Einstein first postulated the notion back in 1916. More recently my countryman . . .' Grenyov leaned forward and lowered his voice to a whisper '. . . Matvey Petrovich Bronstein, who was executed on the orders of our great ruler about ten years ago, tried to quantify the idea. He wrote a landmark paper on the subject published in *Physikalische Dummheiten*. Bronstein's work is banned and must never be mentioned, so in all my studies based on the materials from Legnica I was unable to refer to Bronstein's ideas and constantly forced to backtrack.' With a pained expression, he leaned back in his chair.

'Anyway, I digress. Einstein has been trying to further the idea of unifying relativity and quantum mechanics for over thirty years now. Back in 1935 he was approached by two US naval scientists who had followed the great man's ideas and asked him if there was any way to harness his latest theories as a weapon of war.'

'That's surprising,' I commented.

'Indeed. As you know Einstein is a militant pacifist, if you will excuse the oxymoron.' He laughed for a moment then leaned forward once more. 'Apparently, he was on the point of throwing the men out of his office when he suddenly stopped and said: "Would a defensive device help?"'

It was my turn to laugh. 'Wonderful!'

'Yes. I have a friend of a friend who knows Einstein, and according to him Einstein has often said that he would like to make a machine that neutralized weapons and therefore saved lives. He believed this could be done by harnessing what he called "quantum gravity". It is clear this interest began after the visit by the navy scientists, and from sources close to the man, he thought about little else for the next few years, a fascination that came to its climax in 1937 with his experiments to create a protective shield.'

'He really did try it then?'

'Oh yes. I know that for a fact. The Americans

have done everything they can to hush up the experiments, but information has leaked out. It seems certain Einstein and his team conducted at least one experiment early in 1937, but it went wrong so disastrously that they did not try again. Well at least that is what we thought at first.'

'We?' I said.

'The NKVD.'

'Russian Intelligence? OK, so what do you think now?'

'We still think only one test was conducted, but it wasn't just because it went terribly wrong; it was also because Einstein couldn't solve the problems it presented alone.'

'And that's where the Kessler Document came in?'

'Yes. I have learned that Einstein and Kessler worked together on a form of unified theory. They knew each other back in the early thirties and spent some time together in Cambridge when Einstein was in transit – an émigré from Nazi Germany – on his way to live in the United States. The Kessler Document turns out to be part of the key to explaining what went wrong with Einstein's test and how to set it up in a better way.'

'Part?'

Grenyov sighed heavily. 'What the Germans retrieved and we . . . inherited, was encoded. Some of the Nazis' best brains spent years trying to crack the code. They made little headway, just scratching the surface of what they thought the two scientists had been visualizing. They blended these clues with cutting-edge knowledge of quantum mechanics and expansions of Einstein's theory of relativity. The Germans did their best, but failed utterly.'

'And you, my friend,' I said. 'You have fared better?'

He shook his head, his shoulders slumping a little. 'Some progress has been made. We have approached things from a number of different angles. It is a shame we have no access to the work of Bronstein, the Russian scientist I mentioned earlier. But what we need is the same thing the Germans were searching for, the cipher for the code Einstein and Kessler used.' He gave me an earnest look. 'That is where you come in, Michael.'

I nodded, absorbing the incredible tale Grenyov had unfolded over a few cups of coffee. 'I see,' I said quietly. 'Well, I will try.'

'You have a totally different set of possible leads,' he went on. 'We need a fresh approach. I cannot impress upon you just how important this is.'

'You do not need to, Dimitri. I do understand. Do you have any information on the cipher? Anything at all?'

'As far as I'm aware the Germans made little effort to find it. The war itself diverted attention and resources, but it was also a matter of arrogance I think. They wanted to crack the problem themselves and had no faith in finding where the cipher had gone or what form it may have taken. They set their minds to cracking the code.'

'But you have obtained some new information?' I gave him a searching look.

'You are a very astute young man, Michael. It is only a vague lead; the NKVD again. They learned that, as a security measure, the British got Kessler to encode the document and send it to England via a totally different route to the cipher. The document was hidden on SS *Freedom*, while the cipher was sent to the United States some other way.'

'Clever.'

'Yes, annoyingly so.' Grenyov produced a wan smile. 'The NKVD have gone through every archive to see if the Nazis did try to get their hands on the cipher early on, but they've drawn almost a complete blank.'

'Almost?'

'One reference has been unearthed in a file from Himmler's private office. An encoded message linked with Kessler's people smuggling out the material to England in the spring of 1937. The code the courier had used was a relatively simple one and Wehrmacht Supreme Command cracked it quickly. It was a brief message that made reference to the Kessler Document. It stated that it would be encoded and the cipher sent separately. A single word had been highlighted by one of Himmler's staff, a word that must have held some special relevance. The word was: "Pioneer".'

After this encounter in Moscow I didn't hear from Dimitri Grenyov for over four years. Back in London I set about refreshing my knowledge of physics and in particular the esoteric ideas of relativity combined with quantum theory that lay at the heart of what Grenyov had talked about – the concept of quantum gravity.

I attended seminars at my alma mater, Trinity, Cambridge; I subscribed to *Nature* and the *Journal of Theoretical Physics*; I did as much as I could to use my contacts in British Intelligence to learn whatever I could concerning Einstein's attempted test in 1937.

Although this effort meant I brushed up on my modern physics – which came as a welcome diversion from low-key espionage, rationing and a drab, shared office five days a week – it produced nothing of value in my quest. I longed to share my fascination with others. I always was a great believer in the adage that two heads are better than one, but of course I could not breathe a word of what Grenyov had told me. And all the time the word 'Pioneer' stuck in my mind, but it meant no more to me than it had the day the Russian scientist had half-whispered it to me over a cafe table in Moscow.

Two years after my trip to Russia, I was promoted to the higher ranks of the service and a year after that, in November 1952, I was invited to Washington for a joint services conference with the CIA. It was an important step and it increased my profile with my unofficial employer – the Kremlin. I did my best to extract anything useful from the visit, but the Yanks were in a state of fevered paranoia. The Rosenbergs were in jail and little over six months from execution. I have to admit, the zeitgeist affected me. I often felt as though I were treading a very dangerous path, that the risk was not worth the taking. But another voice in my head kept telling me that I had already gone too far.

Then, on my second visit to Washington, in March 1953, news broke that Stalin had died. I don't know why I was so shocked, but I was. He was an old man, he drank too much and was in bad health, but Stalin? Dead? Impossible, surely?

Lord only knows what the full extent of the repercussions were from this singular death. People died, others were reprieved, policies changed, plans scrapped, new ideas proposed, fresh battles begun, old victors defeated, young ones invited to the fray. And, unknown to almost anyone aside from those directly involved, as Georgy Malenkov grabbed the reins of political power,

Dimitri Grenyov's beloved project to do what Einstein had failed to achieve – the construction of a quantum gravity shield – was shut down, the Movlovyl Research Base decommissioned.

I did not learn of this until June that year; some three months after it happened. I received a letter from Grenyov that he had somehow managed to slip past the censors and the KGB. I later discovered that to get it to me had required calling in favours from the last remaining friends he had in any position of power or influence.

In the letter Grenyov explained that his life had been turned upside down. The new leadership had decided to institute cutbacks in some areas of scientific research and divert money into other projects. Anything Stalin had been particularly supportive of was axed unceremoniously. This meant his project to construct a force shield had been put in the firing line early. At the end of the letter, Grenyov begged me to find my way to Moscow so that we might meet and talk again. He had something very important he wished to tell me.

But this was no easy task. Our countries had few diplomatic ties officially; and although I had been promoted again in the spring of 1953, I was not exactly a mover or shaker. I could not even risk replying to Grenyov's missive, even to tell him there was almost no chance I could see him.

And, of course, there was no way he could risk writing with his secret.

But luck . . . hah! There are two very distinct sides to the concept of luck, are there not? Luck of a black hue, I now know, came my way. Keen to find out whatever they could about the new regime in the Kremlin, my superiors wanted to send a new man to Moscow. Thanks to the intelligence grapevine, my name was mooted because I had done well on my previous information-gathering mission in the guise of a British government trade negotiator years before. So, come November 1953, I was once more in Moscow.

The machinations of my work in an official capacity have nothing to do with this story and are indeed pretty dull, but of course I had a second, covert purpose in being there. During a break in discussions with a pair of junior trade and farming ministers concerning tractor parts and strawberry quotas, I managed to slip away unnoticed to meet Dimitri Grenyov at our previous rendezvous, where again we drank coffee and talked.

The four and a half years since our first visit there together had not been kind to Grenyov. His skin was even pastier than I had remembered it to be, and his wisps of hair lay thinner on his scalp. When he spoke, he sounded weary, as though it were the middle of the night.

'It is good to see you again my young friend.' He shook my hand and indicated we should sit.

In a few minutes it was almost as though the years had been rolled back. The coffee pot stood on the table, hot cups at our fingers, an icy breeze coming from the north-west, patches of sunshine spread out upon ice across the pavement close to the edge of the restaurant forecourt where we sat.

'Do you wish to tell me what has happened?' I asked after a long silence.

'It's hard to know where to start, Michael.'

I let it go and simply waited for the scientist to find the words he wished to use; it would not do for me to push or persuade.

'As I told you in my letter, they have closed down the project.' He took a deep breath and I could see a flash of anger.

'I am sorry.'

He waved a hand in the air. 'Thank you, Michael, but we are beyond words now.'

I felt a ripple of sudden anxiety. 'What do you mean by that, Dimitri?'

He glanced around and leaned forward. 'In a way, I have been fortunate,' he began. 'Some of my colleagues in other departments at the Academy have simply vanished. They were in their labs one day, then . . .' He clicked his fingers silently in the air between us. 'But actually I have been doubly lucky. I am still here, assigned to new, admittedly very dull work, but . . .' he said, lowering his voice a dozen decibels, 'I also had some warning that the authorities were about to shut down my experiments.'

I looked at him slightly confused and then realized what he meant.

'Yes,' Grenyov whispered. 'Two hours. Not long, but enough. I have copies of all the important research, and I have the Kessler Document.'

I shook my head slowly. 'You are a brave man, Dimitri.'

'A desperate man, Michael. I was drawing close, you see. I was on the right path. Six months, that's all I needed, six damn months, and they shut me down.' His face was contorted with fury. He looked around him again. 'I could not throw away my work, the chance to make the discovery of the century . . . Could I?'

'OK, but what do you plan to do with it?'

He drew back and drank some coffee. I watched his Adam's apple bob. Returning the mug to the table, he tilted his head to one side. 'I plan to get it to the Americans.'

'What!' I rubbed a hand over my mouth and glanced around nervously. Part of me wanted to get up, walk away and never look back, but a more powerful aspect of my mind rooted me to my chair.

Grenyov broke into a smile, the first I had seen from him in four and a half years. 'Why so shocked, Michael? What would you do?'

'The Americans, Dimitri?'

'You and I both know there is a higher calling than serving one's country. You of all people know this.'

And for a moment, he threw me. What did I feel? I could not refute the man, but I felt a pang. What was it? Guilt? Shame? I can admit it now, it was a little of each. But then my intellect took command pushing away anything sentimental or emotional. There was no room for those things now, not in the world in which I lived.

'You're going to give them your secrets?'

'I plan to take the secrets to them. They will have greater resources than we ever had here, better than the Nazis. There's even a chance they know enough to decipher the Kessler Document. Einstein knew Kessler, remember. I intend on working closely with Einstein.'

I must have looked horrified because Grenyov paused as he went to speak. He drew in a breath and glanced around the terrace. The other people who had been out there were leaving.

'How on earth are you going to do that?' I hissed.

'That's where you come in, Michael. I need you to organize it.'

I simply stared at him, lost for words.

'You are on the inside. You have contacts in Washington. Wouldn't your people and the Americans grab the chance with both hands? Wouldn't it impress your superiors?'

'Well, yes, but . . .'

'Why any buts, Michael? Is it not obviously a perfect plan? You get me and what I know to America. They obtain a secret lost over sixteen years ago. You receive a pat on the back, perhaps another promotion.'

He had a glint in his eye and his voice was now perfectly calm.

'But don't you think it would be a tad difficult?'

Grenyov was shaking his head and smiling. 'Nothing worth doing is easy, my friend.'

'Oh please, save the clichés.' I felt suddenly angry. How dare this man bring me into his crazy plans? Did I deserve this? Wasn't my life already complicated enough?

Grenyov drew back in his chair and eyed me dispassionately. 'Perhaps I have misjudged you.' He started to rise. 'Forgive me.'

I let him turn and start for the path beside the terrace. Then I got up from the table. By the time I caught up with him my shock had evaporated and I pulled alongside him as he strode quickly towards Red Square. 'Dimitri, wait,' I said and tugged on his arm.

He stopped and whirled on me. 'I know what I'm doing.'

'I'm sure you do,' I replied and held his eyes

for a second. It started to snow, huge feathery flakes drifting down from the leaden sky.

'I have tried to think through the alternatives.' He looked into my eyes and I had the sense that he was already wondering who else he could turn to.

'Fine, Dimitri,' I said. 'You just surprised me back there. I didn't . . . well, I didn't expect that. What do you say we walk and you tell me how you think this could work?'

On the plane back to Croydon Airport I came to the conclusion that I would hand over what I had learned to my superiors and that they would assign tasks to the appropriate departments, contact the Yanks, and that would be the last I would hear of it.

I could not have been more wrong. Within forty-eight hours of arriving in London I was flying to Washington for a rigorous debriefing. Forty-eight hours after that I was assigned as chief liaison officer for what was quickly dubbed 'Operation Retrieval'.

It sounds glamorous, but it really wasn't. My unenviable task was to plan and implement getting Dimitri Grenyov and his invaluable information out of Russia.

I learned very quickly that for all the surface palliness and talk of 'cousins across the pond' there was almost no mutual trust between London and Washington. We, that is, MI6, had not passed on the knowledge of Grenyov's work out of gentlemanliness; it was simply that the Americans had done a lot of the ground work and that Einstein, the chief architect of applying quantum gravity to creating a force shield, still lived and worked in Princeton. Reports indicated that the great man was not the figure of genius he once was and that many of his colleagues believed he was messing around with flaky notions beyond what might be considered 'empirical science'. But then other scientists worked on the principle that an ailing and unfocused Einstein was worth a dozen lesser physicists.

The upshot was that we gave the CIA the nod, they got me over to Washington, grilled me . . . politely, and then refused to share anything more they learned about Grenyov and Einstein. The only reason they had me assigned to the operation was that Grenyov knew me and would not have trusted anyone else.

Communication via letter was impossible of course; telegram or telex were out of the question and telephones were assumed to be bugged and unusable. The only thing we could do was to contrive another plausible excuse for me to return to Moscow and then to make personal contact with Grenyov.

It took two months, during which time there was no contact between Dimitri and me. Indeed, I had no idea what progress was being made in getting me to Russia. In the event, I was given just eight hours' warning that everything had been arranged and I was booked onto a BOAC flight.

It was February 1954. Croydon Airport looked utterly desolate and I felt only anxiety as I boarded the Comet. A mere four weeks had passed since a plane identical to this one had broken up on take-off from Rome Airport. I thought I was used to flying, but I was jumpy the whole way, first to Paris, then Copenhagen and on the final leg to Moscow. It was only later as I dived into the vodka in my hotel room that I realized my nerves were shot, not just through fear of flying, more important was my growing unease with the course my life was taking. I had started out in purity, working for my country. Then I had taken the leap and the money, convincing myself that I was motivated solely by integrity and by political conviction. Now, here I was drawn into a complex intrigue that was way out of my league. I resolved that when this operation was over I would say goodbye to my Russian paymasters and keep my head down.

Based on the concept that the simplest, most basic plans work the best, I just walked from my hotel to the Academy of Sciences. I was in disguise – a dark wig and moustache, a walking stick and appropriate limp. Cleared through the security check at the main entrance using a carefully faked ID, within a few minutes I was at the door to Grenyov's office.

He reacted with admirable calm, but I got the sense that the man was only just managing to hold together his sanity. He felt bored in his current position, frustrated, angry. When I told him of the plan to get him and his work out and halfway across the world to New Jersey, his eyes came alive as though he had been in a coma for months.

The next morning, Dimitri Grenyov walked out of his office, through the main doors as though en route to a regular monthly meeting at the Institute of Soviet Sciences. Instead of turning right at the junction of Nitali and Stolski Highways he walked quickly to the closest Metro station, travelled three stops, changed lines and slipped down a side street to where a car was waiting for him. This car took the scientist overnight to the border with Finland. Aided by Finnish military personnel, he was smuggled over the border a few miles south of the crossing at Niirala where the forest is dense and only a minute fraction of the natural barrier between the two nations can be manned.

From just inside Finland, Grenyov was taken to a safe house overnight. The next day, he was driven across the country avoiding Helsinki, passing close to Tampere and on to the port of Rauma on the west coast. There, a US Navy submarine, USS *Phoenix*, was waiting.

By the time Grenyov reached neutral territory, I was tying up the loose ends of a contrived meeting that had been my cover in Moscow. Twenty-four hours later, I was on a mid-morning flight to Copenhagen. It was not until I reached London the evening of the following day that I learned the *Phoenix* had been lost.

There was an immediate communication blackout over the matter, but I could not simply let things go. I was at least partly responsible for Grenyov's death. Escaping to America had certainly been his idea but I had been instrumental in organizing the route, the method. Now both the Yanks and my own people had shut down. Something about it stank.

It took months of effort and calling in every favour I had from old friends and colleagues but I did eventually unearth the truth . . . the sub had been sunk by the Royal Navy. This alone, I realized, was a fair enough reason for going silent on the operation.

Phoenix had been in the North Sea heading west, very close to the Norwegian coast when it was attacked and sunk by HMS *Swordfish*. Upon returning to port, the British vessel reported the engagement and logged the precise position as 59° 58′ 03″N 4° 05′ 26″E. The submarine commander, a Captain John Henry, was questioned and gave a perfectly clear account of the circumstances.

According to his report, *Phoenix* failed three

times to identify itself. Captain Henry attempted a direct comms link with the American sub; it was ignored. It was only after the unidentified vessel launched a torpedo that *Swordfish* engaged, launching a battery of torpedoes that sank *Phoenix*.

When questioned as to why the Royal Navy vessel was in Norwegian waters in the first place, the commander refused to explain and the matter was swiftly dropped. After some further digging, I learned that the sinking of *Phoenix* boiled down to a horrible confluence of unrelated actions. The American commander had inadvertently entered a clandestine British experimental site. The Royal Navy was testing a new submarine design. The experimental vessel had suffered catastrophic engine failure, lost its way and drifted into Norwegian waters. HMS *Swordfish* had been mobilized to rescue it before the Soviets could get wind of the incident. Captain John Henry had his crew on high alert and responded the only way he could when fired upon by a vessel that would not identify itself.

Phoenix was lost in the deepest part of the North Sea, the Norwegian Trench, which can reach depths of over two thousand feet. There was no chance of rescue of course, and all evidence of the incident was lost for ever.

I hate to think of how Grenyov died. I like to think he was killed in the attack by the Royal

Navy submarine, caught perhaps in the explosion, or knocked unconscious somehow. But sometimes, in the dead of night, most especially in this godforsaken hellhole in which I will die, I see the poor man's face contorted with pain as he descends into the abyss.

And so I draw close to the end of my story and the circumstances that led directly to my new identity, prisoner X-R34, and this, the venue for my imminent death, Camp 16, Kemerovo, Siberia.

I still do not know how my secrets were exposed. I can only conclude that I had pushed too hard, dug too deep to find out what had happened to *Phoenix* and my friend Dimitri Grenyov; but exposed they were.

I was called in to a debriefing to give my side of what the brass were already calling the 'Grenyov Affair'. I gave a good account of myself and left the meeting feeling positive. After all, I concluded, I was their golden boy, was I not?

I had no idea what was actually going on. The night of my interview with my superiors at MI6 HQ I was visited at home by a man I had never seen before. He turned up on my doorstep at 11 p.m. just as I was preparing for bed and more or less invited himself in. He told me his name was Ernest Wainwright.

Please don't consider me a fool, Wainwright had sound enough credentials. He was a friend of an acquaintance of mine and claimed to know my sister, who had gone to St Swithun's in Winchester, the same school as his younger sibling. I offered him a drink and pushed him to get to the reason for his visit – I was tired, you see.

After a bit of prodding, he came to the point. He knew I had been turned and that I was a double agent. He convinced me he was on my side and shared my political views, that he was also a man with unconventional allegiances. He related facts only another such as I could have known and he shared information only someone with the same handler as I could have been privy to. He produced dates, times, places, people. He had photographs of me speaking with KGB operatives, and he could cite which valuable documents I had passed on to the Soviets.

Thanks to Wainwright, I had a few hours of wriggle time and I was able to get out of London just as my erstwhile colleagues and superiors began to close the net.

Having an escape route was all part of the job in my line of work and I had been diligent enough to keep fake passports up to date, carefully hidden cash, a sophisticated miniature radio and scrambler, along with several sets of ID including a driving licence and ration book in the name of Graham Frayne, a lawyer from Manchester.

I shall not bore you with the details of how I slipped out of the country into France. Suffice it to say, in Lyon I made contact with my Soviet boss and explained what had happened. I told him that I had valuable information concerning Grenyov and the experiments he had conducted at Movlovyl. I could tell by the man's reaction that I had taken him by surprise with my suggestion and I accepted that I would have to wait to hear back from him while he contacted his superiors to see what could be arranged.

I spent a week kicking my heels in Lyon until I was given the green light. Three days later, I was crossing the border into the Soviet Union. That night, I was debriefed again, giving the KGB officers at the meeting everything I knew about Grenyov, the force shield and the fate of *Phoenix*. In particular, I emphasized that the authorities need no longer worry about the Americans or anyone else having all the pieces of the jigsaw required to build Einstein's dream. I was expecting this to segue into a formal discussion about what could be offered to me in Russia.

And indeed, that was exactly what did happen, but it did not take anything like the form I expected. I was told that the matter of my future employment and usefulness to the Union of Soviet Socialist Republics was still under discussion and that a decision would be made very soon. I rose to leave the meeting, walked to the door and felt the barrel of a rifle between my shoulder blades.

So, now we come to the end of this sorry tale.

Well, to me it is sorry, perhaps to you it is not. I freely admit my foolishness, what I have called my litany of errors. I would be lying if I said I had no regrets; that given my time again, I would change nothing. Of course I would change things if I could.

I have had plenty of time to think, to ponder my fate, my role, my purpose. I understand that we only have a small degree of control over our lives. We are not truly free, nor are we in any sense able to command the tides of fate.

At least I was involved in something of significance. That is a rare thing, and perhaps you will allow me this boast, for my life has been cut very short by such involvement. In the dark hours before the dawn, I often become morose, but one thought that always helps me overcome the existential shadow is the realization that, yes . . . I will die shamefully young, but perhaps it is better to die in one's prime having already made a mark upon the world than to wither and wilt and crumble to dust at the end of a long life in which nothing of value is accomplished; a life that is a mere blip in time, a life that changed nothing, neither for the better nor for the worse.

37

'I'll need to check this with London,' Fleming said, closing the file after they had all finished reading Caithness's account.

'How're you going to do that?' Lou said.

'I'll make sure my people dig deep to find out if the facts about *Phoenix* tally; whether a Michael Caithness ever existed and worked for us at the times he claims he did.'

'Then what?' Kate asked.

'Then, if this is authentic . . .' He waved the file in the air between them. 'I can do business with Sergei.'

They started back towards the huge door. 'Just out of interest,' Fleming said. 'Check your phones again.'

Lou and Kate tapped at the screens.

'No outside line for phone. Internet's gone,' Kate said.

Fleming looked to Lou.

'Same.'

Fleming was nodding. 'No flies on Sergei.'

They were close to the doors when a wall-phone started to ring. Fleming picked it up.

'Yes. Yes, OK. I understand.' He put the receiver back. 'The man himself,' he told Lou and Kate. 'He must have been watching us in here.' He glanced up to see if he could find a camera. 'He said it's fine for me to talk to London, but he has to be there every moment of the call.'

*

Kate and Lou returned to their room and slept. There was nothing for them to do but hope Fleming's staff in London were as good as he seemed to think they were. Later, a soldier in fatigues brought them lunch – bread, a selection of cheeses and ham, good strong coffee. Lou was about to watch a Lakers game on ESPN when there was a tap at the door and Adam was there holding the file.

'Come in,' Kate said.

'No, we've got work to do.'

'I take it it's genuine,' Lou said, flicking off the TV with a remote and coming over to the door.

'Looks very much like it.'

*

'So, you wanted us to know the full story behind the Kessler Document,' Kate said.

They were sitting in Sergei's sumptuous quarters. The Russian was seated opposite her, his big arms folded across his chest. To his left Fleming was perched on the edge of a large leather armchair.

Sergei nodded. 'I did, yes . . . purely for personal reasons. That's why I didn't just give you the coordinates. Dimitri Grenyov was my great uncle on my mother's side. My father, Igor, was fascinated by the whole affair and spent years researching what had happened to his wife's uncle. It was he who unearthed the Caithness document, made a copy and filed it in the government archives. If you succeed in rescuing the Kessler Document I would like the whole story told. I wish to see my great uncle's honour reinstated and his genius recognized.'

'And you learned we were after the document, how?'

'I've already told you, Adam. My intelligence is one of the best. You and your superiors might be surprised by our abilities.'

'So, what is your price?'

'I'm not a greedy man.' Sergei held Fleming's eyes then glanced at Lou and Kate. 'And I imagine you have been authorized to bid to a certain very definite limit. If thirty-five million dollars is within your range that is what I would like.'

Fleming said nothing for a moment, looked down at his fingers intertwined in his lap and then back up at their host. 'A high price for a set of coordinates.'

'No ordinary coordinates.'

Fleming nodded. 'And what is to stop us simply returning to the surface or sending an email with the information?'

'Oh, about five hundred armed men,' Sergei replied. 'Now, I would like half the money upfront, the second payment when the wreck of *Phoenix* is located.' He withdrew a mobile phone from the top pocket of his jacket. Rising from his chair, he walked over and handed it to Fleming. 'It's hooked into our Wi-Fi and it's secure. You arrange the first payment to be made while you are on the phone. If you give them even one digit of the coordinates for *Phoenix* . . .'

Fleming punched in a number. 'Access code beta, nine, seven . . . This is Winter Fox. Who am I through to? Thank you,' he said. 'Reference four, one w, f . . . Yes, I am. We have an agreement . . . thirty-five million dollars . . . No, that will not be possible. Yes, OK. Good. Half paid now to . . .' Fleming looked up as Lou passed him a sliver of paper from Sergei.

The MI6 agent read out a series of numbers. 'Swiss account. Yes, we can hold . . . OK . . .' Fleming handed the phone to the Russian.

'Seventeen point five million dollars deposited into account number . . . *Da, da, da* . . . Good,' Sergei said. Clinking shut the phone, he got up. 'It's a deal. So, now we should cele—'

The room resonated with a devastatingly loud whine, a siren ascending, then descending the scale.

'What is *that*?' Kate shouted.

Sergei sprung to his feet. 'Border breach.'

'What?' Lou snapped.

'The authorities. It is one of the negatives we have to live with.'

Three armed men rushed into the room and fanned out close to the exit. The door opened again and Max appeared along with another armed man in paramilitary uniform.

'Report,' Sergei said.

'Serious, sir,' Max replied. 'Two separate entry points, D12 and N11. A large force at each. We have them on camera. Two of our men made visual contact at N11. They weren't spotted and are back now.'

'I want to see the men right away,' Sergei said. He turned to one of the soldiers near the door. 'Mobilize Defence Force to D12 and N11. Implement Shutdown Code Alpha Three.' The soldier clicked his heels and ran through the doorway.

'You three have to leave . . . now,' Sergei said, spinning round to his guests. 'Max, will you . . .?'

Max nodded and turned to Fleming. 'We'll stop by your rooms for twenty seconds, then we have to go. Understood?'

'What's the rush?'

'We cannot guarantee your safety, Adam. These intrusions are dealt with, but we live precariously. We can never know—'

'Let's just go,' Kate cut in.

Sergei waved to them, turned and walked to a rear exit with two of his men.

Max took them out into the wide corridor. A soldier brandishing a Kalashnikov fell in behind them. They saw people moving around in an orderly fashion. There was no panic. Everyone – men, women and children –

each seemed to have a precise role to play and knew exactly what was required of them.

Kate and Lou followed Max as he darted silently along the corridor, and they were soon in the quarters they had stayed in the night before. It took almost no time to gather up their things and then they were hurried along a succession of winding passageways.

'Where are you taking us?' Fleming asked, eyeing the armed guard.

'A way back to the surface that will take us as far as possible in the opposite direction to the breeches at D12 and N11.'

They slipped into a narrow tunnel. The only light came from the main path they had just left. Ten paces in, they reached a steel door. Max fished out a key and nudged the door outwards. It creaked on its hinges.

Directly in front of them a spiral staircase ascended. Max led the way and they followed in single file, Lou, Kate, Adam and the guard. Taking a dozen turns, they began to tire, but they each noticed the air growing fresher and cooler.

Reaching a metal platform, they followed Max into a large square space. A pair of closed doors stood in the centre of the far wall.

'We're almost there,' the Russian said. 'These doors lead onto a passage that connects to a disused water conduit. Follow that until you reach the outside. It opens onto a patch of waste ground not far from Michurinskiy Prospekt, the stretch of highway close to the university building where we met.'

'OK,' Fleming said and glanced back to where they had emerged from the staircase. 'How bad is it?' He flicked a glance downwards.

'It is a regular occurrence, but . . . this seems to be a particularly serious one.'

'You seem pretty philosophical about it,' Lou said.

Max shrugged. 'It is a fact of life. Although . . .' He paused and looked away. '. . . the attacks are growing more frequent.'

'And if they get through sometime?' Kate asked.

Max looked her directly in the eye. 'I think you know the answer to that . . . but we won't go down without a fight.'

38

Approaching Darwin, Australia. 27 June 1937.

'Darwin Control. We are at . . . one thousand three hundred feet, approaching from the north-north-west,' Amelia Earhart had spoken wearily into the radio microphone of her plane.

'Copy that, NR 10620.'

'Coming in for final approach.'

Beneath them Amelia and her navigator Fred Noonan had seen the tin roofs of the small town of Darwin, Australia, population 1,500. From the air, they could see all of it at once, perhaps five hundred or so buildings, a main street, a few smaller unmade roads, and beyond the town's edge, tracks stretching out across the bush. In the early morning light the white sand of the shore led to the dense green vegetation, and beyond that, the red soil and the distant orange horizon.

That had been ten days ago, and now here they were in the Kookaburra, the dusty ramshackle pub in which they had waited, hemmed in by a tropical storm. They had used the time for much-needed repairs to the Electra – new tyres, rear plating and tailplane. And as they approached the final legs of the journey, the incident in Senegal seemed like a lifetime ago. Only three weeks had passed since that strange night, but so much had happened it was pushed back into fading memory.

Things had not been the same since Dakar. She had promised to tell Fred what was going on and she had stuck to her word, but she could only relay as much as she knew. She showed him the cylinder in its box, but she had been economical – no, frugal – with the truth, and she sensed that Fred had known that. She had been given the box by a stranger, she had told him, a man from British Intelligence. She had no idea of its contents, nor its purpose. All she knew was that it was of enormous importance to America and that she must guard it with her life. As a consequence, she had taken it with her everywhere she went. It lay at her feet in the cockpit of the plane and under her pillow each night. And, give Fred his due, he had accepted her story. He was clearly not thrilled, but he respected her and that was enough for him to stay schtum.

Amelia looked around the bar. They had got to know a few locals a little, but they were reserved and distant men, content to contemplate their beer and talk sheep, mangoes and crocs with their mates. She was about to take a pull on her drink when she smiled.

'What's funny?' asked Fred.

'Oh,' she produced a small laugh. 'I was just thinking how different this is to the Imperial in Dakar.'

'Not to mention the Raffles,' Fred replied. 'Best sleep I ever had in my life in Singapore.'

'Well, I'm sure glad I won't have to put up with another night in that lumpy thing upstairs they call a bed. I just saw Clem Newton from the workshop on the field. They've got the old girl fuelled, triple-checked and ready to soar. Oh, and the boys here have taken the luggage.' She glanced in her shoulder bag, a nervous habit since Senegal. The slim box was there, nestled in the bottom.

'And the weather has cleared nicely,' Fred observed.

They did not notice the new arrival until he reached the bar and ordered a beer. He was a tall, well-built man in khaki shorts, heavy work boots, plaid shirt and worn leather hat. He looked over and caught Amelia's eye. Picking up his drink, he walked along the bar, placed a small piece of paper at her elbow and strode on to take a seat in an alcove at the back of the bar. Amelia opened the paper and read it quietly: *May I speak with you?*

They dropped into the alcove opposite the man. Amelia held tight to her bag while Fred scrutinized the fellow and said: 'How may we help you?'

He glanced around, removing his hat and placing it on the table between them. The nearest drinkers were well out of earshot, but still he leaned forward. 'My name is Eric Matheson.' He had a British accent, the first they had heard since leaving Singapore. Looking directly into Amelia's eyes, he said: 'I would like you to come with me. I have something important to pass on.'

'Hang on a minute,' Fred began.

Amelia touched his arm and his protests withered away. 'I don't usually go off with strange men,' she said.

Matheson nodded. 'Naturally. He withdrew a small leather wallet, opened it out and gave them just enough time to see his British Army ID.

Fred shrugged. 'So?'

'Miss Earhart? I wonder if I may have a word with you, alone? It's connected with Senegal.'

Fred Noonan went to speak, but Amelia shifted in her seat. 'Fred? Could we . . .?'

He sighed and walked back to the bar.

'What is this all about?' Amelia demanded.

'Unfinished business.'

She closed her eyes for a second and then said: 'More cryptic messages?'

'I'm sorry. I'll try to be clear. What you were given by my colleague in Senegal is only a part of the consignment. I need to take you to the other part and then you must leave Darwin immediately.'

'Wait. I'm a bit lost here.'

'It was deemed too dangerous for you to be given the entire delivery in one go, in Senegal. There was a serious danger you could be intercepted by the enemy between here and there. Indeed, you still have some way to go, but we felt here would be the best point for you to collect . . .'

'The other part of the "consignment".'

'Exactly.'

'I see. And where is it?'

'That's why you need to come with me.'

'How do I know I can trust you?' Amelia said. 'How do I know you are working for us?'

'Ah,' Matheson said and for the first time he changed expression and almost produced a smile. 'I would have been worried if you had not asked. There aren't many you may trust. I know there are spies here, but although I have a few suspicions, no one has played their hand . . . yet. In Senegal, you met an Englishman. He did not give you his name. He passed on a package with which he had been entrusted. It came from the MOD in London. You were asked to volunteer for this mission by your personal friend FDR himself.'

'That much would not be that difficult to find out. It's information any number of spies could possess, is it not, Mr Matheson?'

'They could, but how many of them would appreciate you so much as to refer to you as a . . . pioneer?'

She held Matheson with a steady gaze. He had used the agreed code word. 'What do you want me to do?'

'My car is outside. We need to take a drive out of town, maybe ten miles south. There's a clearing in the bush where Mr Noonan can land the plane. He should meet us there.'

'OK.'

They walked over to where Fred was halfway through a fresh beer. He downed it and they left. Outside on the street, Amelia explained the plan to Fred and Matheson quietly handed him a folded map. 'Don't open it now, Mr Noonan,' he said. 'Head straight for the airstrip. I understand the plane is ready and waiting. The clearing is marked on here.' He tapped the map. 'It will take us perhaps twenty minutes to reach by car. We have some things to do, but if you head off immediately. That would be . . .'

Fred looked to Earhart. 'You sure about this, Amelia?' She simply nodded, turned and followed the Englishman to his old wagon parked across the street.

The road was tarmac only up to the last building on the street; from there it was nothing but baked red soil and gravel. The flat-bed truck bounced and jolted over the pits and potholes, the thick bush was cut back only a yard or two either side of the road.

Amelia felt wary and uncomfortable. Part of her wished she had passed her bag containing the box on to Fred, another, stronger part was confident that she could take care of herself if this Matheson character turned out to be rogue.

'I could ask you how your flight has been,' the man said, half turning from the road.

'You could,' Amelia replied. 'But I get the feeling you're not really one for small talk.'

Matheson exhaled through his nose – what may have passed as a laugh for him – and they stayed silent for a few minutes.

'May I ask who else is interested in our "package"? Who are the spies you believe to be here in Darwin?' Amelia asked.

'Why, the Germans of course. Who else?'

'I see. I was told nothing in Washington.'

'I know little more than you do, Miss Earhart. But I was at least told whose hands we are to stop the package falling into.'

'And you think there are actually German spies *here*?'

'Why not? After all, they know your itinerary. I think those who pursued you in Africa and killed your contact were Nazis. Here though, they are either extremely good actors who have worked their way into this tiny community – which is possible, they would be government-trained pros after all – or the Germans have bought off some locals. I'm inclined towards the latter.'

'We had no more trouble after Senegal.'

'Which makes me extra concerned,' Matheson responded.

They approached a sign and a track east. The sign said: *Maninunup*.

'A small Abo community,' Matheson said. 'And a big ranch owned by a very wealthy Englishman called Timothy Langley. He migrated here two decades ago. He's a real philanthropist, paid for half the construction in Darwin.'

Matheson drove carefully, the road narrowing and descending through a steep incline between dense undergrowth and impressively tall palm trees heavy with fruit. And then suddenly they were out in the open. A clearing about half a mile long and a few hundred yards wide had been cut into the bush and a clutch of buildings stood off to one side.

'I've rented one of the huts over there,' Matheson said. 'I've buried the package behind the back wall. Follow me.'

He jumped from the wagon, slammed the door shut, then walked round the vehicle, retrieving a shovel from the open back. 'This way,' he said and strode off towards the hut a few yards away.

'There's no one here right now,' he explained. 'It's Sunday. Church . . . Langley insists upon it.'

'What goes on here?'

'It's a small township. Or at least it will be,' Matheson said. 'Langley finances it, the natives are building it. Langley sees it as the best way to empower the Abos.'

'You sound doubtful,' Amelia said.

Matheson just shrugged.

They had reached the single-room hut. The window overlooking the strip of land was shuttered. Like every other building in Darwin, it had a tin roof.

They turned the corner. 'Here we are.' Matheson stopped behind the rear wall of the hut and pointed to a spot in the sand. Amelia leaned against the wall as he started to dig.

They both heard the plane at the same moment. Amelia stepped round to the front of the building, raised her hand to shield her eyes and saw her Electra approaching the field. It swayed slightly in the wind and followed a smooth arc, touching down close to the middle of the strip of land and slowing quickly. Fred then let the plane taxi towards the buildings, stopping about thirty yards from Amelia. She waved and walked back to Matheson.

He was lifting a padlocked metal box from a hole in the sand. Placing it on the ground, he rummaged around in his pocket for the key.

They saw the policeman before they heard him. He stepped out of the bush a few feet from where Amelia and Matheson stood, a chubby, ruddy-faced man holding a pistol. He pushed the last of the leaves away with his free hand and stomped onto the sand, his gun steady at waist height.

'Ah! Of course! Sergeant Ampstle,' Matheson said. 'I should have guessed it would be you.'

The policeman was wreathed in sweat, lines of moisture running down each flabby cheek. 'Open it,' he said, nodding towards the metal box.

'That's just what I was about to do.' The Englishman crouched down and slotted the key into the padlock. Lifting the lid, he reached in and pulled out a cloth bag.

'Empty out the bag,' Ampstle said, his voice trembling. With his left hand he wiped the sweat from his eyes.

'I was about to do that too, sergeant.' Matheson straightened. He looked remarkably relaxed as he pulled the fabric bag away and let it drop, empty to the ground. In his hand he was holding a metal tube a little under a foot long.

'I'll have that,' Ampstle snapped.

'Not so fast.' Matheson held it up and turned it end

to end. 'Such a lot of fuss over something that looks so ordinary.'

'I said hand it over.'

'And what if I don't?' Matheson hissed. Without a hint of warning, he tossed the cylinder to Amelia and dived forward stunningly fast, sending the fat cop flying backwards.

Matheson was on Ampstle before the man had time to even cry out in surprise. Landing his fist in the sergeant's face, he screamed, 'Run, Amelia . . . Go!'

39

'At fucking last!' Hans Secker said when he heard the Afrikaans-accented voice of Herman Toit coming down the line.

A cold silence.

'What happened?' Secker asked.

'Meaning?'

'Meaning, asshole . . . what the fuck happened? You've been off the grid for three days.'

'Mr Secker, with respect . . . shove a fucking fork up your ass.'

Another cold silence, then Secker said: 'The Boss has been considering other options.'

'Well, that's up to her. I have other demands upon my time. Shall we call it a day?'

Secker could hear Toit's voice quieten as the man moved the receiver away from his face.

'Wait!'

A cold silence.

'Where are you?'

'I'm in Moscow, doing my job, Mr Secker.'

'OK, Toit, I apologize. Bring me up to date . . . please.'

Toit paused for a moment, turning the screw a little. 'The scientists are here, watched over by MI6 and the CIA. They have made a breakthrough with the Kessler Document, but I have no definite information . . . yet. I believe that the document was spirited out of the Soviet Union in the early fifties. Word has it that it was placed aboard an American submarine.'

'"Word has it" sounds fucking vague, Toit.'

'Surely you wouldn't expect me to give you my sources, would you, Mr Secker?'

'So, what now? I assume you have a plan?'

'I always have a plan. I have been forced to improvise to a degree; things on the ground here are . . . well . . . changing very fast. I am almost certain the scientists have precise information relating to the location of the document.'

'We must acquire that knowledge and then dispose of Bates and Wetherall.'

'I think that would be nearly impossible, and actually completely futile,' Toit replied.

'Explain.'

'I believe it is possible they have already passed the information on to MI6, although I cannot be certain. Also, killing them would both be a logistical nightmare and send up a red flag. A better solution would be to force the information out of them. And, I hate to disappoint you, but even then it will not be possible for you and your boss to have exclusivity: as I just said, I think it very likely MI6 have the facts already.'

'She'll not be happy about that.'

'Happiness is a rare commodity these days, Mr Secker. Very rare indeed.'

40

Moscow. Present day.

Kate leaned down and planted a kiss on Lou's cheek. 'I'll start packing,' she said and waved as she stepped between the tables and out through the ornate doors into the foyer of the Grigovna Zempska Hotel.

'So the next step is to locate the sub, right?' Lou leaned across the breakfast table and lifted his coffee cup as Adam Fleming spread marmalade on his croissant.

'Yes, and that's no easy task. The coordinates narrow it down to a couple of hundred square yards, but the Norwegian Trench is the deepest part of the North Sea. As of first thing this morning my government has clearance from Norway, but that was just a matter of diplomacy. Finding a fifty-year-old wreck in two thousand feet of water is quite different.'

'I think I know that, Adam.'

'Yes, sorry, of course you do. That's why we need to get you to London asap.'

'Our real work can begin at last.'

'Quite.'

Lou glanced back to where Kate had left the room. 'So what's the story with you and Kate back in the day?'

Adam stopped chewing for a second, swallowed and lowered the rest of the croissant to his plate. 'We were friends, Lou. Surely she told you that.'

'Exactly what she said.'

'I can't lie though. I wanted it to be more.'

'I can understand that,' Lou commented and sipped his coffee. 'I imagine she was popular at Oxford.'

'Certainly was. I was way back in the queue, and well . . . I guess I just wasn't her type. Anyway, long, long ago in a galaxy far, far away.'

Lou nodded. 'I assume you found someone else, Adam.'

He took another bite of his breakfast. 'Yes, I did. Celia. We married in 2009.'

'Must be hard, being married and doing your job.'

Adam took a deep breath. 'She died, three years ago.'

'Oh, man, I'm so sorry.'

Adam shook his head. 'It's all right. I've learned to talk about it. You're not the first . . .'

Lou raised his eyebrows and exhaled through his nose. 'Well, I've probably ruined your morning.'

Adam grinned. 'Of course not. Celia was also in the service. She was quite brilliant. I met her at Oxford. Kate never knew her. Kate and I sort of drifted apart and I ended up with a different set – different parties. You know the sort of thing.'

'Yep.'

'Celia was killed in an anti-terrorism operation. I had a rough time of it for a while. I guess I blamed the service. I was angry. But, I worked it out of my system, found a new balance, got back on with the job.'

'Even the blackest clouds can have a silver lining apparently.'

'So I've heard.'

'Right, well I'd better give Kate a hand, I guess.' Lou drained his cup and pushed back his chair. 'What time is the cab?'

'Ten, sharp.'

'Cool.'

Out in the foyer a large group of Japanese tourists had arrived and were checking in. Lou squeezed past, found the lifts swarmed by the new arrivals and took the stairs.

A maid's trolley laden down with toilet rolls, fresh towels and bottled water blocked the corridor two doors short of the room. The maid emerged from the room she was servicing just as Lou tried to move the trolley.

'*Pozhaluysta* . . . Please,' she said and stepped over to guide the trolley out of the way. Lou gave her a warm smile, found his door card and slipped it into the lock.

'Kate? How's it going?'

No reply.

He walked through into the small seating area adjoining the bedroom. No sign of her.

'Kate?'

The bathroom was empty.

Lou pulled out his mobile, punched the speed dial and pulled the phone to his ear. The network took a few moments to find the number and then started to purr. After five rings it went to a messaging service.

'Damn,' Lou exclaimed and flicked off the phone.

He gazed around the empty room. His case was on the bed half packed, Kate's stood close to the end of the bed, zipped and locked. His eyes drifted towards the window, the drawn curtains and an ornate occasional table between two armchairs. There was a folded piece of white paper leaning against a fruit bowl in the centre of the table.

Lou walked over. As he picked up the sheet of hotel stationery and scanned it, he felt a tingling shoot up his spine.

ALERT THE AUTHORITIES AND SHE DIES.
KEEP YOUR PHONE ON.

41

'How could you let this happen?' Lou glared furiously at Adam. They were sitting opposite each other at the table in the bedroom, the note on the surface between them.

Adam had his hands raised. 'I told you, Lou, I take full responsibility, OK?'

'So, what are you going to do about it? How do we find her?'

He lowered his hands. 'You saw me call London. My people are on to it.'

'And the note said no authorities.'

'They mean the Russian police.'

Lou gave the agent a poisonous look. 'And how are your *people* going to find Kate without the help of the cops?'

'We have our methods. Leave this to me.'

'Leave it to you?' Lou stood and leaned over Fleming, his face contorted with fury. 'Like I left it to you to protect us here? You're the fucking intelligence agent. Kate and I are scientists!'

'Calm—'

'Don't tell me what to do, Adam.'

Fleming had his hands up again. 'We will do everything humanly possible to find her.'

Lou turned away and pulled out his phone.

'Who . . .?'

Lou ignored him, walked across the room and sat on the edge of the bed.

Fleming strode over. 'Who're you calling?'

'Mind your own fucking business.'

Fleming made to grab the phone. Incensed, Lou snarled at the MI6 agent.

'Jerry . . . yeah, sorry, man, I know.' A pause. Lou started pacing. 'We have a situation here.'

42

Lou caught sight of Jerry before the naval officer saw him and strode over to the revolving door of the Grigovna Zempska. They embraced and Lou turned to the bellboy with Jerry's bag. 'It's OK, we'll take it,' Lou said.

They walked over to check-in and a few minutes later they were in the bar. It was approaching midnight.

'You look tired, buddy,' Lou said as two beers arrived.

'Military transports aren't the most comfortable,' Jerry replied. 'But I managed to grab a few hours on the train after we crossed the border and I was given the third degree by the guards. I got Fleming's report on my phone. Any other news?'

'Adam is doing all he can. I wasn't too happy with him when Kate disappeared.'

'I can imagine.'

'He's out now with another agent. He has to juggle finding her with keeping the whole purpose of our stay here from the Russians. He can't go to the FSB or the FSK.'

Jerry nodded and emptied half his glass in one go. 'And you haven't heard anything from whoever took Kate?'

Lou lifted his phone. 'Not a word, but I have this beside me at all times. Fleming's people have it tapped. So when I do get a call . . .'

They turned to the door and saw Fleming walking towards them. He looked exhausted. Jerry offered his hand, he took it then sat on a stool rubbing his forehead.

'You look like you need a drink,' Lou said and called the barman over. 'News?' he added as he absent-mindedly signed the bill the waiter offered him.

Fleming looked pained. 'Nothing. Nothing at all.'

'What do you mean?' Lou snapped, then checked himself and glanced around. Aside from a couple in the far corner, the three of them were alone in the bar. 'How can that be?' Lou said in a hush.

'Nothing . . . so far, Lou. We are doing—'

'Yeah, you said this morning . . . You'd do everything humanly possible.'

Jerry turned to his friend. 'Lou, I know it is hard . . . fuck, I can't begin to imagine . . . but we have to think constructively here.'

A double whisky arrived for Fleming and Jerry ordered two more beers.

'What I don't understand,' Lou said, a desperate look in his eyes, 'is how anyone could have known we had the information from the archive. I presume that's what they are after.'

'I've been thinking about that too,' Fleming replied. 'There were only a handful of people involved and it makes no sense that Sergei or his people would be behind it.'

'So, it must have been another intelligence leak,' Lou said. He turned to Jerry. 'You heard about the farce with that character Zero?'

'A precis, yeah. He acquired his intel from some leak between agencies, is that right?' Jerry turned to Fleming.

'He was watching MI6 and CIA moves and not reporting anything back to his superiors because he wanted a piece of the action . . . well, actually, he wanted all the action himself.'

'Could it have been him then? Zero?'

'That was my initial conclusion.'

Lou gave Fleming a hard look.

'I didn't say anything because it was just a first theory . . . in my experience they are usually wrong.'

'But?' Lou said.

'I was right not to chase it up. Arseny Valentin, aka Zero, was dragged from the Moskva this morning at just about the time you found the kidnap note.'

'Fuck!'

'It is not public knowledge, and won't be. He was an FSB agent. One of our embedded operatives passed the news on to me.'

'Well, then I don't understand,' Lou said.

His mobile rang. Lou grabbed it and pushed the 'accept' button.

'Yes . . . yes,' Lou said. 'I understand . . . but look, what are . . .?' He exhaled loudly. The other two could hear a man's voice spilling from the iPhone receiver. The blood had drained from Lou's cheeks. 'Yes . . . OK, OK. Right . . . I get it! I want to speak to my wife. No . . . I want to speak . . .'

Lou's head slumped forward, the phone in his lap. Jerry extended a hand and gripped his friend's shoulder.

Lou looked up. 'They want the location of *Phoenix*. A physical, paper map with the precise details – latitude, longitude and depth. They've given me a set of coordinates . . . somewhere called the Khimki Forest, 6 a.m. One chance, they said . . . One chance. Fuck it up and Kate dies.'

43

Lou hadn't slept a wink, just sat in the chair close to the massive window in the room he had shared with Kate. He had watched the night sky, the moon moving across the punctured black, the field of stars seeming to shift as the world turned on its axis.

Now, well before dawn, he sat in the foyer downstairs still feeling small and insignificant. How was it, he thought to himself, that he and Kate had chosen to be scientists, but kept finding themselves caught up in intrigues and inter-governmental conspiracies? How had they become strange bedfellows with the military, the FBI and MI6?

The risks he and Kate took diving hundreds of feet or poking around old and unstable wrecks were one thing, but what the two of them were involved in now . . . this was a different sort of danger; one over which they had no control, one that forced them to be entirely dependent upon others. He hated that, it went against his character.

Jerry appeared as the lift doors opened and strode towards him across the vast Persian rug that covered the centre of the foyer. 'You obviously haven't slept.'

'Impossible,' Lou replied. 'Heard anything about the phone tap? Do we know who we're dealing with?'

''Fraid not. Fleming briefed me ten minutes ago. The call to your mobile was scrambled and triple re-routed . . . No trace.'

They turned and saw Fleming come in through the revolving door bringing a gust of freezing air with him. 'I have the hire car,' he said. His face was pale. Flakes of snow began to slowly melt on his shoulders.

He sat down the other side of Lou, removed a glove and plunged a hand into a pocket of his fur-trimmed parka. 'And here is the camera I was talking about last night.'

He lifted a device between his thumb and index fingertip. It was about a quarter the size of an aspirin and as thin as foil. Leaning forward, he fixed it to the collar of Lou's greatcoat. It was almost the same colour as the fabric and virtually vanished.

'It's on permanently, recording now, and lasts for eight hours. It'll help us ID the kidnappers.'

He removed a laminated sheet of A4 card and handed it to Lou. He glanced at it. It was a map mostly showing the blue of the North Sea. To the right lay a strip of green – the west coast of Norway. A red dot indicated the precise location of the wreck.

'Let's go,' Fleming said.

The roads were quiet. Lou sat in the back, alone; Jerry in the passenger seat; Fleming drove. Before they set off he punched in the coordinates: 55° 56' 6"N 37°

26' 48"E. None of them spoke as Fleming took the Volkswagen Polo east on the E22. The lights of the city began to slip away behind them. At five-thirty the sun was still some four hours from rising and the traffic was thin, building a little on the main roads with early risers heading to work. Lou let the soporific beat of the wipers roll over him as they swept away large flakes of snow from the windscreen.

Twenty minutes after leaving the hotel they reached the inner ring road, Moskovskaya Koltsevaya Avtomobilnaya Doroga, the MKAD. Turning north, they joined heavier traffic and it started to snow harder. Passing Khimkinskiy Lesopark, an expanse of green on their left, they reached the junction of the MKAD and the northbound M10. Taking the freeway, in a few minutes they could see the outlying birch trees of Khimki Forest, a thousand hectare national park that had recently been a battleground between conservationists and property developers, a conflict the green groups had won.

Fleming checked the GPS. 'The meeting point is in view on the screen now,' he announced and tapped the panel on the dashboard. Lou leaned over Jerry's seat as they both peered at the display.

'Looks like a junction of two tracks about four miles to the north-east of here.'

Pulling off the main road, they took a narrow eastbound unmade road, the Polo bouncing on the ice-hardened track, its suspension complaining loudly. They stopped a hundred yards along the path. Fleming jumped out and Lou took the wheel. Derham lowered himself into the passenger footwell, pulling a Beretta 9mm from his pocket. Fleming squeezed into the narrow space between the back and front seats.

Lou took it slowly, one eye on the GPS, watching the red cursor marking the car's position as it moved along the representation of the track on the screen, drawing closer to the agreed meeting point.

He turned the car left off the track onto a narrower, rougher path, the hard ground making the vehicle bounce and grind. A minute later they reached a clearing and stopped. On the GPS screen the red cursor hovered over the meeting point. He peered through the snow-edged windscreen, keeping the engine running, the wipers swishing.

'See anything?' Derham asked.

'Nothing.'

Lou's mobile trilled.

'Yes.'

He flicked on the Bluetooth and a deep, accented voice spilled from the speakers.

'You should be able to see us now.'

Headlights appeared along the track. They bounced as the approaching car navigated the rutted frozen track.

'I see you. You have my wife?'

'We ask the questions, Dr Bates. You are alone, I hope?'

'Yes.'

The lights came closer and stopped moving. The car was a black Lexus four-wheel drive. In the stillness Lou could hear the purr of its large engine.

'You have the coordinates?'

'I do. And a map.'

'Open the door slowly and take two paces directly in front of your car.'

Lou eased the door open, stepped out, walked slowly, leaving the door open and carrying the map encased in a plastic folder.

Two paces in front of the Polo, he stopped, and with his left hand he shielded his eyes from the bright car beams. He strained to catch a glimpse of Kate, but he could see nothing inside the car.

Two men stepped from the front seats. Another, armed, hands outstretched, the barrel of a pistol pointed directly ahead, emerged from the back. The two men from the front walked towards Lou. One of them removed a gun from under his leather jacket, held it with both hands, pointing it down at his side. He wore Aviators, and lank, greasy hair hung to his shoulders. The other man was older, short and thickset. He was wearing a Crombie over a suit and tie; his business shoes were polished to a mirror finish. They stopped four paces in front of Lou.

'You said you had my wife. Where is she?'

The man in the Crombie lifted a gloved hand. 'All things at the appropriate time, Dr Bates.' He was the man who had spoken on the mobile.

Lou waved the folder in front of him. 'I want to see my wife first.'

The man considered him for a few seconds, his face completely expressionless. Then he turned to the driver. 'What do you think, Uri?'

Uri lifted his arms and pointed the gun at Lou.

'I think that's a "no".'

Lou turned and started to walk back to the car.

'Dr Bates.'

Lou ignored him, kept walking. Uri fired, a bullet hit the ground an inch from Lou's left boot, snow spraying up his coat. Lou dived to the frozen ground, hands over his head.

The passenger door and the offside rear door of the Polo flew open simultaneously. Derham fired his Beretta between the door frame and the car body. Fleming opened fire from the left side of the car.

Uri flew backwards, a stream of blood gushing from a wound in the centre of his chest. The man in the Crombie dived for the driver's side of the four-wheel drive.

Lou scrambled across the snow. More shots rang out. A bullet hit the windscreen of the Polo, another slammed into the near-side front door. Lou turned and saw the man who had been close to the back door of the Lexus slumped on the ground, a plume of blood flying up from his destroyed face.

Uri writhed in the snow, a swathe of pinky-red around him. The Lexus revved and spun on the icy track, the tyres screaming in protest, a wheel caught the side of Uri's head, the left back wheel came round and crushed his body.

Derham and Fleming stopped firing, pulled themselves up just as Lou got to his feet. The Lexus slithered around on the frozen ground in a cloud of exhaust fumes. Lou ran after it, yelling incoherently. And for no more than a second, through the miasma, he saw Kate's face appear at the rear window. She was calling to him, her face contorted with horror.

'Kate,' Lou bellowed, the sound consumed by the damp air and the snow. 'Kate . . .' The sound bounced back to him. He dropped to his knees, sinking into the whiteness. Crumbling forward, he collapsed into the snow, hot tears streaming down his face and onto the frozen ground.

44

The phone rang three times before Lou came to, grabbed for it blindly in the darkened room and heard its dull thump on the carpet. He scrambled across the bed, reached down and found the receiver.

'Yes?'

'I'd like to help.'

Lou was instantly awake, pulling himself up against the headboard. He'd recognized the voice immediately.

'Max. What do you mean?'

'What I said, Lou.'

'How?'

'We told you . . . Sergei has an intel network at least as good as the SVR. We know where Kate is being held.'

Lou was silent for so long Max said: 'You still there?'

'Yes. Why would you help?'

'It is right that you should be cautious, my friend, but it is simply that Sergei likes you and he likes your wife. He feels a sense of responsibility. Kidnapping in his city . . . not good.'

Lou glanced at the clock. It was 3.24. He turned to stare at the faintly lit wall opposite. Shadows and strange patterns of reflected neon played on the wallpaper. From far off in the freezing night he could hear the rumble of traffic cut through by the shallow screech of a siren.

'What do you have in mind?' Lou said, his voice little more than a mumble. He felt nauseous, his mouth dry.

'Come alone. Don't involve Fleming.'

'Why?'

'We don't trust British Intelligence, Lou. You understand, no?'

'Where?'

'Entrance of the hotel. Ten minutes.'

He heard the phone click, closed his eyes for a second and felt the room spin. He reached over and switched on the light, then pulled himself out of bed. As he dressed he punched in Jerry's number and put the phone on speaker. It took a few moments before Derham's drowsy voice spilled into the room.

*

'You did the right thing calling me, Lou,' Jerry remarked as they descended in the lift.

'They said I should come alone.'

'Let me do the talking.'

They crossed the reception. The night staff were busy

at computer screens and paid them no attention. Emerging into the night, the cold hit them hard.

Max was standing beside a car, the doors open. He extended a gloved hand and gave Jerry a hard look. 'I said come alone, Lou.'

'That will not be possible,' Derham replied.

Max stared into the captain's eyes.

'I'm . . .'

'I know who you are, Captain Derham.' Max turned to the car. 'Both of you get in, please.'

The streets were almost empty. Fresh snow had settled; only a few tracks sliced the powdery ice. The pavements were deserted. They saw half-a-dozen police cars doing their rounds close to Red Square. At a junction a few hundred yards from the hotel two army trucks, each carrying soldiers in greatcoats and fur hats, pulled in front of them. Two streets on, they turned off east.

'Where is Kate being held?' Lou asked, leaning forward. He felt overwhelmingly despondent.

'A district in the south-east, Kapotnya.'

'Who has her?'

'Unknowns. By that I mean we can't find any links with them and any of the major gangs . . . yet.'

'We came to the conclusion that Kate was taken by someone connected with Russian Intelligence, the SVR,' Jerry said.

'Possible,' Max replied.

'We considered Sergei, briefly,' Lou said flatly.

Max shrugged without taking his eyes from the

road. 'No sense in it. Sergei wants his second payment. He's hardly likely to alienate Fleming and his people by doing such a thing, is he?'

'That's what we decided. Why didn't you want us to alert Adam?' Derham asked.

'I told Lou, we don't trust MI6. Why should we?'

'But you trust us?'

Max exhaled through his nostrils. 'Lou wants his wife to be rescued alive, doesn't he? We will meet my people in an apartment close to where she's being held. Sergei has put two of his best men onto it. They are excellent. You can trust them.' He gave Lou a reassuring look. 'This is not a good . . . what do you say? Scene? Not a good scene.'

Lou stared out at the ice and snow-strewn streets lined with grey rectangles, faceless monolithic slabs like tombstones against the leaden sky.

They drew into a square car park in front of a residential block. There were three other vehicles there, two derelicts and a tatty, orange Moskvitch van. From the car they made their way over a stretch of waste ground hard and rutted with frozen mud and ice. Across a stretch of pitted tarmac stood a ragged tower block. It had been thrown up in the sixties and was already falling apart; cladding missing, windows smashed. Behind it in the dark morning, they could see, stretching across the horizon, the spindly columns of the Kapotnya oil refinery, red and yellow tongues of flame dancing atop three of the refining towers.

Max walked briskly across the snow, his boots

crunching on the frozen ground. They reached the decrepit entrance to the building, steamy breath swirling around their faces.

'The lifts don't work, of course. Our men are in apartment 184, on the fifth floor. It is directly over 154, where Dr Wetherall is being held.'

Lou's face was red. He had not shaved, and ice crystals clung to the stubble. 'They're here?' he said. 'How, did you . . .?'

'What's the plan?' Jerry asked quickly.

'Wait until we get to 184. The guys will brief you both.'

The flat stank of fast food, cigarettes and sweat. It looked as though the place had not been lived in for some time before Sergei's men had arrived. In the living room, a pair of 1970s suedette sofas, worn to the foam and covered in cigarette burns, formed an 'L' around a scored coffee table covered with McDonald's wrappings and boxes smeared with ketchup. An overladen ashtray took pride of place in the centre. In the corner of the room stood an old boxy TV, the screen smashed in.

Sergei's men sat on one of the sofas. Max introduced them as Yegor and Ilia. Ilia looked in his mid-twenties with black curly hair. Yegor could have been his father; late forties, muscular build. He had the same unruly black hair but it was cut shorter and sprinkled with grey, a stern face, a pink scar running down his face. Lou did not like to ponder how he had come by it.

Ilia offered them a half-empty bottle of vodka. 'It'll warm you up,' he said and produced a gappy grin.

Lou was about to decline, but changed his mind. Taking a swig, he felt the fiery liquid rush down his throat, spreading burning fingers inside his stomach. 'Jesus!' he exclaimed.

Ilia chuckled. '*Da!* Good!'

'OK,' Yegor said quietly. 'This is the situation.'

He swept aside the McDonald's cartons and spread out a sheet of grubby white A3 on the table. A floor-plan had been roughly sketched on the paper in felt tip.

'This is 154, the apartment below us. Basically the same as this charming place.' His English was almost perfect with barely a trace of accent. 'There are three men in there now.' He looked up to hold Lou's eyes. '. . . and your wife, Dr Bates.'

'How do you know?'

Yegor glanced at Max. 'It's irrelevant, but we have sophisticated surveillance equipment that can pick up body heat and translate it into approximate images of the individuals. As well as this we have listening devices. We have been able to hear every word spoken in there from a few minutes after we arrived last night.'

'And Kate?' Lou asked, the pain clear in his face. 'Is she . . . OK?'

'We can't see her, of course, but they haven't harmed her while we've been here. She has spoken a few times and sounds anxious and angry; as you'd expect. But we've heard no sign of violence or distress, so we believe she is unharmed.'

Lou held the man's eyes for a long time then looked down at the paper on the table. 'What's your plan?'

*

Max, Jerry and Lou left the apartment first. Exiting through the front door, they closed it behind them. Jerry had been given a two-way radio, an earphone in his right ear, a coiled cable running down his neck to a receiver at his belt. He and Max had their guns out: Jerry primed his navy Beretta, Max carried an old Luger.

They took the stairs slowly, Jerry in the lead. Keeping close to the wall, they twisted round into the walkway, front doors to the apartments on their right. On their left, a shoulder-high wall stretched the length of the passage. Over the wall they could see the car park beyond the rutted waste ground. Two inches of dirty snow ran along the top of the wall.

The walkway was deserted. The sound of a TV from one of the apartments further along drifted towards them. They pulled close to the wall of the building a few feet from the door to 154.

'*We're ready to descend onto the rear balcony.*' It was Ilia through the two-way.

Jerry nodded to Max and Lou. 'They're ready to go.'

On the far side of the apartment, the rear door led onto a stark narrow concrete balcony. It was identical to dozens of others the length and height of the tower block. Yegor and Ilia were poised to drop a floor from the balcony of 184, ropes attached through pulleys and keyed into the brickwork. They held Kalashnikovs close to their chests.

Yegor gave Ilia a signal and he dropped through the chill air to land silently on the balcony wall of apartment 154. A few seconds later, Yegor joined him five feet along the wall.

'Ready on your signal,' Yegor whispered into his radio.

At the front of the apartment, Lou stood a pace behind Jerry and Max as they took up position either side of the door. Jerry leaned in and pressed the bell.

A fraction of a second later, Ilia and Yegor launched themselves from the top of the balcony wall and smashed through the rear window of apartment 154, glass scattering around the tiny kitchen beyond.

One of the kidnappers was at the stove cooking breakfast. He began to turn, his hand reaching down for a pistol tucked into his belt. Ilia shattered his face with a burst from his assault weapon. The man crumpled over the frying pan and onto the lit ring.

It was just two steps from the kitchen into the boxy low-ceilinged living area. Kate was not there, but the other two men were slouched in front of a TV in a pair of La-Z-Boys. One of the men had a shotgun in his lap. He reacted with incredible speed. Spinning to his right and off the chair, he brought round the gun and emptied both barrels. Yegor opened fire, killing him as Ilia flew backwards and crashed to the floor. The unarmed man in the other chair raised his hands.

Jerry came round from the hall, his gun at arm's length. Yegor dashed over to Ilia.

Crouching low and moving fast, Lou made it past the opening and found a pair of doors to the left and right of the hall. He tried the first one – an empty room with sleeping bags on the floor. Whirling round, he pulled on the other door and almost fell into a blacked-out room. Kate was sitting on the floor against the far wall tied by ropes at her ankles and wrists, a gag over her mouth. She looked terrified, her eyes huge in the half-light from the hall.

45

Within minutes two cars, a Mercedes 600SL and a dark-blue BMW, had pulled up outside the apartment block. People were emerging terrified and sleepy from their flats. Max played it down, flashed a fake ID to show he was a member of the FSB, the state police, then escorted four of Sergei's men to apartment 154.

From the bedroom where Kate had been held, she and Lou could hear the coming and going of the men. Kate was still shaking, sipping a bottle of water.

Jerry Derham stood in the hall just beyond the closed bedroom door and watched the men remove the dead – two of the kidnappers and Ilia, his face hidden by a sheet. Yegor glanced at the captain, his expression rigid, then he followed the men out onto the balcony and down the concrete stairs.

Two men stood over the surviving kidnapper, Max was seated behind them in the main living area. Derham followed Kate and Lou out onto the balcony and down to the snow-strewn patch of tarmac that served as a parking area. The car carrying the dead was disappearing around a corner about a hundred feet from the tower block, the dark-blue BMW stood with the engine running, exhaust fumes billowing into the freezing air.

'I think you should go to the local hospital,' Lou said as he helped Kate into the back of the car and nodded to the driver holding open the door.

'What I need more than anything is a hot bath, a cup of strong tea and about three days' sleep,' was the last thing Derham heard her say to Lou as the door of the car closed. He waved them off and returned to the apartment.

The surviving kidnapper was bleeding, a stream of red running down his arm and dripping onto the cheap velour of the chair. The muzzles of two Kalashnikovs hung inches from his face. Max was leaning forward in his chair talking to the man in Russian.

'Max, this man needs medical attention,' Derham said and stepped over. The prisoner was a youth, barely out of his teens. He had a spotty, red face. Sweat ran down his cheeks. He said something in Russian, his voice anguished.

'Please, Captain Derham, let us . . .' Max said.

Jerry leaned down over the kid. 'Let me see,' he said, pulling the prisoner's arm up and inspecting the wound. The kid winced.

'He has a bullet wound in his forearm. It's bleeding badly, Max.' He lowered the arm gently.

Max nodded to one of the guards. He grabbed Derham's arm. The captain cursed, jerked free and the man shifted position to get a fresh grip.

'Please! Captain Derham!' Max snapped and strode over. 'Please . . .' He pulled free Jerry's arm and the guard stepped back.

'You can't just—'

'Captain, we have our methods. Please try to remember you are a guest in our city. I would hope you would respect that.'

Derham pulled back and sat down in a chair the other side of the tiny living area. The kid gave him a desperate look.

'Name?' Max began again in Russian, standing over the young man.

He ignored the question.

'Name?'

Max counted a beat then smashed his fist into the kidnapper's face. His head snapped back against the chair, blood jetting from his shattered nose.

Derham spoke little Russian, but he could guess approximately what was being said.

'Name?'

'Vasily . . . Vasily Komonech.'

'Who are you working for?'

The kid shook his head, snot and blood dripped from his nose.

'It's a simple question, Vasily.'

'I don't know!' the youth hollered.

Max leaned in and grabbed the man's injured arm, twisted it roughly and found the entry point of the bullet. In the dim light the boy started to scream. Max pushed his thumb hard into the gaping wound.

With his free hand, he clamped the boy's mouth as he struggled.

'Max! Stop!' Jerry was out of his chair. One of the armed men spun round with his rifle and Max jerked up as Vasily Komonech's piercing screams reverberated around the room.

'No more chances, Vasily. Tell me who you are working for.'

Komonech was struggling to draw breath. Derham could see he was about to pass out. His face was bloodless, albumen-like. He tried to speak, but his voice cracked. 'A woman. Rich woman. Don't know her name,' he gasped in Russian. Max translated for Jerry.

Max gave Derham a questioning look and Derham got it. 'Buckingham? Glena Buckingham?'

'*Da, da*. Buckingham.'

'Fuck!' Derham exclaimed.

'Who is your boss here?' Max asked the kid. 'You know you have to tell me one way or the other.'

'Vladich.'

Max smiled. 'Good.' He turned to Jerry. 'He's working for Vladich.'

'Vladich?'

'An arsehole. Heads up one of the smaller gangs we hadn't yet looked into.' He straightened up from the chair. 'Get rid of him,' he snapped.

The guards yanked the youth to his feet. His legs gave way and they half-dragged, half-carried him out into the narrow hall.

'What are you going to do with him?' Derham flicked a glance towards the outside.

'That is our business, Captain. Please don't try to interfere.'

Derham made to reply, but Max had a hand up. 'Please. I have something very important to discuss with you.' He looked furtively towards the hall. They both heard the front door smack against the wall and Komonech pleading pathetically.

'What?'

'We have received some significant information that I believe you should be told about . . .'

46

Lae, Papua New Guinea. Early hours of 2 July 1937.

Lae, steamy hot and wet, as it always was. Thirty degrees centigrade both night and day.

The scruffy hangar lay on the outskirts of the tiny town, part of a privately owned airfield belonging to a wealthy Asian importer. This late at night the whole complex was almost deserted with just the swish of palm fronds in the sticky breeze stroking the west-side windows of the hangar like the fingers of an amorous lover.

Amelia was there, tinkering with the port-side engine of the Electra 10E. She had the metal object in her right hand and with the left she pulled aside a bundle of wires to expose the perfect spot to locate the container.

They would be setting out on the final long haul of the circumnavigation at day break tomorrow. The plane was fuelled and ready, checked and double-checked.

She tugged the wires under the manifold and heard a sound from behind. She turned, saw nothing.

The wires were catching on the base of the object. She leaned in closer, twisted the offenders out of the way and repositioned everything.

The noise came again. This time she whirled round.

Two men were walking towards her. They were both tall and dressed in dark suits and ties. One of the men had cropped blond hair, the other wore a black Fedora. The former held a Beretta at waist height, the stumpy muzzle pointed at Amelia. She raised her grease-smeared hands slowly.

'Where is it?' the man in the hat asked. He had a strong German accent.

'Where is what?' Earhart screwed up her face.

'All right, this is what we are going to do, Miss Earhart,' the gunman said. His English was clearer, crisp with an Oxbridge affectation. 'Our time is limited. We are . . .' and he nodded towards his colleague '. . . entirely lacking any form of empathy. Neither of us cares a bit whether you cooperate or not. If you do cooperate and hand over the item you were given in Dakar, we can all be on our way. If you do not, we will torture you, horribly, and we will not stop even after you have told us where we can find the thing we seek. Do you understand me?'

She saw a movement behind the men as the palm fronds made another pass against the window; then a dash of fabric, a flash of white.

'I don't know what you mean,' she lied, feeling a rivulet of sweat slither down her spine, a tight fear in her abdomen.

'Okay,' the man in the Fedora said, the shadow of the brim across his face.

Amelia saw another judder of movement, and in a fraction of a second she knew what it was. The blond man made to take a small step forward, his hand tight on the Beretta. Amelia caught a brief glimpse of something metallic and slender swing down to the right of the gunman's head. The spanner crashed into the man's skull, sending him sprawling across the floor.

Amelia saw Fred. He had frozen like a store front manikin. She dived towards the prone figure on the floor, yanked the pistol from his limp fingers and spun round.

The man in the Fedora reacted with stunning speed. He stepped away from Fred, never taking his eyes from Amelia as she pulled herself up, the gun levelled at him. Fred seemed to snap out of his daze and took a step to his right. The German made a desperate dive towards Amelia's legs. She hopped back, lowered the gun and fired, missed by several inches and started to stumble backwards, catching her balance just in time.

The man looked almost comical, two feet short of reaching his target, one knee on the floor, his hat glancing his shoulder before hitting the floor and tumbling away. Fred Noonan charged him, the German rolled to one side, crushing his own hat. The spanner slammed into the concrete floor, sparks cascading from the point of contact.

Amelia caught sight of the blond man, a spreading pool of crimson around his smashed head, and she stood up straight just in time to see the other German regain his balance and charge her again. This time, he reached her and grabbed her hand. She yanked back with a surge of strength that startled him, lost her balance and pulled the man down on top of her.

The boom of the Beretta was muffled this time. Fred rushed towards them, dropping to the floor between their tangled legs. He pulled at the German and the man rolled onto his side, a startled look on his face, arterial blood spurting between the buttons of his jacket.

47

'You are calling with good news?' Secker hissed down the line from London.

'Depends on your perspective,' Toit replied. He was calling from a public call box. The view through the broken glass was of a uniform drabness, grey upon grey. 'The operation was not a success. The people I hired were less than useless. They did not retrieve the information and got themselves killed in the process.'

'Well that's something! I assume you have other fingers in other pies.'

Toit exhaled through his nose. 'I will get the information to you via the usual route.'

48

Moscow. Present day.

'You had no authority to do that.' Fleming was bearing down on Lou seated in the MI6 agent's room. Kate was asleep upstairs, an armed plain-clothes officer from the British embassy guarding the door.

'So, I should have left Kate with those men, Adam? Is that how you see it?'

'No, but you should have told me. This is a delicate operation. On the one hand we have to keep the Russian authorities off our backs, and on the other I have to assure my superiors in London that we are not wasting time and money . . . a lot of money.'

'Loose change,' Jerry Derham said from the edge of the bed where he was sitting facing the other two.

'That's irrelevant, Captain.'

'Maybe, but it's also irrelevant talking about this now, isn't it?'

Fleming whirled on him. 'Why exactly are you here?'

'Because I asked him to be,' Lou snapped.

'And, in case you have forgotten, we are on a joint-forces operation,' Jerry added, matching Fleming's angry stare. He stood up as the MI6 agent straightened. They were the same height and about equal build.

Fleming turned away, scowling. 'Very well. What's done is done. The only thing that really matters is that Kate is safe and well.' He pulled up a spare chair. 'So run through it all again.'

'Max took us to an apartment in some rag-tag area.'

'Kapotnya,' Jerry said. 'Three men were holding her. Two were shot. One of Sergei's men was killed.'

'And there were no witnesses?'

'Max assured us Sergei would take care of everything,' Lou said.

'And why did he get involved?'

'According to Max, Sergei likes Kate and me, and he felt responsible.'

'Responsible?'

Lou shrugged. 'Does it matter, Adam?'

Fleming said nothing for a moment, just stared at the gleaming leather of his shoes. 'And, so Sergei has lost one of his best men, simply to save someone he hardly knows?'

'That's his problem, isn't it?' Jerry said.

'Maybe. Maybe Sergei will expect favours in return.'

'Nature of the business.'

Fleming went to reply, but Lou cut over him. 'So what now? I assume your people are doing their best to pinpoint *Phoenix*? After all, they have spent a *lot* of money on getting the coordinates.'

Fleming deliberately ignored the sarcasm. 'I received

a message half an hour ago. They've located the sub at . . .' – he checked his iPhone – '59° 58' 03"N, 4° 05' 26"W. They expect us in London as soon as Kate is well enough to travel.'

49

London. Present Day.

The Secret Intelligence Service building, home of MI6, all green glass and cream stone on the south bank of the Thames close to Vauxhall Bridge, glinted in the unseasonable winter sunshine.

The cab pulled up outside. Lou and Kate looked up at the impressive building, with its huge stacked platforms and a fascia like a medieval castle designed by Frank Lloyd Wright. Lou whistled. 'Impressive.'

'They call it Legoland around here,' Kate said.

'I can see why!'

They were met by a barrage of security, body-scanned, IDs checked, their bags passed through sensors and detectors. Only then were they escorted through to the main atrium, where they were met by two men in sober grey suits, given ID badges and led through a maze of corridors that resembled a hotel rather than a government building.

Descending in a lift, the two minders said nothing, just gazed into the middle distance. Down a wide, carpeted corridor, Lou and Kate followed the two suits to a pair of heavy oak doors. One of the men opened the left door and indicated that the two scientists should enter as he and his colleague retreated to the corridor and left without a word.

There were four men and two women in the room. As Kate and Lou entered they all rose from their seats around a smooth maple conference table. They knew Fleming and Jerry would be there and shook hands with them before being introduced to the others.

At the head of the table chairing the meeting was Sir Donald Ashmore, Deputy Chief of the SIS, a tall, wiry man with swept-back silver hair and dressed in a double-breasted Savile Row suit. Next to him, a muscular younger man, handsome, with burnt umber eyes: Ashmore's senior assistant, Seth Wilberforce. The two women were Commander Ester Lamb, the Royal Navy's most experienced submariner and pilot of the experimental submarine *Jules Verne 3* and across the table from her Jeanette Schmidt of the CIA.

'Thank you all for coming today,' Ashmore began and got up from his chair to stand beside a smart-board. 'Now, as you all know, satellite images have located the precise position of the American submarine *Phoenix*, which sank off Norway in February 1954.'

He clicked a remote and an amazingly clear image of the sub appeared on the smart-board. From this distance and perspective the vessel looked to be remarkably well preserved apart from its rear end, where there was damage.

'*Phoenix* was a Balao-type submarine commissioned in 1942 and had a crew of seventy-six,' Ashmore went on. 'The captain on the ill-fated voyage to rescue assets from Finland was Captain Vince Jacobs; by all accounts a very capable officer with twelve years' experience as a commander.' The screen changed to show a man in his mid-forties in US naval uniform.

'USS *Phoenix* was sunk by a British vessel, HMS *Swordfish*, after it was fired upon by the American submarine.

'As each of you know, we are interested in this vessel because the asset was carried onto the sub by the defector Dimitri Grenyov.' A photograph of the Russian scientist appeared on the screen. He was wearing an ill-fitting suit, his thin wisps of grey hair slicked back. He looked unwell, with dark rings under his eyes.

'The asset is a document which the Russian was trying to get to Einstein in Princeton so that together they could work on producing what has been described as . . .' he checked his iPad on the desk in front of him '. . . a defence shield created using an obscure aspect of quantum theory.

'The object of this meeting is to establish the feasibility of a mission to reach *Phoenix*, board her and retrieve the materials Grenyov had with him.'

He clicked the remote again. It showed a schematic of the wreck. 'This has been constructed from thousands of images taken by satellite and using deep ocean probes along with the original diagrams of the ship from US Navy archives.

'As you can see, although the rear is partly destroyed, the main body of the ship remains intact. We are therefore hopeful that the asset will indeed be retrievable. To explain how that may be facilitated, I'll hand you over to Commander Lamb.'

Ester Lamb was a compact woman wearing naval uniform. She moved with confidence and immediately held the attention of everyone in the room.

'Good morning,' she began and clicked the remote. The image changed to show a more detailed schematic of the interior layout of the submarine. 'We have no definite idea what we will find inside *Phoenix*, but what I can describe to you is the method through which we can approach the vessel, board it, and hopefully retrieve the document.'

She clicked the remote again. 'I know that some of you are familiar with *Jules Verne* submarines.' She glanced around the table. 'They were created by DARPA – that's the Defense Advanced Research Projects Agency – and the US Navy have started to use them. The Royal Navy have four vessels currently on trial. We will be travelling to the site of the wreck aboard HMS *Gladstone*, a specially adapted vessel that carries two *JVs*. The submarine is capable of descending to fifteen thousand feet, so the maximum operational depth of approximately two thousand five hundred feet for this mission lies well within its capabilities.

'Doctors Wetherall and Bates will constitute the scientific team.' She turned to them and the others swivelled in their seats. 'You are both of course familiar with the *JVs*,' Lamb continued. 'The tricky part of the operation is not descending to the sub, but what we do once we reach it.'

Lou raised a hand. 'As Sir Donald indicated, the vessel looks well preserved but how stable is the hull? Looks can be deceptive.'

'Fair point. We have conducted infrared and X-ray scans of the wreck and they look promising.' She tapped the remote and a multicoloured image of *Phoenix* appeared. 'The red regions are frail, the green strong, yellow and orange in between those two extremes.'

The black outline of the sub was filled mostly with bands and patches of green and yellow. A few areas of orange lay close to the rear of the vessel. The structures butting up to the engines glowed red. A second patch near the bow where *Phoenix* had come to rest on the seabed showed up scarlet.

'As you can see, the green and yellow regions predominate. We have no need to approach the red section as there is a large fuel and supplies storage area, here, between the living/operational sections and the engines.' She indicated the region immediately aft of the engines smeared in orange and flecks of red.

'The sections of most interest are the command centre, here, and the crew quarters, here and here. From archive material we believe the document is held in a steel attaché case which Grenyov carried aboard *Phoenix* in Finland.' She clicked the remote and an image appeared of the Russian holding the rectangular metal case shortly before boarding the doomed sub.

'Of course, he may have transferred the document and his papers, or had them out of the case when the encounter with *Swordfish* began; but, naturally, we are unable to ascertain these details without boarding the vessel.'

The image on the smart-board changed to display a schematic of a cylindrical object. 'This,' Lamb said, 'is the means by which we will be able to enter *Phoenix*. The airlock on the vessel will be corroded beyond use, but this device circumvents any need to take that route.

'It is a portable access tube or PAT, a nanocarbon tube which connects the lock of the *JV* to any form of submersed structure such as *Phoenix*.'

On the screen the tube rotated and the image opened up. 'One end of the tube is built up on the hull of *Phoenix*. Nanobots connect it to our *JV* and then an opening can be cut in the skin of the old submarine. It is then possible for you' – she turned to Lou and Kate – 'to crawl through into *Phoenix*.'

'Wow!' Kate exclaimed.

'Wow indeed.' Commander Lamb smiled. 'We have DERA, Defence Evaluation and Research Agency, the British equivalent of DARPA, to thank for this. It's really a development of 3D-printing technology. We've shared with the US Navy, just as they have shared the *JV*s we are trialling.'

'That is very cool,' Lou added. 'How long does it take to do the job?'

'That depends upon a few factors – the material of the hull, the stability of the vessel, the depth at which we use the tube. But for this mission, we estimate no more than ten minutes.'

'To build the tunnel from nanocarbon, cut the portal and seal it?'

'Yes.'

Lou looked at Kate. They had both experienced deep ocean nanotechnology at work before during the mission to try to retrieve documents from a storage facility that was part of the *Titanic* wreck eighteen months earlier, but this seemed to be in a different league.

'OK, any questions?' Lamb asked.

'Security,' the CIA officer Jeanette Schmidt stated. 'I'm assuming HMS *Gladstone* will have a full escort?'

Sir Donald's senior assistant Seth Wilberforce spoke for the first time. Leaning forward, he gazed around the room. 'We have liaised with both the Royal Navy and the US military. *Phoenix* is a US Navy asset, but the operation is being led by the Royal Navy and of course Norway is also a member of NATO so there should be no serious conflict of interest. We are all on the same side, are we not?' He spread his fingers on the wood of the conference table and held Jeanette Schmidt's hard face for a moment.

'But that's not my point,' she said.

Wilberforce had a hand up and glanced at Sir Donald before speaking. 'However . . . as much as the Norwegians have been extremely cooperative, they do not want a foreign fleet in their waters, just a few miles from their coast. It is of course a political matter and we are onto it, but, as I'm sure you will agree, time is of the essence. We know we are not the only ones interested in this whole business.' He paused for dramatic effect and fixed Schmidt with an intense look. 'While the diplomats and ministers sort out the Norwegians, we have to tread carefully. *Gladstone* will be the only vessel in the zone of the wreck.'

'Crazy!'

'We feel it is essential that we keep this a low-profile operation.'

'You Brits and your low-profile this and your low-profile that!'

'Would you suggest going in with all guns blazing, Ms Schmidt?' Sir Donald asked calmly. 'You chaps have a penchant for that.'

Jeanette Schmidt exhaled loudly but decided not to pursue the matter.

'Any further questions?' Sir Donald surveyed those around the table.

'When do we start?' Lou asked.

'*Gladstone* sails from Portsmouth at 17.00 hours today. A helicopter is waiting for you on the roof.'

50

North Sea. 6.21 a.m.

HMS *Gladstone* was a small naval vessel. But it was one of the most modern in the fleet. Commissioned only a year earlier, it was a Type-7 nuclear-powered stealth multi-purpose vessel. For the past six months it had been the primary ship used to transport and maintain two *Jules Verne* subs now in their final month of trials with the Royal Navy.

Gladstone had a full complement of thirty-four crewmen commanded by Steve Windsor, who had been its captain since its maiden voyage twelve months ago. During that time *Gladstone* had been on exploratory missions as far afield as the Gulf of Mexico, the Great Barrier Reef and the Bering Strait. After the Israeli attack on the Iranian nuclear plant at Bushehr, it had also seen action as part of the British Task Force in the military stand-off in the Persian Gulf.

From the bridge the view was one of the most striking Kate had ever seen. The water, grey and violent, absorbed snowflakes as though the sea was vacuuming them from the air. To the east lay the icy snow-encrusted Norwegian shoreline: sheer cliffs fading into fog that crept over the water towards the ship. The panorama was bleak and mean.

'We will be directly over the wreck in under ten minutes,' said a young officer facing a U-shape of flat screens, lines and patches of numbers darting across the glass.

'Very good, Thompson.' Captain Windsor scanned the horizon. 'The fog is moving in fast,' he said, lowering his binoculars and turning to Lou and Kate standing a few feet back from the manned control consoles. 'Fortunately, our radar will give us an image almost as clear as a visual.'

The door to the bridge slid open, Derham and Fleming stepped inside. They were wearing white fur-trimmed parkas. The door closed automatically.

'Fog's getting up,' Jerry said.

'Just been talking about it, Captain Derham,' Windsor said. 'It's a nasty one all right.'

The drop in the engine tone was almost imperceptible as the ship slowed and closed in on the site region.

'Prepare to all-stop,' Windsor said quietly to one of the men at an array of screens to his left. Beyond the windows, the cliffs had vanished from view. It was impossible to tell sky from water except for a shimmering and heaving of the North Sea below the fog-bruised grey sky.

'Can we see anything of the wreck?' Fleming asked,

taking a step over to where Windsor leaned in towards one of the operatives.

'Over here,' Windsor said and paced over to a man seated in front of a large flat screen.

'Anything coming through, Taylor?' Windsor asked him.

'It'll take a moment, sir.' The operator tapped at a keyboard and the image on the screen shifted from a featureless dark blue to a flash of shifting patterns. The picture flickered and a blurred patch of black appeared to the left of centre. The officer ran his fingers expertly over the controls and the smudgy image began to sharpen.

'There she is,' Windsor said matter-of-factly.

'Just trying to clean it up, sir.' The officer kept his eyes on the screen, his fingers dancing over the keys. The dark patch on the monitor skittered left, then right. For a second the picture flickered then, taking them all by surprise, a perfect, clear image of the wreck emerged from the confusion.

51

North Sea. 8.15 a.m.

'We good to go, guys?' Jerry Derham asked and looked around the table at Kate, Lou and Commander Ester Lamb. They were in the Ready Room of *Gladstone* two hours after arriving at the site of the wreck.

'Well I am!' Lou replied.

Derham turned to Lamb. '*JV3* prepped and ready, Commander?'

She nodded. 'Absolutely, Captain.'

'You wanted to go through the plan with me first, yeah?'

'Yes.' Lamb walked over to a flat screen on the wall. An image appeared.

'This is the internal layout of *Phoenix*.'

They had seen it before, in Vauxhall. It was a multi-coloured and meticulously labelled schematic. A series of rectangles represented the various sections of the submarine.

'As I said at the meeting in London, we cannot be sure where the case containing the documents may be found, or even if they are still in it but we have to start somewhere.

'We've worked out that the best entry point for the Portable Access Tube is here, close to the base of the conning tower where it connects to the main body of the sub. You can see there is a small, roughly spherical, chamber here where two crewmen operated the periscope. A ladder leads down to the control room directly beneath the conning tower.'

As she spoke and clicked the remote, different areas of *Phoenix* lit up. 'Next to the control room, towards the bow, are the officers' quarters; the crew mess and quarters lie aft. The rest of the vessel is taken up with machinery, torpedoes, engines, batteries, storage areas. We are very hopeful the attaché case will be in one of these rooms.'

'And if it isn't?' Kate asked.

'It won't be far!' Lou responded.

'It's hard to imagine how this metal can could accommodate . . . how many crew?' Kate turned from the screen to Lamb.

'Up to eighty; the living and working areas are tiny. *Phoenix* is three hundred and twelve feet long, but has a beam of just twenty-seven feet. On top of that, a good seventy per cent of the internal space is taken up with machinery and storage.'

'Do you have any idea what condition Kate and Lou might expect to find the interior to be in?' Derham asked. He was tapping a pencil on a pad in front of him.

'We've just got back a series of images from a probe,' Lamb replied.

A cloudy, ill-defined image replaced the schematic on the screen. 'Not that brilliant to be honest,' she said. 'But there is no clear access point to get a probe inside, so these pictures had to be taken through the hull.'

'Couldn't you have used a PAT for the probe?' Lou asked.

'I'm too worried we might compromise the integrity of the hull if we make more than one opening. Which brings me to another thing to consider.' Ester Lamb scanned the faces of Lou, Kate and Jerry. 'We have no way of telling just how stable the structure will be once we disturb the wreck. Our techs have made the PAT as efficient as it can be, but, as you will appreciate, wrecks are unpredictable.'

'So, what are you saying?'

'We'll monitor the structure with thermal imaging from the moment the PAT connects with the hull. We'll keep you constantly informed. But we have to put a time limit of forty minutes' search time once the PAT is connected. First sign of trouble you must get out asap.'

Derham turned to Kate and Lou. 'Any questions, guys?'

Kate nodded. 'Yes. How long do your Liquid Metal Carbon dive suits last now? Has the design been improved since we explored the *Titanic*?'

'You won't be needing them on this trip. The PAT is completely sealed, and besides, there is simply no room inside the sub for you to wear them. Instead, you'll be using highly advanced thermal suits.'

'Oh,' Kate said. 'I don't know how I feel about that.'

'What do you mean?'

'The LMC suits always worried me . . .'

'Because they could not be used for very long?'

'Yeah, but on the other hand, they did make you feel protected.'

'The fact is, though, the section of the sub you'll be going into is completely sealed. If it weren't, the external pressure of the North Sea at that depth would have crushed *Phoenix* long ago.'

Sure, I get that,' Kate said. 'What sort of protection do we have then?'

'The thermal suits will keep your core temperature up. It will be very cold inside the sub; we estimate about minus twenty Celsius.'

Lou whistled.

Lamb nodded. 'The atmosphere will also be unbreathable and almost certainly toxic because the huge batteries may have leaked and . . .'

'And?'

'Well, before the temperature dropped to preserve the bodies of the crew, they may have decayed. There will be dangerous levels of ammonia, sulphur dioxide, and methane.'

Kate looked pale. 'Fantastic.'

52

'This vessel is pretty much the same as the one used on the *Titanic* mission,' Commander Ester Lamb called back to Lou and Kate as they buckled up and sat back in their seats aboard *JV3*. 'We've made a few modifications, but nothing you would notice.'

'As comfy as ever,' Lou quipped.

Lamb laughed. 'Believe me, I've been in worse.'

They descended rapidly, the external view through the remote cameras quickly turning dark. The powerful beams of the sub criss-crossed through the North Sea water picking out the occasional large fish, rocky projections, and once, a swirling vortex of herring.

The wreck came into view, an indistinct black cylinder at first, but as they drew within twenty yards of *Phoenix* the image on the cabin screen showed a sharp outline.

The old sub lay almost level on its belly, wedged between some lumpy rock formations shaped as a V. These held the dead vessel in a rigid cradle. *Phoenix*'s conning tower tilted at a slight angle and the matt-black hull, with lines of rust and patches of algae spreading along its flanks, had started to merge with its surroundings. Looking at it now, some sixty years after it fell, stricken to the bottom of the North Sea, Kate could see this melding process had only just begun. But how would it look in a millennium? Or in a million years from now? *Phoenix* would become a fossil deep inside the sediment and the rock.

Lamb spoke through the comms to the bridge of *Gladstone*. 'We're at designated docking coordinates, control. Twenty-seven point three feet NNW of the conning tower.'

'Copy that, *JV3*.'

'Prepping support nanobots.'

Lou and Kate unbuckled and came forward to the main control panels and guidance modules where Commander Lamb sat. She manipulated the controls, talking as she worked. 'You won't see much at first.'

Punching a series of pads, a sharp cracking sound came through the speakers. 'Bots launched,' she announced through the comms.

On the wreck of *Phoenix* nothing appeared to have changed. Lou scrutinized the image on the screen and glanced at Kate, who was watching intently.

Gradually, a faint pattern appeared as almost a visual glitch, a faint shadow on the metal of the conning tower. As they watched, it grew like a time-lapse film of bacteria in a Petri dish. A faint orange circle appeared and from its rim four steel-coloured lines stretched out from the skin of the wreck and started to grow. The leading edge moved towards *JV3*.

From descriptions offered by techs on *Gladstone*, the scientists knew roughly what to expect. But seeing a nano system grow before their eyes was far removed from any academic translation. It was like an embryo developing in a womb. Four nanocarbon struts grew several inches per second. Within two minutes, they had reached out from the hull of the wrecked *Phoenix* to join up with *JV3*.

'Unbelievable!' Kate exclaimed.

'You used nanotechnology on the *Titanic* mission, didn't you?' Lamb said as she manipulated a set of controls and made fine adjustments to the settings.

'Yeah,' Lou said, 'but it was a lot less sophisticated than this.'

'The technology is developing fast.'

'No kidding.'

Through the remote cameras they could all see the nanostruts reach the hull of *JV3*. There was no sound, no vibration or jolt as the bots made contact and begun to construct a link to the skin of the vessel around the airlock to the starboard side of *JV3*.

'Excellent,' Ester Lamb said, turning to Kate and Lou for a second before devoting her attention back to the controls in front of her. 'The superstructure is there. That's half the battle over. Now we have to construct the skin.'

The commander ran her fingers over a plastic panel of flashing lights and touchpads, turning from the screen to the controls and back again. On the monitor, they could see fingers of orange stretching out in all directions, starting from the circle attached to *Phoenix* and moving outwards to form a tunnel around the struts. It looked for all the world like a playground tunnel. In the light beams of the *Jules Verne*, the surface shimmered like the scales of a fish. Ten minutes later, the skin was complete.

Lamb leaned back and they all looked at the image on the screen. Between *Phoenix* and *JV3* stretched a twenty-foot-long connecting tunnel. It was about a yard across and gave slightly, swaying gently with the current. Through the almost translucent skin could be seen the outlines of the four nanocarbon support struts.

'Control. The PAT is complete. Testing integrity.'

'Copy that, *JV3*.'

Lamb adjusted a few more settings and watched a digital display on the panel in front of her. Numbers and symbols skittered across the monitor.

'How we doing?' Kate asked.

Lamb ignored her for a moment as she concentrated on calibrating a series of parameters. 'Not bad . . . Just need to . . .'

On the screen they could see coloured lines dash left to right. Lamb made a few alterations to the controls, a green line and red line merged. She hit a plastic pad and the lines locked in.

'Done.' She clicked on the comms. 'Integrity green 100, control. All systems check positive.'

'Copy that, *JV3*.'

They could hear a cheer in the background as the voice from *Gladstone* came over the speakers.

'Is that Captain Jerry Derham we hear?' Kate asked, grinning.

'It is he.' Jerry's voice boomed through the speaker. 'Well done, Commander. Now, Lou and Kate – your turn to shine, guys.'

53

The PAT swayed almost imperceptibly as Kate and Lou edged along it. They took it slowly. All they could see was orange nanofibre and, up ahead, the grey rusted metal of *Phoenix*, a circle of hull about a yard across.

Kate was leading the way and as she reached the point where the PAT connected to the sub she removed a small device from a pouch in her suit. The micro-laser was about six inches long, barrel-shaped with a half-hemisphere at the end. Holding it out, she checked a control on a rectangular panel to one side.

'*JV3*, we are at the hull, calibrating the laser.'

'Copy that, Kate. Your vitals are all fine. PAT integrity one hundred per cent.'

'Fully charged,' Kate said to Lou as he pulled up beside her in the narrow tunnel, '. . . and set.' She pressed the micro-laser against the metal of the hull. 'Here we go.'

A muffled throb came from the device and it started to vibrate. Kate held it steady and an intense narrow red pinprick of light came from the end just below the metal hemisphere. The two scientists watched fascinated as a line appeared in the metal surface of the old sub. Kate moved the laser slowly and the line, a deep cut in the hull, moved with her. The beam was cutting through more than two inches of steel as though the sub were made of candyfloss. As the metal dissolved and cooled, wafer-thin curls of metal slithered away and were sucked into the hemispherical end of the device.

It took no more than sixty seconds for the laser to cut a hole two feet wide in *Phoenix*. As the last of the metal vaporized, the section of hull slipped away, tumbling into the sub. It hit the floor of the chamber directly beneath the conning tower.

Kate deactivated the laser and returned it to the pouch in her suit. Lou slipped through the hole and into the wreck, Kate came through immediately behind him.

That was when they saw the first body, a man crumpled against the wall close to the base of the periscope a few feet away. The light from the PAT splashed into the small room. They could see the flesh of the man's hands and the back of his neck had started to decay before the temperature had dropped enough to halt the process. There were crystals of ice over his uniform and in his hair. Kate crouched down and turned the body over. The face was smashed in, pink and red around bloated white flesh.

'I think he died when the sub struck the sea floor,' she said. And flicked on her comms to *JV3*. 'We're aboard. There's a body in the conning tower chamber.

Young guy, partially decayed as predicted. We're proceeding on to the control room.'

'Acknowledged.'

'How's the hull integrity, Commander? I hope I wasn't too rough with the laser.'

There was a momentary silence, then Lamb's voice came down the line. 'Only slight perturbations by the look of things.' They heard her at the control panel. 'I think it was a good choice of location as an entry point.'

Lou found a sealed circular door in the floor and pulled it upwards to reveal a connecting tunnel about six feet long with a ladder bolted to the wall. He led the way, lowering himself into the control room below the conning tower. Reaching the metal floor, he stood aside as Kate came down.

It was completely black. Lou flicked on his helmet light and activated two powerful torches built into each sleeve of his thermal suit. Between them the lights threw out over two hundred watts. Kate did the same. The control room was the largest open space on the vessel, a rectangle about twenty-five feet by fifteen. Every surface was covered with dials, pipes, openings into voids, leather patches, levers and pressed-steel compartments. They noticed a patina of dust over every surface. Some of the metal components were tarnished by the toxic atmosphere in the sub. The ceiling, lined with white and grey pipes, stretched away just a few inches above Lou's head.

There were four dead men in the room. Close to a

secondary periscope and a small panel dotted with levers and dials the captain, Vince Jacobs, sat crumpled, his face eaten away by bacteria. Next to him, the co-pilot's seat was empty. Two bodies lay on the floor between the control stations. It was clear how the men had died, each had a ragged hole where a part of their skull had been. Two pistols lay close by. The fourth body was slumped on the threshold of a narrow passage that led aft to the crew's quarters.

Lou glanced at Kate – she seemed to be transfixed by the horrifying sight.

'You OK?'

She nodded slowly and snapped back to the moment, steely professionalism taking over. 'Yes. So . . . where do we start looking?'

'I guess we should try to find Grenyov.'

The body across the doorway was that of a young sailor. They lowered him back to the metal and stepped into the crew quarters.

Lou was first into the room, the powerful light beams from his suit slicing the black. It was a long, narrow compartment with rows of bunks either side of a gangway. They could see most of the bunks were occupied, frozen humps under brown ice-sprinkled blankets. They walked slowly along the gap between the racks of the dead, checking each corpse.

At the third upper cot on the right, Lou stopped, peered closer at a face turned towards the narrow aisle. The beam from his helmet illuminated the face. It looked waxy, a mask. The stubble on the man's chin was white and glistened with ice crystals. His dark eyes were open, his mouth contorted into a grimace. Skin, grey as a seal's, was stretched taut over the bones of his face.

'Grenyov,' Lou said.

54

London. 9.15 a.m.

Chief Inspector Derek Warminster was seated in the police car with DS Paul Carrington at the wheel. From there they both had a clear view of the SWAT operation without having to don bulletproof vests and helmets. They could see the black painted door of Glena Buckingham's London home, a three-storey white mansion in The Boltons, Kensington. The door was about to be stoved in by the team of four officers charging towards it brandishing a battering ram.

Ten seconds later they were inside. Two of the men charged across the black-and-white tiled hall floor and into a collection of generously proportioned high-ceilinged rooms to each side, sweeping their MP5s before them. As they did this the other two took the stairs to the next floor. Every few seconds one of the officers would shout 'clear' through his radio, and then move on.

Four minutes twenty-two seconds later, they had checked every square inch of the building and the static-laced voice of Team Leader Zero Four One came over the radio of the squad car in which Warminster and Carrington sat.

'Building clear, sir,' the team leader said. 'No one home.'

Warminster cursed and flicked a glance at Carrington. The radio crackled again with a new voice. It was DS Dave Martin.

'Sir. Leaving Eurenergy HQ. The building is clean. Neither Glena Buckingham nor Hans Secker are here. We have taken seventeen individuals into custody for questioning.'

'Fuck!' Warminster exclaimed and brought a bunched fist down on the plastic dashboard.

55

Flotta, Orkney Islands. 9.15 a.m.

Glena Buckingham and Hans Secker stood at the centre of the horseshoe of consoles in the main control hub of Eurenergy's Flotta base off Orkney, precisely where they had been five days earlier.

On the giant screen dominating the centre of the room, Buckingham, Secker, Chief of Operations Dr Cecil Freeman and his staff could all see the sleek grey profile of the Eurenergy stealth ship *Orlando*. The vessel was stationary twenty nautical miles north-west of the *Gladstone*, anchored off the coast of Norway. Those gathered in the main control hub were able to see *Orlando* through a live uplink via the satellite network that had been online now for a week. The projection onto the screen was crystal clear.

'*Gladstone* has remained in position for over two hours, now,' Buckingham said quietly to Secker. 'They must be directly over the location of the American submarine. Toit was true to his word, his information accurate after all.'

'Toit has been briefed?'

Secker nodded.

'We've managed to key into *Gladstone*'s comms and can eavesdrop on their bridge, ma'am,' Dr Freeman said. He nodded to an operative on his right and a voice from the ship spilled from the speaker in the Main Control Hub on Flotta.

'JV3? Come in, Commander Lamb, come in.' It was Jerry Derham's voice.

'This is JV3, over. We have reached the Phoenix *site and are preparing to dock.'*

They've sent one of the *JV*s down,' Buckingham said gleefully. 'That's a good . . .'

She did not finish the sentence. Blood drained from her face and she could not move her eyes from the screen. Several seconds passed before she could bring herself to speak. 'What in the name of fuck is that?'

55

North Sea. 9.15 a.m.

A few feet to Derham's right, a radar tech jerked upright in his chair and leaned towards the two officers. 'Unidentified vessel,' he announced. 'Position nine hundred yards NNW, approaching fast.'

'Why wasn't it picked up earlier?' Windsor snapped. 'It's almost on top of us.'

He had barely finished his sentence when the water beyond *Gladstone*'s bow began to churn. No more than a quarter of a mile away a grey shape appeared in the foam. It expanded with frightening speed, thrusting upwards, water streaming over its sides. The conning tower bore the symbol of a red star inside a red bar. Below this was written: 09–111.

One of the crewmen tapped at a keyboard. 'Sir . . . Shang class sub, People's Republic of China. NATO database designation: Alpha564/D.'

A voice broke through the bridge comms. 'HMS *Gladstone*, stand down, prepare to be boarded.' The English was only faintly accented.

'Put a call through to *Ark Royal*,' Windsor said. He lifted binoculars to take a closer look at the sub.

'Long-range comms down, sir.'

'Oh, excellent!'

The bridge speakers burst into life again, and the voice repeated the message: 'HMS *Gladstone*, stand down, prepare to be boarded.'

'Prep forward gun.'

'Prepped, sir.'

'Fire across her bow.'

A roar filled the bridge as the Mark 42 *5″/54* calibre deck gun fired. The shell whistled over the water, fifty yards off the bow of the Chinese sub, coming down in the sea a mile beyond the vessel.

'HMS *Gladstone*, stand down, prepare to be boarded.'

Derham leaned in towards the comms operator. 'Warn *JV3*,' he said.

Windsor was preparing to send a reply to the persistent commander of the Chinese sub when a buzzer sounded on the No.2 radar monitor to his right. The operator stiffened.

'What is it?'

'*Ark Royal*, sir. Heading this way . . . fast.'

56

MI6 HQ, London. 9.17 a.m.

Prime Minister Nigel Townscliff's face looked huge on the screen. He was rather an ugly man; and as Sir Donald Ashmore, Deputy Chief of the SIS, considered his leader's visage, for a second he wondered how the PM's face had not hindered his electoral success.

'This has to stop, right now,' Townscliff was saying, his gravelly baritone spilling too loudly from the speaker under the flat screen.

Ashmore's assistant, Seth Wilberforce, was seated next to him. Wilberforce flicked a glance at his boss as Ashmore started to reply.

'I understand your alarm, sir.'

There was a buzzing sound and the image on the screen split into three. Two new faces appeared. Ashmore recognized them immediately: Air Vice Marshal Pip Johnson and First Sea Lord Admiral Sir Kenneth Frobisher.

'Sorry, Prime Minister,' Johnson said, '. . . technical hiccups.'

The PM looked disgruntled. 'What's the latest, Frobisher?'

The admiral, a cadaverously thin man who all on the call knew had recently fought and apparently beaten prostate cancer, cleared his throat. '*Ark Royal* has halted twelve miles west of the Chinese . . . visitor, sir.'

'And standing down.'

'On red alert, sir, but holding. The Chinese have gone quiet.'

'Sir,' said Ashmore, 'I assume you have been briefed on the importance of this operation?'

'A retrieval of some documents that have been under the North Sea for . . . what?' Townscliff consulted a sheaf of papers on the desk in front of him. 'Sixty-odd years . . . is that right?'

'Sir, they are not just *any old* documents.'

Townscliff raised a hand and looked down. 'American scientific papers. From Russia . . . I'm confused.'

Ashmore took a deep breath.

'May I, sir?' Seth Wilberforce intervened.

Ashmore waved a hand indicating that the younger man should speak.

'Prime Minister, these papers – and the source document they refer to – were originally intended for Albert Einstein in 1937. The original document was part of something he was developing with the US Navy. It never reached him. It was stolen by the crew of a German U-boat and taken to Germany. After the war it fell into the hands of the Soviets. In 1954, a defector, a scientist called Dimitri Grenyov, who worked on and developed the ideas in the document, was bringing it and his work to the West when the sub he was travelling in, the American submarine USS *Phoenix*, was sunk . . . by the Royal Navy.'

For a moment, the prime minister seemed lost for words.

'What possible relevance does this have today?' the air vice marshal asked.

'As I understand it, the technology at the heart of the research is still extremely important,' Ashmore explained.

'As you understand it?' Townscliff said.

'I'm not a scientist, sir, but we have a team of experts who have been investigating this matter. The CIA are involved and we have been working closely with them.'

'I see,' Townscliff said. He brought a hand to his chin. 'Perhaps it is the Americans' problem then.'

'It is a joint matter, sir,' Wilberforce interjected. 'We sank *Phoenix* in Norwegian waters in 1954. It was a joint British–American Intelligence operation that got Grenyov out of Moscow and MI6 has been involved in tracing the location of *Phoenix*.'

Townscliff had his hand up again. 'Gentlemen, this sounds like the plot to a 1960s B movie. No other way to describe it.'

Wilberforce went to speak, but the PM cut across him. '*Ark Royal* must not take *any* pre-emptive action. You understand?'

Ashmore said nothing. Frobisher and Johnson nodded.

'Understood,' Frobisher said crisply.

'I want to be kept informed of everything as it happens; every detail, nothing is too small. This is delicate, very delicate. Could open up a whole bloody can of worms. The last thing we all need is a major international incident. I'll have to talk to the White House . . . and the Norwegians. Christ!'

'Sir?' It was Seth Wilberforce.

The prime minister settled his gaze on Ashmore's assistant.

'Perhaps we haven't made it clear just how important the document could be.'

'You don't need to, young man,' Townscliff replied. 'The all-important word in that sentence was "could".'

57

North Sea. 9.17 a.m.

Kate looked down at Grenyov's frozen body. 'He died from hypothermia. His flesh is well preserved, and that expression – I've seen it before in old photographs from Scott's expedition.' Her voice was shaky.

'You sure you're OK, Kate?' Lou asked.

She nodded and swallowed hard. 'Yes . . . let's just get on with it.'

They searched the bunk for the attaché case, but there was no sign of it.

'Give me a hand,' Lou said, bracing himself by standing on the lower bunk and pushing back on the top bed across the passage a few feet away. Kate reached round and gripped the dead man's shoulders. Between them they lowered the corpse to the floor. He was as stiff as a plank.

It was awkward manoeuvring in the narrow space, but they managed to remove the Russian scientist's clothes, his thick overcoat, threadbare suit, shoes. They opened up the pockets that had frozen shut, the fabric laced with ice. Finding nothing, Lou removed a knife from the belt of his suit and ripped open the lining of the overcoat. Again nothing.

Lou handed the coat across Grenyov's body to Kate. She tossed it into the space behind her. Lou was just getting up when they felt the first explosion and the sub juddered. He stumbled forward, went to grab one of the struts supporting an upper bunk, missed it and crashed onto the body lying on the floor.

'Mayday, Mayday.' The sound spilled from their comms, the voice of Commander Ester Lamb. 'Lou, Kate . . . Mayday, Mayday. Please respond.'

'*JV3*? Come in, Commander,' Kate responded.

'We have a situation on the surface. A Chinese sub has shown up.'

'Fuck!' Lou exclaimed.

'Suggest you abort the mission and get back immediately, over.'

'No,' Kate said. 'Not yet. We haven't been able to locate the document.'

'We have a second problem,' Lamb said. 'Hull stability . . . Levels are falling.'

'How bad?'

'Some parts of the sub are reaching dangerous levels. According to my scans, *Phoenix* has shifted almost five feet inside the rock formation it is caught in. There's a real risk of her breaking free. If that happens . . .'

'Yeah, we get it,' Lou responded. 'How long have we got?'

'It's impossible to—'

'Ball park?'

There was a brief silence down the line. The two scientists could hear Lamb's breath coming fast and loud through the receiver. 'Five, maybe ten minutes.'

'OK. The living and operations sections are so small and interconnected, we can get outta here in sixty seconds if we have to. We've got to find the document, or it's all been a waste of time.'

'Yes but—'

'Sorry, Commander.' Lou clicked off the comms.

'We'll have to go through the corpses one by one,' Kate said. 'I'll take these three pairs of bunks, you take those.' She pointed across the gap. 'If we have no luck, we'll move on to the next set, agreed?'

Lou didn't answer, just started on the nearest bed.

It was a difficult and extremely unpleasant task. The first two bodies Lou tried were particularly awkward to search, the men had wrapped their arms about themselves in a futile attempt to stave off the freezing cold. Pulling an arm back, Lou heard the fragile bones snap. Feeling a sudden rush of nausea, he was forced to blank his senses as he shifted from bunk to bunk, from corpse to corpse until he had finished his three sets.

'Anything, Kate?' He turned to see her straighten up from her last body and shake her head. She looked very pale through her visor.

It was the same story for the next set of six, and the six after that.

Kate paused for breath, leaning back on the enamelled steel frame of the end bunk. 'Nothing,' she said.

Lou searched through the last body on his side, pulling off the blanket tucked under the corpse, stripping away the coat, two sweaters, a shirt and a thermal vest. He felt around the flesh, rigid against the gloves of his suit. Finally, he checked the sides of the bunk and under the pillow, running his fingers along an alcove in the wall adjacent to the bed. There he found a Bible and a photograph of a dark-haired woman in a flowery dress clutching two small children to her legs.

'Nothing,' Lou sighed.

A tremor passed through the crew quarters. Kate grasped a steel strut to steady herself as the sub shook from bow to stern. A loud grinding sound stuttered through *Phoenix*, rumbling around like a thunderclap in their headsets. She lost her grip, stumbled and started to fall back against the nearest bunk. Lou managed to grab her arm. She spun round, slipped and they both crumpled to the metal floor.

Another burst of sound, louder this time. It ricocheted around the walls. A terrifyingly squeal like a thousand fingernails scraping down a blackboard crashed into their headsets.

'Kate? Lou? Come in.' Ester Lamb sounded desperate. 'You have to get to the PAT.'

Lou dragged himself upright and helped Kate to her feet. 'You OK?'

She nodded then spoke through her external comms. 'Commander. How bad?'

'My sensors are screaming at me! The sub is close to breaking up. You have to—'

'Understood, Commander. We're heading back into the control room.'

Kate led the way, pulling herself forward as fast as she could go, using the struts of the bunk beds to help her along. In a moment, they were back in the control area. Taking a side each, they searched under seats, behind pipes and in every crevice of the sub's infrastructure. Lou pushed Captain Jacobs's body to one side and searched around his seat. He could find nothing resembling papers, or a case of any sort.

'Shit!' he exclaimed. 'Come on.'

Another crunch, a scream of metal grinding against rock. The sub lurched. A steel box came free from its support straps a foot above Lou's head. It started to shake free.

'Lou!' Kate screamed through her comms.

He glimpsed the box and slid aside as it smashed to the floor a foot away.

Gradually the squalling faded, the shaking subsided.

'Go!' Lou shouted.

It took only a few seconds to reach the room below the conning tower. They stumbled over to the body of the first dead sailor they had seen. The sub started to rock again.

This time the movement was almost soporific.

'Kate? Lou? The sub is caught in a resonance wave. The structure won't hold. The oscillations will keep building . . . Get out . . . Now!'

'We're going,' Kate gasped and dived into the opening of the PAT. 'Lou . . .'

He looked away, scouring the room.

'Lou! Now!'

Kate pulled him towards her and crouched down, keeping her eyes on him. Shifting to her left, she started to crawl. Lou lowered himself and swivelled round, to get through the portal. He turned, cursing with frustration as he scanned the room beneath the conning tower one last time. He saw something.

Bracing herself against the sides of the PAT as it swayed with the movement of the sub, Kate started to move a few feet back towards *JV3*. She glanced back and saw Lou stop, crane his head and start to move back towards the stricken vessel.

'No!' she bellowed through her comms. 'Lou . . . stop!'

58

North Sea. 9.30 a.m.

Commander Ester Lamb exhaled heavily, cut the comms and buried her head in her hands. 'Bloody scientists!' she hissed.

She had a throbbing headache and a ball of anxiety in her stomach. On her screens she could see parts of *Phoenix* breaking away from the main body of the sub. Along the port side a gash at least six feet long had appeared. A vortex of water slithering inside the hole flooding the sealed-off chambers towards the stern. The hull could crumble at any moment. *JV3*'s sensors did not lie.

She pushed the comms button on her control panel. '*Gladstone*? Come in, *Gladstone*.'

Nothing but static.

'*Gladstone*? This is *JV3*. Do you copy?'

Hiss and noise.

'Damn it!' She slammed a hand down on the edge of the panel.

A buzzing sound came through the speaker below

the monitor. A light shone red, blinked. Lamb ran her fingers over the controls, clicking pads. A small monitor among the LEDs and controls lit up. A green trace appeared in the top left corner of the screen.

'What is that?'

Lamb changed the uplink to the external cameras. The image of the *Phoenix* vanished. Two other camera angles flicked on, then off. A third image from the external cameras slid into view. It showed the seabed and the expanse of water directly behind *JV3*. The commander stared at the screen in disbelief.

'Good God!' she breathed, her voice trembling.

59

'Sir . . . comms with *JV3* have just gone down.'

Windsor and Derham strode across the bridge of *Gladstone* to a tech at the comms desk.

'Sir, I'm picking up something,' a second operative at the deep-sea sonar said.

'What sort of something?'

'Look, Captain.' The man pointed at the flat screen. 'Just came into range. A mini-submarine.'

'Sir?'

Windsor spun round towards the comms officer at a control module. 'The mini-sub has just sent a transmission to the Chinese Shang class submarine on the surface. Must be through a set of signal boosters.'

'It was the same transmission code the Shang used to send its warning to us earlier.'

'What's the surface comm situation?' Windsor asked.

The tech fell silent for a few moments as he concentrated on his screen and tapped a series of keys. 'Yes!' he declared and turned to Windsor, a small smile on his face.

'Sir, *Ark Royal* has blocked the Chinese interference.'

'Blocked their block?'

'In a manner of speaking.'

'But still nothing between us and *JV3*?' Derham said.

The tech turned back to his screen again. 'No, sir, nothing.'

'Well it's something,' Derham said and turned to Windsor. 'Perhaps we should talk to the prime minister again, Captain.'

'Agreed,' Windsor said. 'Get me the prime minister's office.'

'Sir?' It was the sonar tech. 'The unidentified mini-sub is closing in on *JV3*.'

'Let me see,' Derham said.

He studied the monitor. 'How fast is that thing moving?'

The tech typed in parameters. The image shifted, a set of numbers and symbols skittered across the screen.

'Around thirty knots, Captain. Looks to me like it's on an attack course.'

60

Lamb saw the streak of white shimmer across her monitor and a momentary flash of grey as the torpedo passed six yards off *JV3*'s bow, shot past the port side and came within a whisker of *Phoenix*. *JV3* rocked from the shockwave.

'Holy . . . !' Lamb stabbed at the controls and split the view screen so she could see the PAT. She let out an audible sigh of relief. The tunnel was intact.

She threw herself back in her seat and tried *Gladstone* again. 'Mayday . . . Mayday.' She had her finger on the comms button but all she could hear was static. 'Hell!' She flicked a switch. 'Mayday . . . Mayday. Lou? Kate? Get out now. We are under attack. Repeat . . . We are under attack.'

61

North Sea. 9.31 a.m.

'Captain Windsor, I need precise details.'

The commander of *Gladstone* stared at the screen on the wall of the bridge. It was split into two. On the left was the pale face of the British prime minister, Nigel Townscliff; on the right Admiral William Hornbee, commander of *Ark Royal*. The bridge of *Gladstone* was preternaturally quiet, the techs and crew concentrating on their screens.

'As I said, Prime Minister, the enemy vessel has launched a mini-submarine and opened fire on *JV3*. I believe the orders were that *Ark Royal* must not take pre-emptive action. Is that not correct, Admiral?'

Townscliff cut across the admiral as the man went to speak. 'When you say opened fire, precisely what does that mean, Captain?'

'*Phoenix* is extremely delicate,' Derham interjected. 'In fact, it is falling apart. The two scientists, Dr Bates and Dr Wetherall are still aboard. The Chinese mini-sub fired a torpedo across the bow of *Phoenix*, missing it by a few feet. It has destabilized the old vessel even more. That is the *precise* situation . . .' He looked at his watch. '. . . as of ninety seconds ago.'

'And there has been nothing more from this mini-submarine?'

'It has moved in close to *JV3*.' Windsor glanced at a tech. The man mouthed something. 'Fifty feet to starboard, captain.'

'I see,' Townscliff said. 'Hornbee? What is your gut feeling?'

'Not good, Prime Minister. We are in an extremely vulnerable position.'

'Explain.'

'The enemy has moved an asset close to the wreck and to our unarmed research vessel, *JV3*. Both the Shang submarine and the mini-sub are stealth vessels, that's how they have come so close without being picked up by radar or sonar. It makes me wonder what other tricks the Chinese have up their sleeves.'

'Perhaps none, Admiral.'

'Indeed, that is quite possible. But, the action is over two thousand feet beneath us on the floor of the North Sea. There is nothing we can do to stop the mini-sub.'

'Do either of you have any idea what the hell the Chinese are doing?'

Derham could think of several answers, each of which would have caused trouble. He glanced at Windsor and said: 'Thanks to the proximity of *Ark Royal* just outside Norwegian waters, they are clearly outgunned up here. They are after the same thing as we are and they are going in hard where we can't reach them.'

'Admiral?'

'I couldn't have put it better myself.'

'I see. So the question is: what do we do now?'

'Would you like my candid opinion, Prime Minister?' Hornbee asked.

'I'm sure I won't like it; but yes, I would.'

'We should fire upon the Shang submarine, NATO designation Alpha564/D.'

'But that would be construed as an act of war.'

'Or self-defence,' Windsor offered.

'Would it not be considered an excessive use of force? An escalation? After all, the mini-sub only fired across the bow of a wreck.'

'Deliberately endangering lives,' Hornbee said.

'We have no way of knowing the Chinese are aware how fragile the wreck is.'

Admiral Hornbee gave the prime minister a hard stare, his silence speaking volumes.

'Admiral Hornbee, *Gladstone*, hold your positions. Do not. I repeat. Do not open fire unless either of you are fired upon.'

'But, Prime—'

'I will not fire the first shot,' Townscliff snapped. 'I will not be responsible for starting a war.'

His image disappeared from the bridge screen.

62

Kate heard Ester Lamb's Mayday message, but she had no time to respond. She spun in the PAT and headed back the five yards to *Phoenix*. Lou had disappeared into the darkness of the old sub. All Kate could see were a pair of darting light beams from Lou's arm and helmet torches bouncing around in the chamber under the conning tower.

'Lou?' she called through the comms.

'No, Kate. Go back. I got this.'

She was in the room and could see him crouching down, pulling something from the floor under an unravelled length of rope.

'You've found it?'

The sub shook. Kate glanced anxiously at the opening in the hull and the PAT beyond.

Lou lifted the object. It was a small attaché case.

'Right. Now we go!' Kate barked. Lou could see her eyes ablaze through the suit mask as she grabbed his free arm.

The sub shuddered violently again. All around them

reverberated the painful rasp of metal against rock, metal against metal.

They heard a boom from the starboard side. *Phoenix* rocked again. A support beam collapsed from the ceiling and smashed to the floor of the room inches from them. They were thrown sideways, Kate tumbling on top of Lou as he collided with a bulkhead.

'Jesus!' He staggered to his feet.

Another violent jolt and they were at the opening into the PAT. Through the comms they both heard Ester Lamb. She sounded utterly desperate.

'Mayday. Mayday. Lou? Kate? We are under attack. Repeat, under attack. GET BACK NOW!'

'We're in the PAT, Commander,' Kate's voice broke.

They crawled as fast as they could along the tunnel. It swayed and groaned under the strain.

'Come on Lou! Faster!' Kate screamed.

He ploughed on, propelling himself along the PAT.

A screech came from the conning tower. They dared not look back.

Kate dived into the airlock of *JV3*, spun round and reached out to help Lou. He was two yards away from her outstretched hand.

Another burst of sound from *Phoenix* and Kate saw a rip appear in the inner skin of the tunnel. It shot along the barrel of nanocarbon, spreading tendrils ten yards long.

'Lou!'

Kate felt the tips of his gloved fingers. He half dived, half ran the final few feet and tumbled into the airlock.

Kate grabbed the rim of the door and started to pull it back when the far end of the PAT gave way.

The tunnel slipped away from the hull of *Phoenix* like a sucker detaching itself. Lou grabbed the door handle and between them they pushed the door back the last few inches. Lou pushed down the locking lever and Kate slammed a bolt into place.

'We're in, Commander.'

Water slammed against the ocean side of the door as the PAT was ripped away by the swirling currents around the two submarines.

Lou and Kate were thrown backwards as *JV3* accelerated away. They clambered through the tiny connecting passage, up a ladder and scrambled into the control room, grasping at any hold they could find as the submarine zigzagged. Pulling off their oxygen packs, they slid into the passenger seats, yanked over the safety belts and locked themselves in.

A few feet ahead, they could see Lamb. She was running her hands frenziedly over the control panel, her gaze flitting between the monitors and the array of LEDs and keypads.

And when it happened, they were all taken by surprise. In the half-light from the *JV3*'s headlamps, they saw the *Phoenix* break free from the rocky cradle it had resided in for so many years. It rose a few yards, aft fins scraping the outcrop of stone. A few yards more and it started to crumple, dissolving like a soluble aspirin.

63

They saw the torpedo before they felt the shockwave. It streaked past the bow of *JV3* and exploded in a vortex of water a hundred yards to port.

The surge of water from the blast hit them.

'Holy shit!' Lou exclaimed as Commander Lamb swung the tiny sub hard to starboard.

For a few moments it felt as though *JV3* was completely out of control.

The engines squealed and the turbulence made the vessel shake from bow to stern. Lou and Kate could do nothing but watch Commander Lamb struggle with the controls.

'I can't believe this is happening,' Kate shouted above the noise. She turned to see Lou's face pale as death.

'*Gladstone*, come in please,' Lamb called into the comms. 'Come in.'

Nothing.

A third torpedo came into view, heading straight for them.

Lamb yanked the control column hard left, then

right. *JV3* jolted, the engines roaring. The torpedo slipped past, almost scraped the hull and disappeared behind them. The crunch from the shockwave came two seconds later.

'Jesus Christ!' Lou exclaimed. 'That was fucking close.'

'Commander? Do we have a plan?' Kate yelled over the noise.

Lamb didn't take her eyes from the controls and monitors.

'Nope . . . unless you have some ideas, doctor. I'm just dodging the torpedoes!'

The boom ricocheted around the control room; then came a shrill pulse like a beast vainly resisting death.

Silence.

'The engines have died,' Lamb said. The matter-of-factness in her voice was terrifying.

64

London. 9.34 a.m.

'Prime Minister, we must attack the Chinese . . . now!'

The Right Honourable Nigel Townscliff glared back at the images on his monitor. The screen was again split into two showing the commander of *Ark Royal* and Captain Windsor on *Gladstone*.

'Must we, Admiral? There are always alternatives. Always.'

'With respect, sir,' Windsor interjected, 'I think that is an exaggeration. This is a time when there are no alternatives left. Unless, of course . . .'

'Unless what, Captain?'

'Unless you are happy to let our three submariners die and allow the material from *Phoenix* to fall into Chinese hands.'

Townscliff said nothing, lowered his head and rubbed his temples. Those on the bridge of the aircraft carrier and the small research vessel could hear the British prime minister breathing heavily.

'And you are absolutely sure . . .' Townscliff said,

'the Chinese mini-sub has actually opened fire on our vessel down there?'

'It has, sir. We have detected three torpedoes. *JV3* has been taking evasive action.'

'I see.'

'Sir?' A tech to Windsor's left turned, his eyes wide. 'The heat image of *JV3* has changed.'

Captain Derham was standing on the bridge next to Windsor and turned away from the faces on the video screen. 'What does that mean exactly, Lieutenant?' He strode over to the tech and stared at an infrared image of *JV3* showing the heat distribution through the vessel.

'It means the engines are down, sir. *JV3*'s a sitting duck.'

65

North Sea. 9.36 a.m.

The Chinese mini-sub filled half the screen.

'One hundred and twenty yards and closing,' Lamb said.

Lou gripped Kate's hand. Both of them knew that any instant their lives could end. They would barely have time to register the firing of a torpedo from the sub before *JV3* was obliterated.

'One hun—'

The unimaginable was happening. They could all see it on the screen over the control panel . . . the Chinese sub turning starboard, moving at high speed out of view and away from them.

For several moments, Kate, Lou and Ester Lamb stared mutely at the screen. Then Lou exhaled heavily, whooped, 'Un-fucking-believable!', and turned to kiss Kate on the mouth.

'What the hell is happening?' Kate asked Ester as she pulled away from Lou.

'They've called off the attack,' Lamb said. She was

focusing on the control panel in front of her and tapping illuminated plastic tabs. 'And if I'm not mistaken . . .'

A loud buzz was followed immediately by a deep whirring, churning sound. 'We have power back to the engines.'

'How?' Kate asked.

'The Chinese must have used an electromagnetic pulse to knock out the power. Everything, well almost everything, is back online. We don't have comms . . . yet.'

Lou was unbuckling.

'What're you doing?' Lamb asked.

He lifted the attaché case retrieved from *Phoenix*. 'Checking this out. It was not easy to get our hands on!'

He placed it on his seat. The metal edging was heavily corroded. The lock had partially disintegrated and it took no effort to lever up the latch and open the lid.

'Easy,' Kate said, getting out of her seat.

From the case, Lou lifted an old tan-coloured cardboard file. With enormous care, he opened the front cover and they saw typed Russian text. He turned back the first few pages, holding them from underneath with his spare hand so that they could see lines of mathematical formulae and Cyrillic sentences.

'Grenyov's work.' Kate said taking the file and placing it on her seat.

At the bottom of the case lay a rectangular object sheathed in brown paper. Lou found a seam in the paper and prised away with expert care. Inside was a single sheet of metal foil etched with a complex array of symbols, letters and numbers.

'This is it,' Lou said in hushed tones, barely able to believe what lay before them, '. . . the original Kessler Document.'

66

North Sea. 9.36 a.m.

Wing Commander Geoff Anderson, operations code name Acer 1, pulled on the pair of joysticks of his F35 fighter and the newly commissioned jet tore away at an angle of almost ninety-five degrees, screaming skyward, accelerating to Mach 1.2 in a matter of seconds. Through his cockpit windows he could see three of his squadron, but the remaining two were just out of sight, their signals blinking on the head-up display he wore showing a range of detailed information.

'All systems green, *Ark Royal*,' Anderson said into his comms.

'Copy that, Acer 1.'

Anderson studied the complex array of information before his eyes. The HUD included altitude, attitude and speed meters, a radar sweep and a detailed set of coordinates giving the precise position of the Chinese Shang sub in relation to his F35.

Anderson tapped at the display panel a few inches from his armrests, his other hand steady on the left joystick. The parameters in the HUD shifted accordingly. The plane banked and levelled off.

'Acers 2 to 6. I'll make a solo pass before we go in. Over?'

The other five pilots acknowledged the command one by one and swept through a predetermined broad arc as Acer 1 dipped its nose and began a sharp descent.

The fog had entirely cleared, but in places the cloud line was as low as six hundred feet.

On his HUD, Anderson watched a computer representation of the enemy sub, then breaking through the cloud, he saw it for real, immobile on the surface, its nose two hundred yards from *Gladstone*'s bow.

'Have visual of Shang,' Anderson said. He moved the joysticks, banked to the west and streaked over the submarine ninety-six point seven feet above the conning tower.

Even through the triple-plated steel of the Chinese sub's hull, those aboard the Shang heard the scream of the F35 as it shot overhead.

'Status please, *Ark Royal*.'

'Unchanged, Acer 1,' came the reply from the bridge of the aircraft carrier. 'No word from the Chinese. Orders from London unaltered.'

'Copy that, *Ark Royal*. We're going in.'

Anderson's plane cut through the clouds and into the bright afternoon sunshine. The other five F35s slipped into view. Anderson caught up with them and they swept east, then north.

'Acer 3 and Acer 5, follow me. Formation Gamma

9-A. Acers 1, 2 and 4 hold back for second wave, maintain altitude and course.'

The squadron leader pulled away and saw the other two planes fall in behind him. His fingers tapped a series of patches on the flat screen at the centre of his control panel. 'Weapons armed and ready.'

'Armed and ready,' Acers 3 and 5 responded.

'*Ark Royal*, preparing for attack mode 9443.'

'Copy that, Acer 1.'

'Good luck, gentlemen,' Anderson said into his plane-to-plane comms and with a delicate nudge of the joystick, he was pulling round and down. The nose of the F35 dipped into the clouds once more.

'Keep close and wait on my command,' Anderson said.

They were through the clouds. There was the Shang sub, the water grey about its black serpent shape.

'Final sequence patched in,' Anderson said.

'Copy that,' came the response from Acer 2 and Acer 5.

'Remember. Wait for my command.'

Six miles east of the Chinese vessel and travelling close to one thousand miles per hour, Acer 1 and the two other planes descended to three hundred feet. Twenty-one seconds to target.

A red light flashed on Anderson's display. He knew the same thing would be showing on the displays aboard Acer 2 and Acer 5. It was the warning light indicating a pair of Storm Shadow cruise missiles were now primed.

'Target locked,' Anderson announced. 'Distance 3.5 miles and closing. Nine seconds to target. Eight . . . seven . . . six.'

'Acer 1.' It was *Ark Royal*. 'Abort, Acer, abort.'

Anderson had his finger poised a fraction of an inch from the fire button.

'Acer, abort. Call off attack.'

Anderson lifted his finger and thundered over the Shang, Acers 2 and 5 a fraction of a second behind as the three aircraft rocketed up towards the low cloud and the clear blue, sun-soaked sky beyond.

Thousands of feet below, the Chinese sub began to turn slowly to starboard and accelerate away north, pulling away from *Gladstone*, *Ark Royal* and the other NATO ships.

67

North Sea. 10.05 a.m.

As *JV3* docked with *Gladstone*, the bridge crew watching it all on the wall monitors erupted into applause. Jerry was there clapping along with the Royal Navy officers and Adam Fleming, who was seated towards the back of the control room sporting a big grin. They could all see the look of incredible relief on the faces of Kate, Lou and Ester Lamb as the engines of *JV3* powered down and the hatch into the docking bay opened.

'Permission to leave bridge, sir?' Jerry asked Captain Windsor. At the captain's word, he headed for the door and the corridors and stairways leading him down to the dock.

Two minutes later, he met his friends a few steps ahead of Commander Lamb. He saluted Lamb and hugged Kate and Lou. 'God, it was touch-and-go there for a while, guys,' he said.

'You're not kidding,' Lou replied. He was clutching the object he had retrieved from *Phoenix*.

'And that's definitely it?' Derham said, nodding towards the silver-foil encased rectangle.

'Checked it on the way to the surface,' Kate said. 'After the Chinese backed off. It's the real deal.'

They were walking along a grey corridor. Lamb had dashed on ahead to report to the engineer giving *JV3* a check-over.

'And speaking of the Chinese,' Lou commented. 'What the fuck was all that about?'

Derham stopped abruptly and held up a hand. Lou and Kate stood still giving him a puzzled look.

'I'll explain about that later. First though, there's something I need to tell you.'

'Can't it wait, Jerry? We need to get this material photographed and analysed asap.'

'No it can't. Just listen . . .'

*

Lou and Kate came onto the bridge to more applause from the crew.

Fleming stepped forward. 'Well done, you two. Well done! So, you retrieved the Kessler Document?'

Holding the case, Lou walked slowly to the centre of the bridge where a small metal table stood. He walked around it, facing the back of the bridge and the exit to the rest of the ship, the bow and the expansive grey sea behind him. Kate came round beside him. Lou opened the case and removed the cardboard file and the sheet of foil.

'So, this is really it?' Fleming looked down at a small sheaf of papers, frayed at the edges and discoloured in places.

'Doesn't look much . . .' Lou began, before raising his eyes and seeing the muzzle of a Glock a few inches from his face. He looked straight into Adam Fleming's eyes and began to shake his head slowly.

'Adam?' Kate glared at him.

'Oh, Katie, dear Katie. I'm sorry you had to be dragged into this.'

Captain Windsor took two steps towards them, reaching for his holstered pistol.

'Please don't,' Fleming snapped.

Windsor pulled the gun an inch away from its resting place and Fleming fired, the bullet shattering the man's forehead in a spray of red, his body crumbling in mid-movement.

Kate screamed.

'Get up and put your guns on the floor,' Fleming shouted to the three crewmen. Two were still seated at their consoles, the third poised half out of his chair. They obeyed silently, let their guns fall, and raised their hands.

'Thank you. Now, who's in charge here?'

'Me. Lieutenant Taylor,' said the lead operator.

'OK, Lieutenant, we shall try to get this right . . . yes?'

The young man nodded.

'Fuck, Fleming! I never liked you.'

'Shut up, Lou,' Fleming said quietly. He turned back

to the lieutenant. 'Right, Taylor, I want the chopper warmed up.' He flicked his head back an inch to indicate aft where the helipad was situated.

'Who are you working for, Adam?' Kate asked.

Fleming kept his eyes on the naval officers. 'Long story, Katie. Perhaps we can chat about it when you and hubby come on a chopper ride with me.'

'I don't think I'll be able to persuade Admiral Hornbee on the *Ark Royal* to let you do that,' Taylor said.

'Don't you, Lieutenant? Well, in that case you must make Hornbee understand that for every five-minute delay one of you dies . . . OK? Now get on the phone.' He nodded to the receiver nestled up against the nearest monitor and Taylor stepped towards it gingerly.

'Tell us what this is all about, Adam. Now!' Kate cried.

Fleming drew breath. 'I was working for Eurenergy. You have heard of them?'

'Of course,' Kate replied. ' "Was"?'

'I accepted a better offer.'

'The Chinese,' Lou said coldly.

'I wasn't sure which way the wind was going to blow in this little escapade. So I kept my options open. Evidently, the Chinese are better organized than Eurenergy.'

'But they backed down.'

'Indeed, they did. So Plan B has kicked in. I take the document and you two as hostages and then I consider the options . . . Who will pay the most for Kessler and

Grenyov's work? Maybe the Yanks!' He snorted contemptuously.

A noise came from the door.

'Put the gun down, Fleming.' Jerry was poised in the doorway, his gun grasped double-handed, at arm's length.

Fleming did not flinch. He had his back to Derham, his gun covering all five people in front of him, Lou, Kate and the three naval officers. 'Ah, Jerry, old boy.'

'Drop it.'

'Why should I, Captain? You go to shoot me, I'll shoot Lou, or Kate. You willing to risk that?'

'Now,' whispered Derham into his comms.

A burst of light came from beyond the starboard window of the bridge and *Gladstone* rocked. Fleming lost his footing and Derham fired. The MI6 man screeched as the Glock flew from his shattered fingers and he was thrown to his left. Jerry was across the bridge in a fraction of a second, standing, feet apart, the barrel of his gun pointed down at Fleming's head.

Fleming's contorted face was spattered with his own blood, his right hand a mess. He made to get up.

'Don't,' Derham barked. 'Move another inch and I swear it will be the last fucking thing you do.'

Bending down, he picked up the Glock, thrust it into his belt and looked towards Lou and Kate. 'You two all right?'

They nodded in unison. Taylor picked up the phone again.

'They know already, Lieutenant,' Derham said.

The door onto the bridge slammed inwards as three Royal Marines in flak jackets carrying MP5s ran in. Two of the bridge officers retrieved their pistols. Taylor knelt beside Captain Windsor's corpse. One of the Royal Marines pulled Fleming roughly to his feet, gripping his arm. Fleming shook him off.

Lou stepped forward and landed his fist in the centre of Fleming's face, smashing his nose and knocking him backwards against a console. Fleming straightened, gripped his nose with his good hand and gave Lou a poisonous look.

'Been dying to do that from the moment I met you,' Lou panted, shaking his hand out.

One of the Royal Marines snatched at Fleming's arms, yanked them back fiercely and snapped on cuffs.

'How did you know, Captain Derham?' Fleming said, blood streaming down from his nostrils and over his lips.

'We have Sergei to thank for that. Turns out he has a better intelligence network than any of us. He learned you had been working for Glena Buckingham at Eurenergy. You used the name Herman Toit, a man with a completely fabricated identity – a South African ex-mercenary. It is important to Sergei where the Kessler Document and Grenyov's work end up. Yes, a multi-billion-pound enterprise such as Buckingham's may have been able to make good use of it, but he would have preferred that either my guys or your official employers got it. He cared because Dimitri Grenyov, the scientist who managed to get the document out of

Soviet Russia, was his great uncle, he told us that. It is understandable that he wanted the man's work completed.'

'Unreal,' Lou interrupted. 'So you knew something would happen out here?'

'There's more, Lou. Sergei's people learned that our friend Adam Fleming was being paid by at least two separate groups – Eurenergy and the Chinese. He was playing both ends against the middle.'

Fleming managed a small twisted smile. 'And it nearly worked.'

'Nearly,' Derham said. 'But when Sergei learned about your Asian pals, Fleming, he really wasn't happy. In fact, he was really pissed. The last thing he wanted was for the Chinese to get their hands on the Kessler Document, because with them holding it and the West in possession of the other half of the information – what Einstein knew – there would never be any chance that Dimitri Grenyov's work would be completed, and therefore his great uncle would have died in vain.'

Derham sighed. 'I couldn't do anything. I just had to wait. Max was given the task of informing me – just after we rescued you from the apartment, Kate. I had to keep it quiet because I needed proof.' He nodded towards Fleming. 'I needed him to make a move. I didn't know when he would act. I realize now he was waiting to see what the Chinese would do and was improvising towards the end.'

'And the guy, Zero, in Moscow? Fleming killed him?'

'His own people, the FSB, bumped him off.'

'And the kidnap?' Kate hissed. 'That was . . .?'

'A delaying tactic, I believe. He needed to put the brakes on you getting out here – to give his Chinese buddies time to make arrangements. As I said, improvising.'

'Not exactly improvising, Jerry,' said Fleming. 'Respect where respect is due.'

'Respect?' Kate hissed. 'Respect you . . . a traitor. You make me sick.'

'Ouch, Katie. I have feelings, you know.'

'Get him away from me . . .' she said, her face contorted as though she was coping with a very bad taste, '. . . before I smack him in the face too.'

68

Flotta, Orkney Islands. 10.09 a.m.

On the giant screen in the Main Control Hub of Flotta Base, Glena Buckingham and her team had seen the F35 fighter jets scrambled from *Ark Royal*; seen them swoop down towards the Shang-class submarine and pull back seconds away from destroying it.

And now, thirty minutes after the stand-off, *JV3* had returned to the safety of the submarine bay of *Gladstone* and she could hear the marine archaeologists Kate Wetherall and Lou Bates walking onto the bridge.

'Toit, or Fleming as they know him, must be about to make a move,' Buckingham hissed half to herself. '. . . he must . . .'

'*So, this is really it?*' came Fleming's voice from the bridge.

'*Doesn't look much . . .*' Lou's voice replied.

'*Adam?*'

'He's done it!' Buckingham said.

'*Oh, Katie, dear Katie. I'm sorry you had to be dragged into this.*'

In the main contròl hub, they heard shuffling, voices, a gunshot, a scream. More shouting.

There was a dead silence on Flotta. None of the technicians dared to move. Then a burst of interference shimmied down the line from *Gladstone*. Buckingham turned and gave the nearest technician a deadly look. He scrambled to correct the problem. A confusion of sounds came through the speakers, then the crack of a pistol shot.

Buckingham spun on her heel. 'Prep the chopper, Freeman. Sounds like Toit's fucked. Get me off this pisshole of an island . . . NOW!'

She had not moved so quickly for a very long time, having grown accustomed to making other people move at top speed for her and was wholly unused to the role. Buckingham reached the lift with Secker close behind and Freeman trailing a few yards back looking scared and more than a little confused.

She stabbed at the lift button and hollered over her shoulder to the chief of operations. 'I want us off here without delay!' She ran into the lift as the doors opened. Freeman extricated his mobile and tapped in the number for the chopper pilot, whom he assumed was still out in the helicopter with it refuelled and ready for take-off at a moment's notice.

'No!' Freeman exclaimed into the phone as the lift shifted through the floors. 'What do you mean, you aren't ready?'

Buckingham looked daggers at the man and snatched

the phone. 'MacBride. You can't be serious! How long for God's sake?'

The two men could hear the muffled sound of a reply.

'WHAT!' Buckingham exploded, stabbed at the phone and tossed it back to Freeman. 'Other choppers? There must be others fuelled and ready.'

Freeman called a number nervously, avoiding direct eye contact with the head of Eurenergy. He talked quietly and gave nothing away before terminating the call. 'Thirty minutes,' he said.

Buckingham was terrifyingly silent. Secker and Freeman heard her take deep breaths as the lift doors swished open.

'Give me the phone back,' Glena Buckingham said, striding quickly out of the lift along a corridor heading towards the departure/arrivals room close to the helipad. 'MacBride. We just need enough fuel to get to the mainland. We can radio ahead. Yes . . . yes . . . I know. For God's sake, listen, man. I'm giving you ten minutes, not twenty. Do it, or you will be signing on come Monday.'

They reached the white-walled waiting area and could see the helipad through the glass. A fuel truck had just reached the chopper and MacBride was out of the aircraft hurrying along the technicians and ground crew.

Buckingham started to pace, Freeman kept out of the way the best he could. Freeman's phone tinged. He read the screen, his face incredibly pale in the harsh whiteness of the room.

'What is it?' Buckingham hissed.

'Erm, not sure you want to—'

'WHAT IS IT?'

'Newsfeed. Police have raided central office, and . . . erm . . . your home, Ms Buckingham.'

The head of Eurenergy simply stared into Freeman's face, her eyes as black as the Grim Reaper's.

'I'm sorry . . .' Freeman spluttered.

They all turned to the glass as a sound broke through the glazing. For a vain moment, they each hoped it was the chopper engine sparking to life, but it was not. It was the sound of F35s screaming low over Flotta.

69

Norfolk Naval Base, Virginia. Ten days later.

Kevin Grant pushed the hair out of his eyes and stared at the words he had written on a piece of paper: 'REMEMBER JOAN'S PLACE?' They were the three words presumably written by Johannes Kessler and placed in the cylinder found aboard Amelia Earhart's plane.

On the monitor in front of him the single continuous line of symbols and notation Kate and Lou had discovered on the inside of the same cylinder ran across horizontally in three neat rows. For two weeks now, since Grant had been given this material, he had tried, in vain, to match the prosaic three-word sentence with the confusion of text in front of him.

'"Remember Joan's Place?"' he muttered for perhaps the hundredth time. 'What the fuck does it mean?'

Clearly it was a 'key to the key'; those three words meant something that would unlock the meaning of the lines of symbols found inside the cylinder.

He had spent the first ten days searching for some

mathematical relationship, employing every technique he had acquired during his eight years as an encryption analyst, everything he had learned as a mathematics PhD at MIT. Nothing worked, nothing. But he would not be beaten. He had cracked every code he had been called upon to solve. He would not be defeated by this, even if it had been contrived by two of the cleverest scientists in history.

As he worked, Kate and Lou had tried to find out anything they could about the Kessler Document they had retrieved from *Phoenix*, but without the key anything they could do was peripheral – just as Grenyov's work had been. A week after returning from the North Sea they had flown to the Pacific to supervise the retrieval of the remains of Amelia Earhart's plane.

On day eleven, Grant reached breaking point and went fishing.

It was perhaps an unlikely hobby for the encryption genius who wore Grateful Dead T-shirts and spent far too much time in front of a computer screen, but fishing relaxed him, gave him a sense of purpose far removed from mathematical abstractions. But this time the exercise had failed and Grant had returned to the naval base still seeking a breakthrough.

Back in the bare-walled office he stared at the blank face of his iPad resting on his paper-strewn desk.

He picked it up and opened his library. He had purchased two dozen titles, each relating to Albert Einstein. There were no surviving letters between Einstein and his colleague, Kessler, but their relationship was mentioned in most of the books. Sadly, none of these references had led to any sort of clue.

Glancing at the screen, he saw a notification from an e-book seller, Truman and Co., a company that, a week earlier, had located one of the less well-known biographies of Einstein from the 1970s. It was a short message informing Grant that they had managed to track down a copy of another, even more obscure, book called *Chatting with Einstein*, a collection of conversations from 1951 between the scientist and a respected journalist of the day, Winslow Mortimer.

Grant shrugged and tapped the link, approved payment of a dollar ninety-nine, and a few minutes later he had the e-book on the screen.

He flicked through abstractedly, pausing at a few of the exchanges before moving on. His finger stopped on the glass and he felt a pulse of excitement shoot through him as he read.

'Professor, you spent some time in Oxford before you arrived in the States in 1933. Was that rewarding?'

'Oh, yes, indeed. I was there with my wife, and my dear friend Johannes Kessler was visiting for a semester. He had a wonderful time too. I remember many stimulating conversations with Johannes. Also, there was a woman we knew, Joan Sinclair. She was a widow, her husband James had died in 1930. She was a Professor of Botany at New College and hosted lovely gatherings of like-minded people at her home.'

'And you and Kessler often met there?'

'Indeed we did; our wives too. Joan was a very versatile individual and an excellent scientist, a keen painter and a very accomplished pianist. I remember she lived on Iffley Road, number 1001; that was often a source of merriment for Johannes and me.'

Kevin Grant did not notice how much his hands were shaking. 'My God!' he announced to his empty office. 'Oh . . . My . . . God. I'm a genius, a fucking genius!' He plucked up his phone and called Jerry Derham.

70

'You really think you've cracked it, Kev?' Derham said, sitting at Grant's desk five minutes later. He could not disguise completely the edge of scepticism in his voice.

'Do I hear doubt, Captain?'

'No,' Derham said earnestly.

'OK, so this is how it works. "Remember Joan's Place?" wasn't some silly message or a red herring. I had a strong feeling about that from the start. I had a sense it was actually integral to solving the puzzle. But I was getting nowhere with it until ten minutes ago.' He nudged his iPad across his desk and twisted it so Jerry could see the highlighted passage from the e-book *Chatting with Einstein*.

'And?' Derham said after he had finished reading it.

'1001 Iffley Road.'

'Yeah. What caused Einstein and Kessler a chuckle over that, Kev?'

'It's binary. 1001 is 9. An in-joke. The number 9 must be the key to the text from the inside of the cylinder and that will then unlock the Kessler Document. I wanted you to be the first to see it happen.'

Derham was shaking his head. 'That is, well . . . unexpected.'

'Yep. Now watch.' Grant shunted his laptop so that they could both see the screen and flicked the mouse to drag the computer from hibernation. They both studied the lines of symbols, numbers and letters as they ran across the screen.

'The simplest thing would be to extract every ninth figure, taking the first letter – "M" – as number 1. Yeah?'

Grant's fingers stuttered across the keyboard and a succession of symbols were lifted from the lines and placed in a fresh section of the screen. There were three hundred and fourteen figures in all. This produced a fresh line containing thirty-four letters, numbers and symbols.

With the last number in place, Grant sat back and considered the screen. It made absolutely no sense.

'OK, we'll try something else,' he said. 'Let's extract every ninth figure, starting from the end and working backwards.'

He tapped at the keyboard again and a fresh line of thirty-four appeared.

They both considered the screen.

'Sorry, Kev, that makes no sense either.'

Grant was staring, unblinking. Derham could see the man's jaw muscles working. What was that? he wondered. Frustration? Anger? A nervous twitch?

'Ah!' Grant exclaimed and pulled in close to the desk, gripped the ends of the keyboard and brought it a few inches nearer to himself before stabbing at the keys. 'First, take out all the symbols and numbers from this sequence of thirty-four figures.'

Half of them disappeared to leave seventeen letters that read: 'NICE TRY BUT NO CIGAR'.

71

Pacific Ocean. 2 July 1937.

Amelia and Fred had barely exchanged a word. They had acted on impulse, moving mechanically, speechless, thinking about nothing beyond the moment, the next move, the next requirement.

Back in Lae, Papua New Guinea, they had opened the doors of the hangar, each barely able to look back at the two dead men on the floor. From twenty feet away, the Germans looked as though they were relaxing on red mats, glossy red mats that caught the electric ceiling lights shining down from above the Electra.

There would be some serious questions to answer, Amelia knew that. Why had they run? Why had they not gone to the local police? They would be accused of murder. But then that had to be better than being dead . . . or worse. How could they know for sure that there were no other German spies ready to torture them for information?

But then again: what evidence could be used against them? Amelia realized they had every right to fly when they wanted to. Who was to say with any certainty that the two men were killed by them? Where was the proof to say the aviators were not a hundred miles away in the skies over the water by the time these men died? Who was to say the two had not killed each other?

But Fred was angry, Amelia knew that. And that was perfectly understandable. What had she got him involved in? That's what he would be thinking, and that's what she was thinking also.

Neither of them had sensible answers. She could say nothing more about the things she knew, even now, even after Noonan had saved her and killed for her.

They flew on in silence. Flew on for twelve hours, well over halfway to Hawaii. From there, Amelia mused, they would begin the final leg. The news of the deaths in the hangar would not travel as fast as them. The government of Papua New Guinea was a flimsy fragmentary thing, any form of police force almost non-existent. No, they would leave Hawaii, and after that they would soon be home. There they might be asked questions, but by then they would have formulated answers. Everything would be deflected by the fact that they had achieved something truly amazing. No one would care about some strange, unsubstantiated event on an obscure Pacific island. Everything would be all right.

*

Six hours later and they were both utterly exhausted. The ocean, almost totally featureless, had become a boring nothing. They could almost imagine it was not there at all, and as night crept in, and the hours slipped away, it felt as though they were flying through a vacuum. The only sound came from the engines and from the air rushing over the wings, the same beat, the same tempo.

Amelia checked the chronometer. It was 20.13. She yawned. Eighteen hours in the air, and they were still flying through an eternal void, or so it seemed. They had been warned of a storm along the designated flight path, taken a detour south, and now they were back on the original course.

'How we doing, Fred?'

'Running good, Amy. Plan?'

She knew exactly what he meant. For how many hours could they just keep on flying without rest? Neither of them could tell for sure. But she stayed silent for a long time and Fred surveyed the dials in front of him, and without registering it, he heard the air over the wings.

'You got our position, Fred?'

He gave her the numbers. She flicked on the radio and cleared her throat. 'We are on the Line of Position 157–337. Will repeat this message on 6210 KCS.' She paused for a moment. 'Wait listening on 6210 KCS . . . We are running north and south . . .'

There was no response. She expected none. She took a breath and was about to say something to Noonan. They both heard the sound; it came like the crack of a whip.

The plane seemed totally unaffected.

'What was that?' Fred Noonan asked.

'Hell if I—'

A much louder crack.

Fred looked down out the window and saw a piece of metal tear free from the port wing. 'Holy fuck!' he screamed.

A third crack and a section of the port-side engine cover broke away and shot over their heads. A sheet of flame thrust into the night, lighting up the hidden ocean. The fire swept towards the cockpit before being extinguished in the rush of air over the wings. Amelia screamed and was thrown back in her seat as the engines shrieked and a series of bolts shot out from the control panel. One of them passed through the flesh of her arm.

The plane slipped to starboard, the wing dipping, the engines whining, disengaging like a car that had slipped out of gear. Amelia, unaware of her injury, pulled on the controls, but nothing responded. She saw the rip in her jacket and her blood staining the bulging lining red; but she felt no pain.

The plane flipped over and the sea and the sky merged, indistinguishable. Sound and light became one.

The Electra 10E scythed the water, the ocean consuming Amelia Earhart and Fred Noonan; taking them in as most welcome guests.

72

Off Howland Island, Pacific Ocean. Present day.

The sun was so dazzling even Lou's expensive sunglasses did little to diminish the glare. He shaded his eyes with a hand and gazed up to the winch suspending the remains of Amelia Earhart's plane as it swung round slowly to bring it onto the deck. Only twenty minutes earlier he and Kate had returned from the wreck after triple-checking the pulleys, cables and restraints that would enable the salvage crew to retrieve the remains of the plane without it suffering any further damage.

It touched down gently on a large sheet of air-filled plastic, taking up most of the open space of the deck to the rear of the bridge. Lou and Kate stood close by with their three assistants, Gustav, Connor and Cherie.

Kate was the first to reach the wreckage and she started the process of carefully unlatching the clasps and braces that had caged the fuselage, the inner parts of the wings and the engines as they had been raised from the ocean floor.

In the cold light of day the plane looked far smaller than it had seemed when they first spotted it two weeks earlier. It was covered with slime, some of the paintwork stripped back to the metal. One side of the fuselage was ripped open to reveal rusted cables and springs. The tailplane had gone and the stubs of the wings left behind a tangle of wires, and strips of metal.

Kate ran latexed fingers along the degraded surface of the Electra 10E.

'Pretty sad,' Lou said standing a few feet to Kate's right.

'You can say that again.'

'It'll take a long time to get all the pieces to the surface,' Kate added and walked to the front of the plane. The cockpit glass was shattered, the cockpit itself filled with water, seaweed and a few crustaceans; everything distorted, corroded, warped.

Gustav and Connor were inspecting the rear of the plane while Cherie filmed and photographed the wreckage from every angle. Kate walked slowly around the remains of the aircraft, now not much more than a collection of truncated pieces of metal.

Lou stopped close to the port engine. The cover was contorted and buckled. Very gently, he prised it up. It creaked and groaned. A chunk of corroded metal about a foot square fell away to the cushioned floor.

Inside, the engine was a mess. The central block was coated in algae and rust. Exhaust pipes looked like tree roots where they had snapped, partially dissolved over time and tangled together.

Kate came round and stared into the engine cavity. Lou stepped close, put his head under the propped-open cover and started to poke around, trying to get a clearer understanding of what almost eighty years of ocean life had done to the plane.

That was when he saw it.

He moved aside a bunch of wires and thrust both hands into the mess.

'What is it?' Kate asked. She had worked with him long enough to know when he had spotted something interesting.

He ignored her and stretched the fingers of his right hand, just managing to reach the cylindrical object. Leaning in as far as he could, he clasped the metal, his fingers closing on it and weaving it upwards, negotiating a muddle of wires and cables. He made a twist left, down and then right and his arm was free. Holding up the cylinder, he squinted at it. It was almost identical to the one they had found two weeks earlier in the plane's cockpit. The only differences were the streaks of oil and the electrical burn marks running from one flat end to the other.

73

Somewhere in England. Two weeks later.

There was a long list of conditions placed upon Kate's visit to her old friend from Oxford days, Adam Fleming. She was not allowed to record the meeting, she had to sign a non-disclosure agreement which covered every aspect of who he was and what he had done, and she was not permitted to know where the man was being held. To facilitate this last requirement Kate had agreed to be transported to the site in a windowless vehicle driven by an anonymous chauffeur.

The building was a nondescript concrete monstrosity, huge and cold and resting in a flat windswept landscape many miles from the nearest habitation. The journey from London had taken a little over three hours and Kate had no idea in which direction they had travelled. It was not enough time for the vehicle to reach Dartmoor or the Yorkshire Moors; the landscape here was too flat and bleak for the Welsh borders, so she concluded the detention complex was somewhere in East Anglia, perhaps near King's Lynn or Lowestoft.

She was searched, asked to walk through a scanner, had her bag thoroughly checked, mobile temporarily requisitioned and her shoes removed. On stockinged feet, Kate was led to a featureless waiting area, a long, narrow room painted gunmetal grey with a stone floor. From there, flanked by silent armed guards, she was shown into a smaller, low-ceilinged space with one wall taken up by a darkened window. The room contained just four things: a table, two chairs, and Adam Fleming.

He was dressed in a bright orange one-piece, his blond curls cut brutally short. He had a cut under his left eye and he was chained to the table by his wrists and his ankles. His right hand was in an aluminium cast. In the two weeks since the bizarre series of events aboard *Gladstone*, he seemed to have lost some weight and his face had a haunted gauntness about it.

'Come to gloat have we, Katie? I'm surprised at you.'

She stared back at Fleming across the dull and scratched metal table, her expression neutral. 'Not at all, Adam.'

'I'm sure hubby isn't too delighted you should choose to visit your old pal though.'

She ignored the remark.

'So why then, if not to rub in that you won?'

'I just want some answers, Adam. I'm confused about something.'

'Clever Katie, confused? Goodness me!' He squinted at her and she could see through his hubris, through the pain he was feeling, to the numbness that had become the key feature of his life.

'People don't do what you did without reason, Adam.'

'Maybe it was simply about money. Thought of that?'

'Of course, but I'm not so sure you were ever that interested in vast wealth.'

'And you purport to know me do you, clever Katie?'

There was a long dull silence between them.

'I imagine a lot has happened during the past two weeks, has it not?'

'Yes, it has. The head of Eurenergy, Glena Buckingham, has been arrested, as have a dozen of her top people. Buckingham has tried plea-bargaining, sold you down the river.'

'Naturally.'

'And we have tied up the loose ends over the questions surrounding Einstein's work and the Kessler Document.'

'Oh?'

Kate looked around her. She knew this conversation was being taped, and although she could not see them through the darkened glass, she knew the armed guards were there along with perhaps several senior staff.

'Obviously I can't go into details, but suffice it to say, things did not turn out as simply as we had hoped. The cylinder we recovered from the cockpit proved to be a decoy. By sheer fluke, we found a second cylinder that had been secured inside one of the Electra's engine casings. Except it had not been secured well enough.' She paused again. 'Hell, there's no real secret about it – Lou and I are scheduled to attend a press conference to announce the news tomorrow afternoon.'

Fleming gave her a puzzled look.

'We are pretty sure the second cylinder became dislodged during the final leg of Amelia Earhart's fateful flight and that it shorted the electrics of the port engine, causing the plane to crash. We could tell by electrical burn marks along the length of the cylinder.'

Fleming looked startled for a moment. 'And this second cylinder carried the real message?'

'Yes. We're close to cracking the code.'

Fleming shook his head slowly. 'That is, well, quite surprising. If I were in a better mood I would congratulate you – two mysteries solved simultaneously.'

There was another long silence.

'So why did you do it, Adam? Why betray your country, your friends . . . and even Eurenergy?'

'Perhaps for the fun of it, Katie.' He pursed his lips and looked down at the table.

'I know about your wife, Celia.'

Fleming did not look up.

'Did her death . . .?'

'You know nothing about me,' Fleming hollered, pushing himself forward as far as he could, the chains clinking under the strain. Kate thought she heard movement from behind the glass.

'I'm sorry,' Fleming said and sighed heavily.

'At Oxford you were a patriot extraordinaire,' Kate said. 'Your family history, your upbringing. You were imbued with it all. And then, the army, the intelligence service. Is it any wonder I might think Celia was the catalyst?'

'You didn't know me that well.' There was an edge to his voice, a touch of resentment. 'But, look, OK. I won't deny it. We are all slaves to what happens to us . . . it's all very Nietzschean, is it not?' And he produced a sliver of a smile that vanished as fast as it appeared. 'It was all so simple and straightforward when we were kids, wasn't it, Katie? When did it all start to get so goddamn complicated?'

'Our lives become progressively more complicated the older we get.'

'Pedestrian of you, but yes, you're right. Celia's death was a catalyst. How could it not have been? She died for nothing. Her death changed nothing. She believed in her country, but her country had no interest in her, not in who she really was, the woman she was. To them, she was a statistic, a number, a series of numbers, just as we all are. I carried on, I carried on for years after she died; went on doing what I did, believing still, never really questioning. But then, I don't know . . . something snapped, I suppose.'

He held Kate's gaze, his voice calm, as though he were talking about a book he had enjoyed, or an innocuous incident from schooldays. 'I was in Karachi. It was eighteen months after Celia died. I didn't really realize it at the time, but I was working flat out; classic displacement of course, and something . . . well, you get the picture, something gave. It really did. I felt it. It was almost a physical thing, I swear I heard it go, heard it snap, some cord, a connection, an empathy. It was a link between the old me and the new me. A link between the person who had been brought up in the Fleming family, with all our long, proud heritage, and the evolved Adam Fleming, if you will.'

He paused for breath and looked around the soulless room. 'There. Does that satisfy you? Or do you want me to beg forgiveness? Feel remorse?'

'Do you?'

'Do I feel remorse, Katie?'

She looked at him and could see nothing in his expression. He was either extremely good at concealing his feelings – or maybe there really was nothing there to conceal.

'You killed people, Adam.'

'Yes, I did. I killed people for queen and country, many people. And then I killed for myself. Is there really any difference? I was patted on the back for the former, sent here for the latter.' He gazed around again, pausing for a moment as he glanced past the darkened window. 'Moral relativism . . . a strange beast. A unicorn perhaps. Nothing more than a legend, a figment of the imagination.'

Kate suddenly felt tired and part of her no longer wanted to be there, no longer wanted to ask questions, find out things. She had a momentary vision of being curled up on a sofa with Lou, watching their favourite TV show.

'Did you really come here just to ask me questions?' Fleming said.

'I'm not altogether sure now.'

'I was being disingenuous when I accused you of wanting to gloat. But you did not come here for me, nor to satisfy prosaic curiosity. You have asked me these questions for yourself, Katie.'

She was shaking her head. 'How do you possibly . . .?'

'How do I work that out? It's really not that difficult. You and I, we knew each other, albeit briefly at a time in our lives when we were each emerging from childhood. Neither of us stayed the adults we grew up to be initially. When I knew you, you were more mature than me in many ways, but I could never have visualized you then as a married woman, settled, with a career and a domestic future lined up. And me, well, I changed even more, didn't I?' He allowed himself another vague smile.

'But I scared you, didn't I?' He tilted his head slightly. 'Oh, don't look so surprised. Drop the guard a second, be honest, at least with yourself. You saw how thin the veneer of education, upbringing . . . even morality can be. You saw me, the product of a "good" family and an Oxford education, followed by the army and MI6 discipline. You saw me change . . . change hugely. That frightened you. You wanted some deep, meaningful answers. That's why you came here today.'

'If that is true, I will go away empty-handed.'

'Yes, you will.'

'Because you can't, or you won't, answer?'

Adam Fleming did not reply; just gave her that thin smile one last time.